PENGUIN CLASSICS

THE BOOK OF DEDE KORKUT

ADVISORY EDITOR: BETTY RADICE

GEOFFREY LEWIS, originally a classicist, taught himself Turkish during five years in the RAF and came back to Oxford in 1945 to read Arabic and Persia ~~~~~~~~~~~~~~~~~~~~ rer in Turkish and Arabic, S~~~~~~~~~~~~~~~~~~~~~~, and finally Professor of Turk~~~~~~~~~

His other books include~~~~~~~~~~~~~~~~~~~~~~~*ürk I Knew* (1981), *Teach Yo~~~~~~~~~~~~~~~~~~~~mmar* (1988) and *Thickhead and~~~~~~~~~

He is a Fellow of the British Academy and an Emeritus Fellow of St Antony's College. Besides his Oxford D.Phil., he holds honorary doctorates of Istanbul University and Bosphorus University, and has twice been honoured by the Turkish Government for services to scholarship and the advancement of British–Turkish relations.

senior Lecturer in Islamic Studies and

Modern Turkey (1974), *The Atatürk*

Turkish Grammar (1988), *Turkish* and *Other Turkish Stories* (1988)

THE BOOK OF
DEDE KORKUT

*Translated, with an Introduction
and Notes, by Geoffrey Lewis*

PL 248 .K54 E5 1974
Kitabi D˘ad˘a Gorgud.
The book of Dede Korkut

PENGUIN BOOKS

PENGUIN BOOKS

Published by the Penguin Group
Penguin Books Ltd, 27 Wrights Lane, London W8 5TZ, England
Penguin Books USA Inc., 375 Hudson Street, New York, New York 10014, USA
Penguin Books Australia Ltd, Ringwood, Victoria, Australia
Penguin Books Canada Ltd, 10 Alcorn Avenue, Toronto, Ontario, Canada M4V 3B2
Penguin Books (NZ) Ltd, 182–190 Wairau Road, Auckland 10, New Zealand

Penguin Books Ltd, Registered Offices: Harmondsworth, Middlesex, England

First published 1974
7 9 10 8 6

Introduction, translation and notes copyright © Geoffrey Lewis, 1974
All rights reserved

Printed in England by Clays Ltd, St Ives plc
Set in Linotype Plantin

Except in the United States of America, this book is sold subject
to the condition that it shall not, by way of trade or otherwise, be lent,
re-sold, hired out, or otherwise circulated without the publisher's
prior consent in any form of binding or cover other than that in
which it is published and without a similar condition including this
condition being imposed on the subsequent purchaser

FOR LALLY AND JOB

CONTENTS

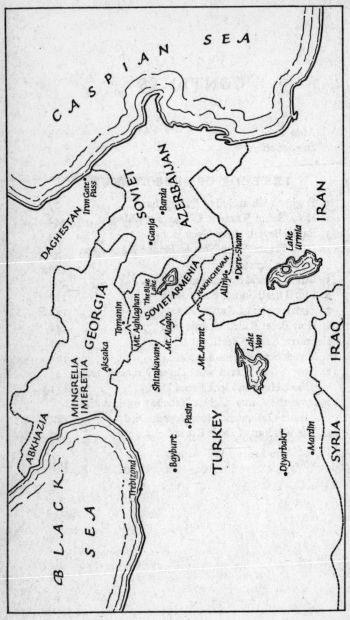

Principal places mentioned in the text and notes. The political boundaries are modern.

INTRODUCTION

THE BOOK OF DEDE* KORKUT is a collection of twelve
stories set in the heroic age of the Oghuz Turks. The oldest
monuments of written Turkish are the inscriptions found in
Siberia and Mongolia, the earliest dating from the eighth century AD. In these, 'Oghuz' and 'Turks' appear as the names of
two distinct communities, sometimes at war with each other,
sometimes in an alliance in which the 'Turks' are the dominant
partner. Later, however, the Oghuz are referred to as a Turkish
tribe (for example, by Mahmud Kashghari, the eleventh-century
lexicographer); this is because the name 'Turk', originally
applied to the most powerful segment of the people, was subsequently applied to the whole people.

In the ninth and tenth centuries, the Oghuz migrated westward, from the region of the Altai Mountains and Lake Baikal,
to the lands between the Syr Darya and Amu Darya (Jaxartes
and Oxus) and east of the Caspian. In their new home, they
came under the influence of Islam, for this land was within the
dominions of the Arab Caliphs of Baghdad. Still moving westward, the Islamicized Oghuz formed the bulk of the forces led
by the family of Seljuk, who conquered Iran in the eleventh
century and Anatolia in the eleventh and twelfth. The Ottoman
dynasty, who gradually took over Anatolia after the fall of the
Seljuks, towards the end of the thirteenth century, led an army
that was also predominantly Oghuz.

It is clear that the stories were put into their present form at
a time when the Turks of Oghuz descent no longer thought of
themselves as Oghuz. So in Chapter 3†: 'In the days of the

---

* The word is pronounced as two syllables, with both vowels short.

† Of the thirteen chapters of this book, 1–12 are the twelve stories, while
13 contains the material, mostly of later date than the stories, which I have
called 'The Wisdom of Dede Korkut'.

BALDWIN-WALLACE COLLEGE

Oghuz the rule was that when a young man married he would shoot an arrow and wherever the arrow fell he would set up his marriage-tent.' 'Among the Oghuz nobles, lying was unknown.' In Chapter 6: 'In the days of the Oghuz there was a stout-hearted warrior called Kanli Koja.' Now it is known that the term 'Oghuz' was gradually supplanted among the Turks themselves by *Türkmen*, 'Turcoman', from the mid tenth century on, a process which was completed by the beginning of the thirteenth. The Turcomans were those Turks, mostly but not exclusively Oghuz, who had embraced Islam and begun to lead a more sedentary life than their forefathers (although it must be noted that the evidence is not unequivocal and that the modern Turcoman tribes are still largely nomadic). We may therefore suppose that the stories were given their present form after the beginning of the thirteenth century. But there is no possible doubt that the basic material of the stories is far older.

The Oghuz in the stories live off their flocks and herds, and the whole tribe migrates from summer-pasture to winter-quarters and back. The society depicted is aristocratic. At the head of the Oghuz is the Great Khan, Bayindir, though he tends to remain in the background, the control of affairs being in the hands of his son-in-law Salur Kazan. With only two notable exceptions, commoners do not play much of a part; a shepherd fathers the monster Goggle-eye in Chapter 8, and in Chapter 2 we find another shepherd, the brave, garrulous, humorous and supernaturally strong Karajuk. The principal characters are the nobles or princes (*begler*) and their ladies. Salur Kazan's wife, Lady Burla the Tall, presides over the women's gatherings. The stock epithet of the Oghuz ladies is 'white-faced', which because in English it has connotations of fear I have paraphrased as 'white-skinned'; 'delicately nurtured' is what it implies, for in pastoral societies not to be sun-tanned is a sign of wealth and rank. But the Oghuz ladies have great freedom and do not sit quietly in their tents all the time. Prince Bay Bijan, in Chapter 3, prays for a daughter and his prayer is granted. The daughter, the Lady Chichek, is 'purer than the moon, lovelier than the sun', but she is also a first-rate horsewoman, archer, and

wrestler. In Chapter 4, Lady Burla takes an active part in rescuing her son from the infidel; it is she who strikes the enemy standard down with her sword. In Chapter 6, Kan Turali's ideal bride (though admittedly he has to go outside the Oghuz to find her) is one who 'before I reach the bloody infidels' land must already have got there and brought me back some heads.' The 'withering scourge' in Chapter 13 complains that since her marriage to her unsatisfactory husband she has never had a yashmak, but the yashmak could be an aid to coquetry as well as to modesty, and her words do not indicate the existence of a system of purdah. The same applies to the reference in Chapter 3 to the ladies laughing behind their yashmaks, especially in view of what is said there about the behaviour of two of the ladies.

The houses in which the heroes and heroines live are tents, of the type used by the modern Turcoman tribes; they are made of felt, laid over a wooden frame in the shape of a beehive. The tents in the stories are splendid and ornate, as befits their heroic occupants; the very smoke-holes are described as 'golden', presumably meaning that they were surrounded by a golden frame.

Although the stories have been given an Islamic colouring, they are full of references to the most ancient practices, some going back to the time when the religion of the Turks was shamanist. On the death of a hero, his relatives slaughter his horses and give a funeral feast (Chapters 4 and 10). The dying Beyrek (Chapter 12) asks for his horse's tail to be cut off. A boy is not given a name until he has distinguished himself in battle. The antiquity of this last practice is shown by the occurrence in the old inscriptions of such statements as 'my manhood-name is Yaruk Tegin' and 'my young brother's manhood-name became Köl Tegin'. When the characters are distressed they weep bloody tears; this is not entirely metaphorical, for at Turkish funerals in ancient times the mourners would gash their faces and let the blood mingle with their tears.

Not much perspicacity is required to see that the Islamic colouring has been superimposed on stories that are basically pre-Islamic. The enemy throughout is equated with 'the infidel', and when the heroes are in trouble they invoke the Prophet Muhammad and perform the rites of Muslim prayer. But there is no mention of their doing so when they are not in trouble. They are monogamous, they eat horse-meat, which most Muslims will not do (although it is not forbidden in the Koran), and they drink wine and kumis, fermented mare's milk. Several of the Islamic references in the stories betoken a not very profound understanding of Muslim belief and practice (see notes 66, 150, 151), and part of the fun of Chapter 5 is the hero's lack of the most elementary religious knowledge. The verses descriptive of early morning, which occur twice in Chapter 1, include the line 'When the long-bearded Persian calls to prayer'. Although this shows that the Turks were not strangers to Islam when this line was composed, it also shows that they were as yet only newcomers to it.

Dede Korkut, after whom the book is named, is the soothsayer, high priest and bard (*ozan*) of the Oghuz. *Dede* ('Grandfather') is still heard in Turkey as a title of popular saints and holy men. It is he who gives the young men their names when they have proved themselves, it is to him that the Oghuz turn in time of trouble, for advice and practical help. At the gatherings of the Oghuz he plays his lute (*kopuz*), an instrument of which legend names him the inventor. In Chapter 10, Egrek finds his brother sleeping and takes his lute from him. Segrek wakes up and is about to strike him with his sword (the brothers have never met), but sees that he is holding the lute. 'I do not strike you,' says Segrek, 'out of respect for the lute of Dede Korkut. If you were not holding the lute I should have split you in two.'

There is no need to go deeply into the question of whether Dede Korkut was a real person; certainly there is no evidence that he was not. The historian Rashid al-Din (d. 1318) says that he lived for 295 years; that he appeared in the time of the Oghuz ruler Inal Syr Yavkuy Khan, by whom he was sent on an embassy to the Prophet; that he became a Muslim; that he gave advice to the Great Khan of the Oghuz, attended the election of the Great Khan, and gave names to children.

The modern Turcomans and Kazak-Kirghiz have a proverbial saying, 'Don't dig Korkut's grave', apparently meaning 'don't waste time trying to do the impossible', and explained as alluding to his longevity or (a minority opinion, this,) his superhuman stature. Alternatively, the saying may mean 'don't waste time doing what has already been done'; this is suggested by the nightmarish Central Asian legend that he lived far beyond the usual span and wherever he went he saw gravediggers at work. When he asked 'Whose grave is this?' they would reply, 'There is a man called Korkut who is looking for his grave, and here it is.' So he would run away, but in whatever place he sought refuge he would encounter exactly the same scene and the same answer. Eventually, at the age of 300, he died by one such grave. There is a tomb of his near the town named after him, Khorkhut, on the railway between Novokazalinsk and Kizil-Orda in Kazakhstan, about 150 miles east of the Aral Sea. Another of his tombs was reported by at least two seventeenth-century visitors to Derbent in Daghestan. An attempt has been made by one scholar to equate him with the Korghut who led a revolt of some of the Oghuz against the Seljuk Sultan Senjer in Khorasan in 1153. But this Korghut's father was a Muslim, as is shown by his name, Abd al-Hamid, and no one who reads the stories will find it easy to accept our Dede Korkut as a Muslim born. The name Korkut was in fact quite common, which is not surprising in view of the legendary and proverbial fame of this particular bearer of it.

In four of the twelve stories we are expressly told that Dede Korkut 'strung together this tale of the Oghuz'. On the other hand, the stories as written do not purport to come first-hand from him. A study of the final paragraphs of the stories shows this; Dede Korkut puts the stories together out of contemporary events, in many of which he participates, but half of the stories conclude with a verse beginning, with slight variations, 'Where now are the valiant princes of whom I have told ... Doom has taken them, earth has hidden them'; these cannot be the words of Dede Korkut. One could counter this argument by saying that as Dede Korkut lived a preternaturally long life

he might be able to speak of his erstwhile comrades as all being
dead, but his proverbial longevity is nowhere referred to in the
book. His words at the end of Chapter 5 (see also Chapter 7)
are suggestive: 'Let this story be known as the Story of Wild
Dumrul. After me let the brave bards tell it and the generous
heroes of untarnished honour listen to it.' We may infer that
the real narrator is one of the 'brave bards', an *ozan*, who may
or may not have been the *ozan* who speaks, in Chapter 13, 'from
the tongue of Dede Korkut'.

We are unlikely ever to know who it was who compiled the
book. Clearly he was a gifted story-teller, with a considerable
poetic talent. The stories are in prose interspersed with rhythmic, alliterative, and assonant or rhyming passages of *soylama*,
'declamation'. The level of the language fluctuates, now highly
poetic and dignified, now racy and colloquial. I have en-
deavoured to reproduce the effect of this in the translation. The
characters live: Kazan, who cheerfully pretends to necrophily
in order to secure his release from imprisonment; the chivalrous
Beyrek, who goes to his death rather than betray his Khan; the
unpredictable Crazy Karchar, whom Dede Korkut tames with
the help of some voracious fleas; and many more whom the
reader will meet. Even the monster Goggle-eye is not just a
bogyman; he has a distinct personality, which emerges most
clearly in his terrible dying confession 'I meant to ... break my
pact with the nobles of the teeming Oghuz, ... to have once
more my fill of man-meat.' The heroines are unforgettable: the
brave and queenly Lady Burla, the spirited and lovely Saljan
and Chichek, and the not-quite-heroine Boghazja Fatima of the
forty lovers.

Gifted as the story-teller was, however, as an editor he had
his shortcomings. The list of nobles and the description of the
battle in Chapter 4 are almost word for word the same as in
Chapter 2. Kazan kills the infidel King Shökli twice: he runs
him through and cuts off his head in Chapter 2, cuts off his
head again in Chapter 3, and spills his blood and captures him
in Chapter 4, while in Chapter 9 Shökli escapes death by turning Muslim. In Chapter 1, Dirse Khan's son is given his name

by Dede Korkut after he has killed the bull, but it is not until Chapter 3 that we are told 'In those days, my lords, until a boy cut off heads and spilled blood they used not to give him a name.' Nor is there any uniformity about this: in Chapter 4, Uruz is so called at a time when, as we are expressly told, he had not yet cut off heads or spilled blood. So too with Egrek in Chapter 10. Uruz speaks of his mother as 'white-haired' and 'aged', which she shows no signs of being, and Kazan speaks of himself as 'white-bearded' while he is obviously in the prime of life; these must be stock epithets. Beyrek in Chapter 3 mentions his father's 'swan-like daughters and daughters-in-law', though Beyrek was an only son and not yet married. Similarly Begil in Chapter 9 speaks of his 'white-skinned daughters and daughters-in-law', although his only son Emren is not married until the very end of the story.

The story with most loose ends is that of Beyrek (Chapter 3), doubtless because he is a famous folk-hero and elements from several stories about him have been brought together here. He was betrothed in infancy to the infant daughter of Bay Bijan, but still has to wring permission to marry her from her jealous and formidable brother. It then turns out that her father has promised her to the infidel lord of Bayburt Castle, though at no stage does anyone reproach him for this duplicity. After sixteen years of captivity, during which he seems to have been in excellent spirits, Beyrek suddenly decides to escape at the suggestion of his captor's daughter. I shall not spoil the story for the reader by disclosing here the most startling discrepancy of all.

The story of Goggle-eye (Chapter 8) also exhibits some anomalies, which are discussed in the notes.* This story incorporates many elements of the story of the Cyclops as told in Book ix of the *Odyssey*. Much ink has been spilled over the puzzle of how the Homeric tale found its way into the *Book of Dede Korkut*; a summary of the discussion will be found in the paper cited in the footnote. An account of folktale variants

* For a full analysis, see C. S. Mundy, 'Polyphemus and Tepegöz', in *Bulletin of the School of Oriental and African Studies*, xviii (1956), 279-302.

of the Homeric story is given in Merry and Riddell's *Odyssey*
(Oxford, 1886), I, Appendix II, from which we learn, among
other things, that the episode of the magic ring, which
is not in Homer, occurs in a Rumanian and a twelfth-century
Latin version, while the 'No-man' episode, which does not come
in our story, is found only in an Estonian version. Merry and
Riddell, like Wilhelm Grimm before them, thought that the
Cyclops story was not of a piece with the rest of the *Odyssey*,
though they did not go as far as Grimm in asserting that the
folktales (including the *Dede Korkut* version) and the Homeric
story derived from a common source. But as there are some
other clear echoes of the *Odyssey* in the story of Beyrek (Chapter
3), it is simpler to suppose that they and the story of Goggle-eye
derive ultimately from Homer. The alternative is to imagine that
Homer borrowed some themes which he found circulating orally
round western Asia Minor and which, still circulating after
two millennia, were borrowed once more, this time by the unknown Turkish author of the *Book of Dede Korkut* in the east
of the country. Well, it is not impossible.

Another story in our book which appears to have a link with
the classical world is the story of Wild Dumrul (Chapter 5), in
which the hero's wife, like Alcestis, offers to die in place of her
husband; whether this is a genuine link or the result of coincidence is an open question.

It would obviously facilitate the dating if we could positively
identify any character in the book with a historical figure.
Unfortunately this does not seem possible. Bayindir, for example,
may well have been a real person, but when all we have to go
on is a mass of legend and an Ottoman genealogist's assertion
that he was a descendant in the fifth generation from Noah, we
cannot use him as a peg to fix a date on. The same applies to
the statement by a seventeenth-century historian that Salur
Kazan lived 300 years after the Prophet; this could be true, but
we have no way of knowing. The one character who at first
sight appears to be dateable is Kan Turali, in Chapter 6, who
wins the beautiful Princess Saljan of Trebizond.

In the fourteenth century, a federation of Oghuz, or, as they were by this time termed, Turcoman tribesmen, who called themselves *Ak-koyunlu*, 'The Men of the White Sheep' (possibly for totemistic reasons), gradually gained control of the region of Diyarbakr and the Upper Euphrates. Eventually they established a dynasty which ruled eastern Turkey, Iraq and western Iran, until its power was broken, in the west by the Ottoman Sultan Mehmet II (in 1473) and in the east by Shah Ismail (in 1508). In the 1340s, an Ak-koyunlu chief named Tur Ali several times raided the Greek Empire of Trebizond. In August 1352, to avoid further trouble, the Emperor Alexios III Comnenos gave his sister Maria in marriage to Tur Ali's son Kutlugh. It is pleasant to be able to record that the Greek princess and the Turkish prince lived happily ever after; when they had been married for thirteen years they paid a visit to Trebizond, which the Emperor reciprocated in the following year. And in due course their son Kara Ilig (or Yülük), who became the first Ak-koyunlu Sultan, married one of his Greek cousins.

Now if we find a storybook Turali who marries a princess of Trebizond, are we not bound to equate him with a real-life son of Tur Ali who also marries a princess of Trebizond? The reader must judge for himself; my own opinion is that we are not. If the story-teller was drawing on a historical incident, why did he get the names wrong? It may be argued that the names were deliberately changed; however free-and-easy a popular story-teller might be with his chronology, he could hardly put a mid-fourteenth-century couple into the same tale as Dede Korkut who lived 'close to the time of the Prophet', 700 years before. But why in that case should he substitute for Kutlugh's name the name of his father, and above all why should he change Maria into Saljan, which does not even sound like a Greek name? To my mind, this last point alone is enough to show that the story-teller was not writing about a real princess of Trebizond. My belief is that Saljan is the original name of the heroine; that the only substitution has been to put Trebizond in place of the name of some other 'infidel' city a good deal further east, near the earlier homeland of the Oghuz, perhaps because the wedding of Kutlugh and Maria was, so to speak, in the news; but that apart from this there is no reason to suppose the story to be based on any historical incident.

What looks like another possible peg for dating turns out to be equally insubstantial. Bayburt, which is spoken of as an infidel city in Chapter 3, was in Turkish hands from 1071, except for a few years at the end of the eleventh century when it was recaptured by the Byzantines. We might therefore be tempted to say that the parts of the story relating to Bayburt must have been composed before the beginning of the twelfth century, but they could equally well have been composed much later, by someone who was making up a story about the olden days without bothering about historical accuracy. Alternatively, as I have postulated in the case of Trebizond, 'Bayburt' may have replaced the name of some earlier city, similarly without regard for historical accuracy.

Leaving aside Chapters 3, 5, 8, and probably 6, as being timeless romances, the substratum of the stories is the struggles of the Oghuz in Central Asia in the eighth to eleventh centuries against their Turkish cousins the Pecheneks and the Kipchaks (note the reference in Chapter 2 to Kara Budak 'who made King Kipchak of the iron bow vomit blood'). It is significant that the 'infidels' are given Turkish-sounding names: Kara Tüken, Boghajuk, and so on. Incidentally, a Byzantine source mentions a late-ninth-century Pechenek chieftain named Korkut. Whereas the Oghuz were predominantly Muslim by the early years of the eleventh century, the Pecheneks did not accept Islam till the end of that century, and the Kipchaks not for another fifty years or so after them. This does not mean that we can pin down the Oghuz wars against the 'infidel' in our stories to the time in the eleventh and early twelfth centuries when the Pecheneks and Kipchaks could rightly be so termed, because the Islamic word for 'infidel', which cannot be part of the oldest substratum, has no doubt replaced an earlier word for 'enemy'.

This substratum has been overlaid with more recent memories of campaigns in the Ak-koyunlu period against the Georgians, the Abkhaz (see note 60), and the Greeks of Trebizond. The Ak-koyunlu Sultans claimed descent from Bayindir Khan and it is likely, on the face of it, that the *Book of Dede Korkut* was composed under their patronage. The snag about this is that in the Ak-koyunlu genealogy Bayindir's father is named as Gök ('Sky') Khan, son of the eponymous Oghuz Khan, whereas in our book he is named as Kam Ghan, a name otherwise unknown. In default of any better explanation, I therefore incline to the belief that the book was composed before the Ak-koyunlu rulers had decided who their ancestors were. It was in 1403 that they ceased to be tribal chiefs and became Sultans, so we may assume that their official genealogy was formulated round about that date. In sum, I would put the date of compilation fairly early in the fifteenth century at the latest.

Before we leave the question of dating, a word must be said about the two manuscripts on which our knowledge of the book depends. One, in the Royal Library of Dresden, was made known to the modern world by H. F. von Diez in 1815. The second was discovered in the library of the Vatican by Ettore Rossi in 1950; it contains only six of the twelve stories, in the following order: 1, 3, 2, 4, 7, 12. Neither manuscript is dated, but both are of the sixteenth century; Rossi inclined to consider the Vatican MS a little older than the Dresden, on palaeographic grounds. He published a facsimile of his find, with a long introduction and a translation of the complete work, in 1952.* Six years later there appeared the first of two volumes by Muharrem Ergin, in which are given facsimiles of both MSS, and a transcribed text and *apparatus criticus* in Latin characters. His second volume, containing a glossary, came out in 1963.†

Ergin calls his work a critical edition, which it is not and could not be (even if he had not used as his text the readings of one MS, relegating those of the other to the footnotes), since the two, or rather one and a half, manuscripts are not copies of one original which might be reconstructed from them; the divergences between them are far greater than those commonly found

* Ettore Rossi, *Il "Kitāb-i Dede Qorqut"* (Vatican City, 1952).
† Muharrem Ergin, *Dede Korkut Kitabı* (Ankara, 1958, 1963).

between two different manuscripts of a literary text. This is precisely what one would expect if a cycle of stories that had long been transmitted orally, with much time-honoured phraseology but also with variations introduced by different narrators, happened to be twice recorded in writing. Ergin takes the view that the book must have been composed in the middle or second half of the fifteenth century, because the reference in the 'Preface' (my Chapter 13) to the Ottomans suggests a time when that dynasty had begun to grow strong in Anatolia. As we shall presently see, however, the 'Preface' has no relation to the stories beyond the fact that it talks of Dede Korkut. Moreover, the reference to the Ottomans is suspect, to say the least; see note 140. And if we are going to be fundamentalist about the text, the reference in Chapter 3 to Istanbul as a market for infidel goods points to a date before 1453.

Another Turkish scholar, Faruk Sümer, originally believed that the work was committed to writing in the second half of the fifteenth century, but in his recent book on the Oghuz* he prefers a later date, on the grounds that (*a*) in Chapter 4 there is a mention of the Fortress of Barehead Dadian, 'Barehead' being a nickname of Bagrat, King of the Georgians, which occurs for the first time in a sixteenth-century work, and that (*b*) a number of Ottoman administrative terms appear which did not come into use until the sixteenth century. From this he concludes that the stories were written in the second half of the sixteenth century, in the area of Ottoman domination. Even if we accept it as fact that the term 'Barehead' in this context was not used before the sixteenth century, all we can conclude is that neither of the two manuscripts could have been written before the sixteenth century, which we knew anyway. That a given work could not have existed before the date of the earliest extant manuscript is a startling principle, previously unknown to scholarship. For there is a vast difference between saying that a text of an ancient work dates from a particular time and saying that the work itself dates from that time. This is especially so in the case of a book such as this, which is the product of

* Faruk Sümer, *Oğuzlar* (Ankara, 1965, 2nd edn 1972).

a long series of narrators, any of whom could have made altera-
tions and additions, right down to the two sixteenth-century
scribes who wrote our two manuscripts and who may well have
inserted some contemporary words in them. Would one make
assumptions about the architecture of ancient Bethlehem on the
evidence of a sixteenth-century Dutch Nativity?

We in fact know that a version of at least one of the stories
(Chapter 8) existed in writing at the beginning of the fourteenth
century, from an unpublished Arabic history, Dawadari's *Durar
al-Tijan*, written in Egypt some time between 1309 and 1340.
It speaks of

a book called the *Oghuzname* which goes from hand to hand among
the Oghuz Turks. In this book occurs the story of a person named
Dabakuz who ravaged the lands of the early Turks and killed their
great men. They say he was an ugly and loathsome man with a
single eye on the top of his head. No sword or spear had any effect
on him. His mother was a demon of the ocean and his father's
bonnet was of the skins of ten rams so as to cover his head. They
have many well-known tales and stories about him, which circulate
among them to this day and are learned by heart by their sagacious
men who are skilled in the playing of their lute [*kopuz*].

Chapter 13, which I call 'The Wisdom of Dede Korkut',
comes at the beginning of both manuscripts and at first glance
could be taken for a preface to the stories, but it is not, and I
have put it at the end. It consists of five parts. The first tells
briefly who Dede Korkut was and quotes him as prophesying
that the Ottoman dynasty would reign for ever; this portion is
clearly of later origin than the stories. The second is a series
of proverbs attributed to Dede Korkut, at least one of which
belongs to the Turcoman period rather than to the Oghuz period
in which the stories are set. It is the one which runs 'The black
tents to which no guest comes were better destroyed.' In the
stories the tents are normally white; compare note 154. The
third part is a string of gnomic utterances designed to persuade
the bard's audience to reward him generously; this may well
have been a standard conclusion to the bard's performance. The
fourth is a list of 'beautiful' beings and things, the product of a

Turcoman environment whose Islam was more devout than
scholarly. Like the fourth, the final part, with its amusing
description of four kinds of wife, does not seem to belong to
the heroic age.

As to the language of the text, it is consistent with the book's
belonging to the late fourteenth or early fifteenth century. It
exhibits a number of features characteristic of Azeri, the Turkish
dialect of Azerbaijan, side by side with certain western features,
the latter being more frequent in the Vatican MS. The origins
of the text lie back in the time before Azeri and Ottoman
emerged as separate dialects. But it is unwise to try to draw
conclusions from linguistic evidence about the time or place of
the compilation of the book, as we cannot know whether any
given feature is due to the compiler or to subsequent bards and
copyists.

In view of the sometimes wide divergences between the two
MSS, I have felt myself at liberty to range from one to the
other, choosing the fuller version wherever possible. Some of
the more interesting variants are mentioned in the notes at the
end of the book.

When dealing with proper names, I have avoided what one
may call the 'Lady Precious Stream' technique. Most Turkish
names, ancient and modern, are susceptible of translation, but
one would not turn such modern names as Abdürrahman
Aydemir and Taner Olguner into 'Slave-of-the-Compassionate
Moon-iron' and 'Dawn-hero Mature-man', since what these
English renderings connote is not what the originals convey to a
Turkish ear. So I have left Ters Uzamish in Chapter 10 as
Ters Uzamish and have not turned him into Stretched-out
Contrariwise, and the heroine of Chapter 3 is Chichek and not
Flower, while the villain of the same story appears as Yaltajuk
son of Yalanji and not as Little Toady son of Liar. I have, how-
ever, translated *Kara* as 'Black' when it is part of a title rather
than of a name, so 'the Black King' for Kara Tekür. Otherwise I
have departed from this principle only in one instance: the
monster in Chapter 8 is called Goggle-eye and not Tepegöz. The
reason is that this Turkish name is pretty certainly, as Mundy

points out, a corruption by popular etymology of the last three syllables of the Greek *Sarandápekhos*, 'Forty-cubits' and so 'Giant'. Tepegöz to a Turkish ear means 'Head-eye' or 'Apex-eye'; I arrived at 'Goggle-eye' after rejecting 'Top-eye' as sounding too much like Popeye.

One or two other terms call for a word of comment. *Delü*, in later Turkish *deli*, which I have rendered sometimes by 'wild', sometimes by 'crazy', meant something very much like berserker; indeed, were it not for the incongruity of the Icelandic word in a Turkish setting I should have used it. *Koja*, which I have left in its original form, meant 'old'. The two brothers whom Dede Korkut assigns to cook for Goggle-eye are Yünlü Koja and Yapaghilu Koja; being old men they were presumably too tough for him to eat. The vocabulary of abuse in the book is virtually confined to the one word *kavat*, still used in provincial Turkey for 'pimp', 'pander', 'person without honour'. I have varied the translation a little.

The notes at the end include such information and conjecture as is available about unfamiliar place-names, though it will be appreciated that some of the places mentioned in the stories are as mysterious as Camelot or lost Atlantis. The most thorough study of the geography of *Dede Korkut* is M. Fahrettin Kır-zıoğlu's *Dede-Korkut Oğuznâmeleri* (Istanbul, 1952). I have not given a bibliography, because, with the exception of the few books and articles in western languages which I have mentioned in the notes, most of the work on *Dede Korkut* has been done by Turkish scholars writing in Turkish. Any of my readers who knows Turkish and seeks bibliographical guidance will find it in the works of Rossi and Ergin cited above and in Orhan Şaik Gökyay's *Dede Korkut* (Istanbul, 1938). My professional colleagues will recognize my indebtedness to these three scholars and to the many more whose writings they mention in their books. Several problems of translation were resolved for me in the closing stages of the work by the timely appearance of Sir Gerard Clauson's *Etymological Dictionary of Pre-Thirteenth-Century Turkish* (Oxford, 1972). Now let me stand no longer between the reader and the heroic world of Dede Korkut.

G.L.L.

THE BOOK OF
DEDE KORKUT

TELLS THE STORY OF BOGHACH KHAN SON OF DIRSE KHAN, O MY KHAN![1]

ONE day Bayindir Khan son of Kam Ghan rose up from his place. He had his striped parasol set up on the earth's face, his many-coloured pavilion reared up to the face of the sky. In a thousand places silken rugs were spread. Once a year the Khan of Khans, Bayindir Khan, used to make a feast and entertain the Oghuz nobles. This year again he made a feast and had his men slaughter of horses the stallions, of camels the males, of sheep the rams.[2] He had a white tent pitched in one place, a red in another, a black in another. He gave orders thus: 'Put any-one who has no sons or daughters in the black tent. Spread black felt beneath him. Set before him mutton-stew made from the black sheep. If he will eat it, he may; if he will not, he can get up and go. Put him who has a son in the white tent, him who has a daughter in the red tent. But him who has neither, God Most High has humiliated, and we shall humiliate him too; let him mark this well.'

The Oghuz nobles came one by one and began to assemble. Now it seems there was a noble called Dirse Khan, who had no son or daughter.

When the winds of dawn blow cold,
When the bearded grey lark is singing,
When the Arab steeds see their master and neigh,
When the long-bearded Persian recites the call to prayer,
When white begins to be distinguishable from black,
When the sun touches the great mountains with their lovely
    folds,
When the heroic warrior chieftains come together,

at break of day Dirse Khan rose up from his place, called his forty warriors[3] to his side and came to Bayindir Khan's feast. Bayindir Khan's young men met Dirse Khan and brought him to the black tent. Beneath him they spread black felt, before him they set mutton-stew made from the black sheep. Said Dirse Khan, 'What shortcoming has Bayindir Khan seen in me, whether in my sword or in my table? Baser men than I he puts in the white tent and the red tent. What is my offence that he puts me in the black tent?' 'Lord,' they said, 'the order this day from Bayindir Khan is this. He has said, "Him who has no son or daughter God Most High has humiliated, and we shall humiliate him too."' Dirse Khan stood and said, 'Up, my warriors; rise from your place. This mysterious affliction of mine is due either to me or to my wife.'

Dirse Khan came home. He called to his wife, declaiming; let us see, my Khan, what he declaimed.

> 'Come here, luck of my head, throne of my house,
>   Like a cypress when you go out walking.
>   Your black hair entwines itself round your heels,
>   Your meeting eyebrows are like a drawn bow,
>   Your mouth is too tiny to hold twin almonds,
>   Your red cheeks are like autumn apples,
>   My sugar-melon, my honey-melon, my musk-melon.

'Do you know what has befallen? Bayindir Khan rose up and had three tents pitched; one white, one red, one black. He said: "Put the father of sons in the white tent, the father of daughters in the red tent, and him who is father of none in the black tent. Spread black felt beneath him, set before him mutton-stew made from the black sheep. If he will eat it, he may; if he will not, he can get up and go. Any man who has neither son nor daughter, God Most High has humiliated, and we shall humiliate him too." When I arrived they met me and put me in the black tent, they spread black felt beneath me, they set before me mutton-stew of the black sheep, and they said: "Him who has no son or daughter, God Most High has humiliated, and we shall humiliate him too; mark this well." Is it your fault or my fault? Why does God Most High not give us a fine hefty son?' said he, and he declaimed:

> 'Princess, shall I rise up?
> Shall I seize you by the collar and throat?
> Shall I cast you beneath my hard heel?
> Shall I draw my black steel sword?
> Shall I cut your head from your body?
> Shall I show you how sweet life is?[4]
> Shall I spill your red blood on the ground?
> Princess, tell me the reason.
> Mighty the anger I shall now vent on you.'

When he said this, great sorrow came over his wife; her black almond eyes filled with bloody tears and she said, 'My Khan, it is neither from me nor from you, but from the God who stands above us both.' Then she declaimed; let us see, my Khan, what she declaimed.

> 'Dirse Khan, don't be angry with me;
> Don't be vexed and speak bitter words.
> Rise and bestir yourself; have the tents of many colours
> Set up on the earth's face. Have your men slaughter
> Of horses the stallions, of camels the males, of sheep the
>   rams.
> Gather round you the nobles of the Inner Oghuz and the
>   Outer Oghuz.
> When you see the hungry, fill him;
> When you see the naked, clothe him;
> Save the debtor from his debt.
> Heap up meat in hillocks; let lakes of kumis be drawn.[5]
> Make an enormous feast, then ask what you want and let
>   them pray.
> So, with prayerful mouths singing your praises,
> God may grant us a fine hefty child.'

Dirse Khan, at his wife's word, made an enormous feast and asked what he wanted. He had slaughtered of horses the stallions, of camels the males, of sheep the rams. He summoned

the nobles of the Inner Oghuz and the Outer Oghuz. When he
saw the hungry, he fed him; when he saw the naked, he clothed
him. He saved the debtor from his debt. He heaped up meat in
hillocks, he milked lakes of kumis. They raised their hands and
asked for what he wanted. With prayerful mouths singing his
praise, God Most High granted them a child; his wife became
pregnant and some time later she bore him a son. She gave her
baby to the nurses and let them look after him. The horse's hoof
is fleet as the wind; the minstrel's tongue is swift as a bird.[6]
The one with ribs gets bigger, the one with breast-bones grows
greater.[7] He reached his fifteenth year, when his father went to
join Bayindir Khan's horde.

Now it seems, my Khan, that Bayindir Khan had a bull and a
camel. If that bull gored a hard rock it would crumble like
flour. Once in the summer, once in the autumn, they used to
let the bull and the camel fight, while Bayinder Khan and the
nobles of the teeming Oghuz would watch and enjoy themselves. Now, once again, in the summer they brought the bull
out of the palace. Three men held him with iron chains on his
right, three men on his left. They came and released him in the
middle of the arena. Well now, my Sultan, Dirse Khan's young
son and three boys of the army were playing knuckle-bones in
that arena. When the men released the bull, they said to the
boys 'Run!' The other three boys ran, but Dirse Khan's son
did not run; he stayed there watching, in the middle of the
white arena. And the bull charged the boy, bent on destroying
him. The boy gave the bull a merciless punch on the forehead
and the bull went sliding on his rump. Again he came and
charged the boy. Again the boy gave him a mighty punch on
the forehead, but this time he kept his fist pressed against the
bull's forehead and shoved him to the end of the arena. Then
they struggled together. The boy's shoulders were covered with
the bull's foam. Neither the boy nor the bull could gain the
victory. Then the boy thought, 'People put a pole against a
roof to hold it up. Why am I standing here propping up this
creature's forehead?' He removed his fist from the bull's forehead and stepped aside. The bull could not stand on its feet

and collapsed headlong. The boy drew his knife and cut off the bull's head. The Oghuz nobles crowded round the boy, crying 'Well done! Let Dede Korkut come and give this boy a name; let him go with the boy to his father and ask him to make his son a prince. He should have a throne at once.' They called Dede Korkut and he came. He took the boy and went to the boy's father, to whom he declaimed; let us see, my Khan, what he declaimed.

'O Dirse Khan, make this boy a prince!
Give him a throne; well does he merit it.
Give long-necked Arab chargers to this boy
That he may ride; he is resourceful.
Give this boy ten thousand sheep from your folds
As meat for his spits; well does he merit it.
Give this boy red camels from your herds
To bear his burdens; he is resourceful.
Give this boy a gold-capped pavilion
To be his shade; well does he merit it.
Give this boy robes with birds on the shoulder
To be his dress; he is resourceful.

'This boy fought on Bayindir Khan's white arena and killed a bull. Let your son's name be Boghach, Bull-man. Now I have given him his name and may God give him his life.' So Dirse Khan made the boy a prince and gave him a throne.

The boy ascended the throne, and his father's forty warriors were forgotten. Those forty warriors grew jealous and they said to one another, 'Since this boy appeared, Dirse Khan has had little regard for us. Come, let us speak evil of him to his father so that he kills him, and our respect and honour may be great again in the father's eyes, and even greater.'

The forty warriors divided into two groups of twenty. The first twenty went and gave this report to Dirse Khan: 'Do you know what has happened, Dirse Khan? Your son – may he not prosper, may he have no joy of it – has turned out wicked and evil. He led out his forty young men and marched against the teeming Oghuz. Wherever a beautiful girl appeared he

dragged her off, he reviled white-bearded elders, he tore the
hair of white-haired women.[8] The news will cross the limpid
flowing rivers, the tidings will climb the many-coloured mountain that lies askew,[9] the news will reach the Great Khan Bayindir. "Such and such monstrous evil has Dirse Khan's son
wrought," they will say. It will be better for you to die than to
walk alive. Bayindir Khan will summon you, he will be fiercely
angry with you. What good is such a son to you? Better no son
than such a son. Kill him!' they said. 'Go,' said Dirse Khan,
'bring that boy and I shall kill him.' At that moment the other
twenty unmanly scoundrels appeared and they too brought a
lying tale: 'Dirse Khan, your son rose up, he went out to the
chase on the great mountain with its lovely folds. While you
were here he hunted after game, he hawked after fowl, and
brought them to his mother. He took and drank of the strong
red wine, he talked like a lover to his mother, he had designs
on his mother, he laid hands on his mother. Your son has turned
out wicked and evil. The news will cross the many-coloured
mountain that lies askew, the·news will reach Bayindir Khan.
"Such and such monstrous evil has Dirse Khan's son wrought",
they will say. You will be summoned. Wrath will fall on you
from Bayindir Khan. What good is such a son to you? Kill
him!' 'Go,' said Dirse Khan, 'bring him and I shall kill him. I
have no need of such a son.' His vassals replied, 'How are we
to bring your son? Your son won't take orders from us, he
won't come here at our word. Rise up, speak winningly to your
warriors and lead them out. Find your son and take him with
you hunting. While you are hunting after game, and hawking,
contrive to shoot an arrow into your son and kill him. If you
don't kill him in this way, you will not be able to kill him in
any other way, be sure of that!'

When the winds of dawn blow cold,
When the bearded grey lark is singing,
When the Arab steeds see their master and neigh,
When the long-bearded Persian recites the call to prayer,
When white begins to be distinguishable from black,

When the daughters and daughters-in-law of the teeming
   Oghuz adorn themselves,
When the sun touches the great mountains with their lovely
   folds,
When the heroic warrior chieftains come together,

at break of day Dirse Khan rose up from his place. He took his
own dear son with him, he called his warriors to his side and
went out hunting. They hunted game, they hawked after fowl.
One of those forty treacherous scoundrels approached the boy
and said, 'These are your father's words: "Let him chase the
stags and drive them and kill them before me; I would see how
my son rides and handles a sword and shoots, then I shall be
glad and proud and confident."' How was the boy to know? He
was chasing and driving the stags and hamstringing them before
his father, saying, 'Let my father watch my riding and be
proud; let him watch me shoot, and be confident; let him
watch me handle my sword, and be glad.' Those forty
treacherous scoundrels said, 'Do you see the boy, Dirse Khan?
He is chasing the stags over field and plain and driving them
before you. Be on your guard! He will pretend to shoot the
stag, but it is you he will kill. Before he can kill you, see that
you kill him!' As the boy chased the stag, he kept passing in
front of his father. Dirse Khan took up his strong bow, strung
with wolf-sinew. He rose up in his stirrups and drew mightily
and shot far; the arrow struck the boy between the shoulder-
blades and felled him. Deep went the arrow, the red blood
welled forth and his bosom was filled with it. Clasping the
neck of his Arab horse, he slid to the ground. Dirse Khan
wanted to fall sobbing on his own dear son, but those forty
treacherous scoundrels would not let him. He turned his horse's
head and started back to his camp.

Dirse Khan's lady, because this was her son's first hunt, had
them slaughter of horses the stallions, of camels the males, of
sheep the rams, to feast the nobles of the teeming Oghuz. She
gathered herself and rose up, she called her forty slender maidens
to her side and went to meet Dirse Khan. She raised her head

and looked at Dirse Khan's face. She turned her gaze to right and left, but did not see her own dear son. Her inward parts quaked, her whole heart pounded, her black almond eyes filled with bloody tears. She called out to Dirse Khan, declaiming; let us see, my Khan, what she declaimed.

'Come here, luck of my head, throne of my house,
 Son-in-law of the Khan my father,
 Dear to the Queen my mother,
 You to whom my parents gave me,
 You whom I see when I open my eyes,
 To whom I gave my heart in love,
 O Dirse Khan!
 You rose up from your place,
 You leaped onto your black-maned Kazilik [10] horse,
 You went hunting over the great mountain with its lovely
   folds.
 Two you went and one you come; where is my child?
 Where is the son I conceived in the dark of night?
 May my eye which sees come out, O Dirse Khan; dread-
   fully it quivers.
 May my vein of milk be stopped, which suckled my son;
   dreadfully it aches.
 The yellow snake has not stung me but my white body is
   swollen.
 I do not see my only son and my heart is aflame.
 I sent water into the parched channels,
 I gave to the black-garbed dervishes the promised offerings.
 When I saw the hungry I fed them,
 When I saw the naked I clothed them.
 Meat I heaped up in hillocks, lakes of kumis I drew.
 By the people's prayers, arduously, I conceived a son.
 O Dirse Khan, give me news of our only son.
 If you have hurled our only son down from yonder many-
   coloured mountain,
 If you have sent him floating down the rapid swirling
   water, tell me.

If you have let him be eaten by lions and tigers, tell me.
If you have left him captive to the black-garbed infidel of
    savage religion, tell me.
I shall go to the Khan my father,
I shall take loads of treasure and many soldiers,
I shall go to the infidel of savage religion.
Until I am cut to pieces and fall from my Kazilik horse,
Until I have wiped my red blood on the neck of my dress,
Until I am hacked limb from limb and drop on the earth,
I shall not turn back from the road my only son has taken.
O Dirse Khan, tell me what has happened to my only son
And my dark head be a sacrifice for you this day.'

So saying she lamented and wept. Dirse Khan did not
answer his lady, but those forty treacherous scoundrels came to
her and said, 'Your son is alive and well; he is hunting. He'll
come soon, today or tomorrow. Don't be frightened, don't be
worried; your lord is drunk, that is why he cannot answer.'

Dirse Khan's lady turned away. She could not bear it; she
called her forty slender maidens to her side, she mounted her
Arab horse and went in quest of her dear son. She reached
Kazilik Mountain, whose ice and snow do not melt in winter or
summer, and she climbed it. Up she galloped, from the lowlands to the high places. She looked and saw that crows and
ravens were alighting in a valley and rising, settling and flying
up. She spurred her Arab horse and rode in that direction.

Now, my Sultan, that was the place where the boy had been
laid low. The crows and ravens, seeing blood, wanted to settle
on him, but he had two small dogs, who kept chasing them
away and would not permit them to settle. As the boy lay there,
Khizr[11] on his grey horse appeared to him. Thrice he patted
his wound with his hand, saying, 'Fear not, boy, you will not
die of this wound. The flowers of the mountain with your
mother's milk will be salve for it.' Then he disappeared. Suddenly the boy's mother galloped up. She looked and saw her
own dear son lying, bedaubed with red blood. Crying out to
her son she declaimed; let us see, my Khan, what she declaimed.

'Sleep has fallen on your black almond eyes; open them,
    hero!
Your twelve ribs are fallen in; pull yourself together, hero!
Your sweet God-given soul seems to be wandering abroad;
    snatch it back, hero!
If you have soul in your body, tell me, my son,
And my dark head be a sacrifice for you, my son.
Kazilik Mountain, your waters flow –
May they cease their flowing!
Kazilik Mountain, your grasses grow –
May they cease their growing!
Kazilik Mountain, your stags run free –
May they cease their running, may they turn to stone!
How should I know, my son? Is this a lion's doing?
Or a tiger's doing? How should I know, my son?
Whence did this disaster befall you?
If you have soul in your body, tell me, my son,
And my dark head be a sacrifice for you, my son.
A word or two for me from your mouth, your tongue!'

As she said this, her voice penetrated to the boy's hearing. He
raised his head, he suddenly opened his eyes and looked at his
mother's face. Then he declaimed; let us see, my Khan, what he
declaimed.

'Come closer, my lady mother whose white milk suckled
    me,
My white-haired honoured mother, dear as life.
Do not curse its waters as they flow;
Kazilik Mountain is innocent.
Do not curse its grasses as they grow;
Kazilik Mountain is guiltless.
Do not curse its running stags;
Kazilik Mountain is innocent.
Curse not its lions and tigers;
Kazilik Mountain is guiltless.
If you must curse, curse my father.
This crime, this sin is my father's.'

He went on, 'Mother, don't cry. I shall not die of this wound. Don't be frightened. Khizr of the grey horse came to me. Thrice he patted my wound and said, "You will not die of this wound. The flowers of the mountain with your mother's milk will be salve for you."' At these words the forty slender maidens scattered and collected mountain flowers. The boy's mother squeezed her breast but no milk came. Again she squeezed and no milk came. The third time she struck herself a blow and her breast became tight and full. She squeezed, and out came milk and blood mixed. They applied the mountain flowers with her milk to the boy's wound. They set him on a horse and led him to his camp. They handed him over to the care of the physicians and concealed him from Dirse Khan. The horse's hoof is fleet as the wind; the minstrel's tongue is swift as a bird. My Khan, in forty days the boy's wound was healed and he was strong and well. Once again he could ride and wear a sword, could hunt game and hawk after fowl. Dirse Khan knew nothing; he thought his dear son was dead.

Those forty treacherous scoundrels got wind of this and took counsel together about what to do. 'If Dirse Khan sees his son he won't spare any of us; he'll kill us all,' they said. 'Come, let us seize Dirse Khan, bind his white hands behind his back, tie a rope of hair round his white neck, and carry him off to the lands of the infidel.' They seized him, they bound his white hands behind his back, they tied a rope of hair round his white neck, they beat him till the blood flowed from his white skin. Away they went, he on foot, they on horseback, and they marched him off to the lands of the bloody infidel. Dirse Khan became a captive, but the Oghuz nobles did not know that he was a captive.

Yet, my Sultan, Dirse Khan's wife heard about this. She went to her own dear son and declaimed; let us see, my Khan, what she declaimed.

'Do you see, my son, what has happened?
The steep rocks have not stirred but the earth has gaped,

There was no enemy in the land but enemies fell on your
  father.
Your father's forty cowardly comrades seized him,
They bound his white hands behind his back,
They tied a rope of hair round his white neck,
They on horseback drove your father walking,
With him they made their way to the lands of the bloody
  infidel.
My lord, my son, arise!
Take your forty warriors, deliver your father from those
  forty cowards.
Bestir yourself, son; if your father showed no mercy to you,
Do you show mercy to your father.'

The boy did not disregard his mother's words. Prince
Boghach arose, he girded on his black steel sword, he grasped
his strong bow with its white grip, he took in his arm his golden
spear, he had his Arab horse brought and leaped into the
saddle, he took with him his forty young men and galloped in
search of his father. He followed the tracks of those treacherous
scoundrels and when he came in sight of them he put his forty
young men in ambush. The forty cowards had made camp and
were drinking the strong red wine, when suddenly Boghach
Khan came upon them. Seeing him, they said, 'Come on, let us
seize this young man and carry him off and deliver the pair of
them to the infidel.' Dirse Khan said, 'Mercy, my forty comrades! There is no doubt that God is One. Untie my hands, give
me my arm-long lute, and I shall turn that young man back.
Then you can kill me, or let me live and set me free.' They
untied his hands and gave him his lute. He did not know that
it was his own dear son; he advanced on him and declaimed;
let us see, my Khan, what he declaimed.

'If there are long-necked Arab horses, they are mine;
  If there is a mount of yours among them, tell me, handsome
    warrior.
  With no fight, with no battle, I shall give it to you;
  Only turn back!

If there are ten thousand sheep in the folds, they are mine;
If there is meat for your spit among them, tell me.
With no fight, with no battle, I shall give it to you.
Only turn back!
If there are red camels in the pastures, they are mine;
If you have a beast of burden among them, tell me;
With no fight, with no battle, I shall give it to you.
Only turn back!
If there are gold-capped pavilions, they are mine;
If you have a home among them, warrior, tell me.
With no fight, with no battle, I shall give it to you.
Only turn back!
If there are white-skinned chestnut-eyed marriageable girls,
    they are mine;
If your betrothed is among them, warrior, tell me.
With no fight, with no battle, I shall give her to you.
Only turn back!
If there are white-bearded elders, they are mine;
If you have a white-bearded father among them, tell me.
With no fight, with no battle, I shall give him to you.
Only turn back!
If it is for me that you have come, I have killed my own
    dear son.
I deserve no pity, warrior; turn back!'

Then the boy declaimed to his father; let us see, my Khan,
what he declaimed.

> 'Yours are the long-necked Arab horses;
> My mount too is among them.
> I shall not leave it to the forty cowards.
> Yours the red camels in the pastures;
> My beast of burden too is among them.
> I shall not leave it to the forty cowards.
> Yours the ten thousand sheep in the folds;
> Meat for my spit too is among them.
> I shall not leave it to the forty cowards.
> Yours are the white-skinned, chestnut-eyed girls;

My betrothed too is among them.
I shall not leave her to the forty cowards.
Yours are the gold-capped pavilions;
My home too is among them.
I shall not leave it to the forty cowards.
Yours are the white-bearded elders;
I have an old father too among them.
His mind is wandering, he's lost his wits,
But I shall not leave him to the forty cowards.'

So saying, he waved his arm in signal to his forty warriors. They spurred their Arab horses and rallied to the boy. He led his forty men, he charged, he fought and gave battle. Some he beheaded, some he took prisoner, and he freed his father. Father and son embraced each other and wept together, they told each other their stories. Then they turned homeward. The Princess came to meet them and, seeing Dirse Khan and her son together, she gave thanks to God Most High. She offered sacrifices, she fed the hungry, she gave alms. She clasped her son to her breast and kissed his eyes. The Great Khan Bayindir gave the boy a principality and a throne. Dede Korkut told stories and declaimed; he composed and strung together this tale of the Oghuz.

They too came to this world and left it;
They camped and moved on, like a caravan.
Them too doom has taken and earth has hidden.
Who now inherits this transient world,
The world to which men come, from which they go,
The world whose latter end is death?

When dark death comes may he give you a fair passage. May God increase your prosperity, with health and prudence. May that High Lord whom I extol be your Friend and come to your aid. I shall pray for you, my Khan: may your firm-rooted black mountain never be overthrown, may your great shady tree never be cut down, may your lovely clear-flowing river never run dry, may the tips of your wings never be broken,[12] may your grey-white horse never stumble as he gallops, may your black steel sword never be notched in the fray, may your many-coloured lance never shatter in the thrusting. May your white-haired mother's place be heaven, may your white-bearded father's place be paradise. May your lamp which God has lit burn on, may mighty God never put you in need of unworthy men, O my Khan!

2

TELLS THE STORY OF HOW
SALUR KAZAN'S HOUSE WAS
PILLAGED

ONE day Salur Kazan son of Ulash, chick of the long-plumed
bird, hope of the wretched and the helpless, lion of the Emet
river, tiger of the Karajuk, master of the chestnut horse, father
of Khan Uruz, son-in-law of Bayindir Khan, luck of the teeming Oghuz, prop of forsaken warriors,[13] rose up from his place.
He had his ninety capped[14] pavilions pitched on the black
earth. In ninety places he spread silken carpets of many colours.
In eighty places great jars were set up. Golden goblets and
ewers were put out. Nine lovely infidel maidens, black-eyed,
beautiful of face, their hair plaited behind, with red buttons at
their breasts, their hands dyed with henna from the wrists down,
their fingers adorned with henna patterns, were giving the nobles
of the teeming Oghuz cups of wine to drink. Salur Kazan son
of Ulash drank deep, and the strong wine rose up to his forehead. He lurched onto his great knees and said, 'Hear my voice,
nobles, pay heed to my words, nobles. Our sides are sore with
too much reclining, our backs are stiff with too much standing.
Let us go out, nobles, let us hunt game and hawk after fowl,
let us lay the elk low, then let's come back to our pavilion and
eat and drink and have some fun.' Wild Dundar son of Kiyan
Seljuk said, 'Yes indeed, Khan Kazan, a splendid idea!' Kara
Budak son of Kara Göne said, 'A splendid idea, my lord
Kazan!' When they said this, horse-mouthed Uruz Koja lurched
onto his two knees and said, 'My lord Kazan, it is a splendid
idea, but you are living in the mouth of foul infidel Georgia;
whom will you leave to look after the camp?' Kazan replied,
'My son Uruz can stand guard over my tents, with three hundred men.' Straightway he called for his chestnut horse and

leaped on its back. Dundar mounted his white-blazed stallion. Prince Kazan's brother Kara Göne had them catch his blue Arab horse and he mounted. Sher Shemseddin, scourge of the foes of Bayindir Khan, called for his white Arab horse and he mounted. Beyrek, who once came flying out of Parasar's fortress of Bayburt,[15] mounted his grey horse. Prince Yigenek, he who once called Kazan of the chestnut horse 'Christian priest', mounted his red-brown horse. Of counting the nobles of the teeming Oghuz there could be no end; they all mounted. The many-coloured host went out to hunt on the many-coloured mountain.

The infidels' spy espied them and brought the news to the wild infidel beast, King Shökli. Seven thousand infidels mounted their dappled horses, men of foul religion, enemies of religion, the backs of their caftans slit, their black hair streaming down to their waists. Speedily they galloped and at midnight they came to Prince Kazan's encampment. They sacked his golden pavilions, they set his swan-like daughters and daughters-in-law screaming in chorus. They mounted his falcon-swift horses, stall after stall of them, they led behind them file upon file of his red camels. They looted his heavy treasure, his abundant silver. Forty slender-waisted maidens and Lady Burla the Tall went into captivity. Prince Kazan's old mother went, hanging round the neck of a black camel. Khan Kazan's son, Prince Uruz, and his three hundred men, went with hands and necks tethered. Saru Kulmash son of Ilig Koja was killed at Prince Kazan's tent. Kazan knew nothing of all this.

The infidel King said, 'Nobles! We have mounted Kazan's falcon-swift horses, stall after stall of them, we have looted his gold and silver, we have captured his son Uruz and his forty young men, we have led away his camels, file upon file, we have taken Kazan's wife and her forty slender-waisted maidens; these losses we have inflicted on Kazan.' One of the infidels said, 'We have one loss yet to inflict on Prince Kazan.' 'Noble lord, what loss is that?' asked King Shökli. 'Kazan has ten thousand sheep at the Gated Black Pass; if we were to take them too we would inflict great loss on Kazan.' King Shökli at once gave orders:

'Let six hundred infidels go and fetch those sheep!' Six hundred infidels mounted their horses and galloped towards the sheep.

That night, as Karajuk the shepherd lay sleeping, he had a nightmare. He leapt up in terror and called his two brothers to his side, Kiyan Güchi and Demür Ekiji. He strengthened the gate of the fold, in three places he heaped mountains of stones, he took up his sling with its many-coloured handle. Without warning the six hundred infidels were upon him. They said,

'Shepherd, anxious when the gloomy shades of evening fall,
   Shepherd, busy with your flint when the snow and rain-
      drops fall,
   Shepherd, full of milk and cheese and good cream over all!

'We are the men who have torn down Prince Kazan's pavilions with their golden smoke-holes, who have ridden off his stables full of falcon-swift horses, have led away his files of red camels, have taken his old mother, have looted his heavy treasure, his abundant silver, have taken captive his swan-like daughters and daughters-in-law, have carried off Kazan's son with his forty warriors, and Kazan's wife with her forty slender-waisted maidens. Now shepherd, come over here from far and near, bow your head, put your hand on your heart and salute us infidels, and then we shan't kill you; we'll send you to King Shökli and we'll see you made a prince.' The shepherd replied,

'Don't talk rubbish, there's a good infidel dog!
   Rabid infidel, who shares with my dog a dish of my slops,
   Why boast of the dappled horse you ride?
   I wouldn't swap my goat with the spotted head for it.
   Why boast of the helmet you wear?
   I wouldn't swap my cap for it.
   Why boast of your sixty-span lance?
   I wouldn't swap my dogwood stick for it.
   Why boast of your quiver with your ninety arrows?
   I wouldn't swap my coloured-handled sling for it.
   Come over here from far and near,
   See the beating your men will get; and then be off.'

The infidels did not stand on ceremony; they spurred their horses, they showered arrows. That dragon among warriors, Karajuk the shepherd, loaded his sling and shot it. When he shot his first stone he toppled two or three of them; when he shot his second he toppled three or four of them. Terror filled the infidels' eyes. Karajuk the shepherd with his sling-stones laid three hundred of the infidel low. His two brothers fell before the arrows and died. The shepherd ran out of stones: sheep, goats, he didn't care what they were, he loaded them into his sling and shot them out, and began toppling four or five of the infidel at each go. The infidels were panic-stricken, the world became dark about their heads. 'Is this thrice-accursed shepherd going to smash us all?' they said, and turned and fled.

The shepherd committed his slain brothers to their God and piled up the corpses of the infidel into a huge mound. He himself had been wounded in one or two places; he struck his flint and lit a fire, burnt a piece of his cloak to ashes and pressed them on his wounds. Then he sat down at the roadside and wept bitter tears, saying, 'Salur Kazan, Prince Kazan, are you dead or alive? Don't you know anything of this?'

Now it seems, my Khan, that while Salur Kazan son of Ulash, the luck of the teeming Oghuz, the son-in-law of Bayindir Khan, lay sleeping that night he had a nightmare. He leapt up and said, 'My brother Kara Göne, do you know what appeared in my dream? I had a nightmare, I saw my bird, the falcon that flutters in my grip, dying. I saw thunderbolts crashing down from heaven onto my white pavilion. I saw dense fog pouring down over my encampment. I saw rabid wolves rending my tent. I saw a black camel grasping my neck. I saw my raven-black hair grow long as reeds; it grew and grew until it covered my eyes. I saw my ten fingers covered in blood from the wrists down. Since I saw this dream I have not been able to collect my wits. My lord brother, interpret this dream for me.' Kara Göne replied, 'The black cloud you speak of is your might; the snow and rain is your army, the hair is anxiety, the blood misfortune. The rest I cannot interpret; let God interpret it.' 'Do not interrupt my hunt,' said Kazan, 'do not disperse my army. I shall put the spur to my chestnut horse today and in one day make the three-day journey. I shall arrive home before noon; if all is safe and sound I shall be back with you before nightfall. If my encampment is not safe and sound, look to yourself; I shall have gone too.'

Prince Kazan spurred his chestnut horse and set out. He rode and rode until he reached home, where all he saw was crows flying and hounds roaming. Thereupon Prince Kazan asked his home for news; let us see, my Khan, how he asked.

'My people, my tribe, my snug home,
  Neighbour to the wild ass, the elk, the deer, my home.
  Remote from the enemy with his dappled horses;
  How did the enemy come to rend you, my beautiful home?
  There where the white pavilions stood the traces stay,
  There where my aged mother sat the place remains.
  The target stands where my son Uruz shot his arrows,
  The field remains where the Oghuz nobles galloped,
  The hearth remains where the dark kitchen stood.'

Kazan's black almond eyes filled with bloody tears at the sight; his veins swelled, his heart was agitated. He dug his heels into his chestnut horse and went down the road which the infidel had taken. A stream appeared in his path and he said, 'Water has looked on the face of God. I shall ask this stream for news.' Let us see, my Khan, how he asked.

'Water that plashes over the rocks,
  Water that sets the wooden boats dancing,
  Water for which Hasan and Huseyn yearned,[17]
  Water that adorns orchard and garden,
  Water that dowered Ayesha and Fatima,[18]
  Water that the falcon-swift horses drink,
  Water that the red camels cross,
  On whose banks the white sheep lie,
  Have you news of my encampment? Tell me,
  And my dark head be a sacrifice for you, dear water.'[19]

But how should water give news? He crossed the stream and

now he encountered a wolf. 'Blessed is the face of the wolf,'[20] said he, 'I shall ask the wolf for news.' Let us see, my Khan, how he asked.

'You whose sun rises when dark night falls,
Who stand up like a man in the snow and rain,
At sight of whom the well-trained stallions neigh
And the red camels scream.
Swishing your tail when you see the white sheep,
Driving your back against the strong fold and smashing it,
Seizing the fattest of the huddled two-year-olds,
Wrenching off bloody tails and gobbling them,
Whose voice challenges the huge dogs,
Busying the shepherds with their flint and steel all night,
Have you news of my encampment? Tell me,
And my dark head be a sacrifice for you, friend wolf.'

But how should a wolf give news? He passed the wolf by. Then the shepherd Karajuk's black dog came to meet him. Kazan asked the black dog for news; let us see, my Khan, how he asked.

'You who bark when the gloomy shades of evening fall,
Who gulp the sour ayran[21] as it is poured,
Who terrify the night-prowling thieves,
Putting them to flight with your uproar,
Have you news of my encampment? Tell me,
And so long as my dark head is in life and health I shall
    treat you kindly, dog.'

But how should a dog give news? The dog snapped at the legs of Kazan's horse and whined. Kazan hit the dog with a stick, and the dog slunk off by the way he had come. Chasing the dog in front of him, Kazan came upon Karajuk the shepherd. Seeing the shepherd, he asked him for news; let us see, my Khan, how he asked. Kazan said,

'Shepherd, anxious when the gloomy shades of evening fall,
Shepherd, busy with your flint when the snow and rain-
    drops fall,

Mark what I say, hear my words.
The black infidel with his dappled horses has laid waste my
    encampment;
Has he passed this way? Tell me,
And my dark head be a sacrifice for you, shepherd.'

The shepherd replied,

'Were you dead or were you lost, Kazan?
Where were you wandering, where had you gone, my lord
    Kazan?

'Now yesterday – no it wasn't, it was the day before, your
family passed this way. The black infidel with his dappled
horses had looted your white-pavilioned household. They had
captured your tall Lady Burla and the piece of your heart, the
fruit of your life, your son Uruz. The unbelievers were riding
your falcon-swift horses, stables full of them, they were leading
your red camels, file on file of them, they had got all your
treasure of gold and silver. The day before yesterday it was,
they passed this way. I saw your little old mother clutching
the neck of a camel, and your wife, the tall Lady Burla with
her forty slender-waisted maidens, walking before the unbelievers, crying as she went. Among the young nobles I saw
your son Uruz, the beautiful light of your eye, a halter round
his neck, captive in the unbelievers' hands.' When the shepherd
said this, Kazan groaned, his mind departed from his head, and
the whole world became dark in his eye. 'May your mouth dry
up, shepherd!' he cried. 'May your tongue rot, shepherd! May
God write your doom on your forehead, shepherd!' The shepherd replied, 'Why are you angry with me, Lord Kazan? Is
there no faith in your heart? Six hundred unbelievers attacked
me too, my two brothers were killed, I killed three hundred
unbelievers, I fought the good fight, I did not let the unbelievers
have the fat sheep and the thin yearlings from your gate. I was
wounded in three places, my dark head was stunned, I was all
alone; is this what you're blaming me for?' Then he said,

'Give me your chestnut horse,
 Give me your sixty-span lance,
 Give me your shield of many colours,
 Give me your pure sword of black steel,
 Give me the eighty arrows in your quiver,
 Give me your strong bow with its white grip.
 I shall go to the unbeliever,
 I shall rise again and kill,
 I shall wipe the blood off my forehead with my sleeve.
 If I die I shall die for your sake;
 If God Most High allows, I shall deliver your family.'

These words offended Kazan and he abruptly moved on. The shepherd came along behind him. Kazan turned and looked and said, 'Shepherd, my boy, where are you going?' He answered, 'My lord Kazan, if you are going to get your family back, I am going too, to take revenge for my brothers' blood.' Then Kazan said, 'Shepherd, my boy, I'm hungry; haven't you anything to eat?' 'Certainly,' replied the shepherd, 'I've got a lamb that I was cooking all night; come on, let's stop at the foot of this tree and eat.' They stopped there, the shepherd brought out his bag and they ate. Kazan thought to himself, 'If I go with the shepherd, the nobles of the teeming Oghuz will put shame on me and say, "Kazan could never have overcome the unbelievers if the shepherd had not been with him."' Jealous for his honour, he tied the shepherd tightly to a tree, mounted his horse and rode away. The shepherd shouted, 'Lord Kazan, what are you doing to me?' 'I am going to rescue my family,' said Kazan, 'then I'll come back and let you go.' The shepherd said to himself, 'Now, shepherd, you'd better uproot this tree before you feel hungry and faint, or the wolves and birds will eat you here.' Karajuk the shepherd exerted himself, he uprooted the great tree with its earth and all, and ran after Kazan with it on his back. Kazan looked and saw the shepherd coming along after him with the tree on his back and said, 'What's the idea of the tree, shepherd?' 'Lord Kazan,' said the other, 'I'll tell you what the idea is. While you're fighting the unbeliever you might feel a bit peckish, so I'll use this tree for firewood to cook you something to eat.' Kazan liked these words; he dismounted, untied the shepherd, kissed him on the forehead and said, 'If God delivers my family I shall make you my Master of the Horse.' Then they went on their way together.

Meanwhile King Shökli, happy and cheerful, was sitting feasting with the infidel nobles. 'Nobles,' said he, 'do you know what we ought to do to bring shame on Kazan? We must fetch the Lady Burla and make her our cupbearer.' Lady Burla the Tall overheard this, and fire fell on her heart and soul. She went among her forty slender-waisted maidens and instructed them thus: 'Whichever of you they happen upon and ask if she is Kazan's wife, you must all forty of you call out together, "That's me!"' King Shökli's men came and asked, 'Which of you is the wife of Prince Kazan?' From forty-one throats the cry came, and they did not know which was she. They told the infidel King, 'We addressed ourselves to one of them but an answer came from forty-one throats, and we cannot guess which of them it is.' The infidel replied, 'Bring Kazan's son Uruz, hang him on a hook, chop up his white flesh and make a nice brown roast, and offer it to the forty-one noble ladies. Whoever eats it is not the one; the one we want is the one who refuses it; fetch her and let her be our cupbearer.' Lady Burla the Tall went up to her son and called out to him, declaiming; let us see, my Khan, what she declaimed.

'My son, my son, O my son,
Do you know what has happened?
They whispered together,
I heard the infidel's plan.
Son, pillar of my great tent with its golden smoke-hole,
Son, flower of my swan-like daughters and daughters-in-
    law,
My son, my son, O my son,
Son whom I carried for nine months in my narrow belly,
Whom I brought into the world when the tenth moon came,
Whom I swaddled in the gold-framed cradle,

Whom I suckled with my white milk.
Son, do you not know what is going on?

'The infidels have taken monstrous counsel together and said,
"Impale Kazan's son Uruz on a hook, cut up his white flesh
and make a nice brown roast, offer it to the forty-one ladies,
and you may know that whichever of them will not eat it is the
wife of Kazan. Take her and we shall bring her to our bed and
make her our cupbearer." What do you say, son? Shall I eat of
your flesh or shall I enter the bed of the infidel of foul religion
and defile the honour of your lord Kazan? What shall I do, my
son?' Uruz replied, 'May your mouth dry up, Mother! May
your tongue rot, Mother! Were it not that they say a mother's
due is God's due, I should rise up and seize you by your collar
and your throat, I should cast you beneath my hard heel, I
should trample your white face into the black earth, I should
bring the blood gushing from your mouth and nose, I should
show you how sweet life is. What kind of talk is this? Let
them impale me on the hook, but beware of rushing up to me
and saying, "My son!" and beware of weeping for me. Let
them cut up my white flesh and roast it, let them offer it to the
forty ladies. And for every mouthful they eat, you must eat two,
so that the infidels do not guess who you are and detect you, lest
you go to the bed of the infidel of foul religion and become his
cupbearer and defile the honour of my father Kazan. Beware!'
So saying, he wept great tears. Lady Burla the Tall clasped his
neck and his ear and fell down. She clutched and ripped her
cheeks, red as autumn apples, she tore her hair like reeds uprooted. She wailed and cried, 'My son, my son!'
    Said Uruz,

> 'Lady mother, why do you scream in front of me?
> Why do you lament, why do you weep?
> Why do you wound my heart?
> Why do you recall my days that are past? [22]
> Mother, where the Arab horses are
> Is there never a foal?
> Where the red camels are

Is there never a young one?
Where the white sheep are
Is there never a lamb?
Live, my lady mother, and let my father live;
Will there never be a son like me?'

At these words his mother could no longer endure; she walked
hastily away and joined the forty slender-waisted maidens. The
infidels seized Uruz and brought him to the foot of the tree of
slaughter. Uruz said, 'Mercy, infidels, there is no doubt that God
is one. Let me speak with this tree.' Loudly he declaimed to the
tree; let us see, my Khan, what he declaimed.

'Tree, if I call you "wood" be not offended, tree! [23]
The gates of Mecca and Medina are of wood,
Wooden the staff of Moses who spoke with God,
Wooden the bridges over mighty rivers,
Wooden the ships on the black seas,
Wooden the saddle of Duldul, the mule of Ali, King of
    men,[24]
Wooden the scabbard and hilt of Zulfikar,[25]
Wooden the cradles of Hasan and Huseyn.
Tree that terrifies man and woman,
When I look towards your top you have no top, tree.
When I look towards your foot you have no foot, tree.
They are going to hang me on you; do not support me, tree.
If you do so may my manhood blast you, O tree!
You should have been in our own land, tree;
I would have ordered our black Indian slaves
To chop you up in tiny pieces, tree!'

Then he said,

'Alas for my stables full of tethered horses!
Alas for my comrades, who guarded me like a brother!
Alas for my falcon, quivering in my fist!
Alas for my greyhound, overtaking and seizing!
I have not had my fill of being a prince; alas for my soul!
I am not weary of being a warrior; alas for my life!'

And he wept huge tears and wounded his burning heart; and raised his face towards the Court of the Almighty and invoked the intercession of Muhammad of beautiful name. At that moment, my Sultan, Salur Kazan and Karajuk the shepherd came at the gallop. The leather of the shepherd's sling was made of the skins of three-year-old calves, the thongs were of the skins of three goats, and one goatskin made the tassel. At every shot it threw a hundredweight of stone. The stone it fired would not fall to earth; if ever it did fall it would shatter into dust, it would explode like a furnace, and for three years no grass would grow where that stone fell. If the fat sheep and the thin yearlings were left on the hillside no wolf would come and eat them, for fear of Karajuk's sling. Well, my Sultan, when Karajuk the shepherd saw the infidel host, he could not control himself. He loosed his sling, and the whole world became dark in the infidels' eyes. Said Kazan, 'Shepherd Karajuk, have patience. I shall ask the infidel for my mother.' The horse's hoof is fleet as the wind; the minstrel's tongue is swift as a bird. Kazan cried out to the infidel, declaiming; let us see, my Khan, what he declaimed.

'Hey, King Shökli!
You have taken my pavilions with their golden smoke-
    holes;
Let them give you shade.
You have taken my heavy treasure, my much silver;
Let them be yours to spend.
You have taken the Lady Burla with her forty slender
    maidens;
Let them be your slaves.
You have taken my son Uruz with his forty warriors;
Let them be your bondmen.
You have taken my stables full of falcon-swift horses;
Let them be yours to ride.
You have taken my camels, file on file of them;
Let them be your beasts of burden.

You have taken my little old mother whose white milk
  suckled me,
Her of the plaited hair;
Infidel, give me my mother.
With no fight, with no battle, I shall retrace my steps,
I shall turn back and go, be sure of this.'

The infidel replied,

'Kazan!
We have taken your white pavilion with its golden smoke-
  hole;
It is ours.
We have taken Lady Burla the Tall, with her forty slender
  maidens;
She is ours.
We have taken your son Uruz with his forty warriors;
He is ours.
Your stables full of falcon-swift horses,
Your camels, file on file of them,
We have taken them all;
They are ours.
Your little old mother we have taken;
And she is ours.

'We shall not give her to you. We shall give her to the son of
Yaykhan the Priest. The son of Yaykhan the Priest will have a
son and we shall make him your enemy.' At these words Karajuk
the shepherd was infuriated, his lips drew back in a snarl, and
he said,

'Godless brainless infidel,
  Witless disordered infidel!
  Yonder snowcapped black mountains have grown old,
  No grass grows on them.
  The blood-red rivers have grown old,
  No water flows in them.
  The falcon-swift horses have grown old,

They give no foals.
The red camels have grown old,
They give no young.
Infidel! Kazan's mother has grown old,
She gives no sons.

'If it would please you, King Shökli, to improve your breed
with the help of an Oghuz sire, if you have a black-eyed
daughter, fetch her, give her to Prince Kazan. Then, infidel, a son
of his may be born of your daughter, and you can make him an
enemy to Kazan.'

Now it seems that the Oghuz nobles had heard of the disaster,
and they had followed Kazan's tracks. At that moment they
arrived. Let us see, my Khan, who they were who arrived. Kara
Göne galloped up, he whom the Almighty set at the narrows of
the Black Valley, the coverlet of whose cradle was of black bull-
hide, who when he was angered made black rock into ashes,
whose moustaches were knotted seven times at the back of his
neck, that dragon of heroes, the brother of Prince Kazan. 'Wield
your sword, brother Kazan!' said he, 'Here I am!' Let us see
who came next. Wild Dundar son of Kiyan Seljuk galloped up,
he who kicked in and destroyed the iron gate at the Pass of the
Iron Gate,[26] who transfixed men on his sixty-span lance, who
three times unhorsed so great a hero as Kazan. 'Wield your
sword, my lord Kazan!' said he, 'Here I am!' Let us see, my
Khan, who came next. Kara Budak son of Kara Göne galloped
up. He it was who smashed the fortresses of Diyarbakr and
Mardin, who made King Kipchak of the iron bow vomit blood,
who came and won Kazan's daughter by his valour, whom
despite his youth the white-bearded Oghuz elders praised whenever they saw him. Red silk trousers he wore, and his horse, born
of the sea,[27] was decked with a golden tassel. 'Wield your sword,
my lord Kazan!' said he, 'Here I am!' Let us see, my Khan,
who came next. Sher Shemseddin son of Gaflet Koja galloped
up, with snow still on his grey-white horse's mane, he who
swooped down on the enemies of Bayindir Khan without so
much as a by-your-leave, who made sixty thousand unbelievers

vomit blood. 'Wield your sword, my lord Kazan!' said he, 'Here
I am!' Let us see, my Khan, who came next. Beyrek of the grey
horse galloped up, he who once flashed forth from Parasar's
fortress of Bayburt and arrived in front of his many-coloured
bridal tent; he the hope of seven maidens, the darling of the
teeming Oghuz, trusty minister of Prince Kazan. 'Wield your
sword, my lord Kazan!' said he, 'Here I am!' Next, Prince
Yigenek son of Kazilik Koja galloped up; he who swaggered as
he glared about him, brave as an eagle, tightly belted, with
golden earrings in his ears,[28] who could unhorse the Oghuz
nobles one after another. 'Wield your sword, my lord Kazan!'
said he, 'Here I am!' Next, Prince Kazan's uncle galloped up,
horse-mouthed Uruz Koja. If he made a fur coat from the skins
of sixty two-year-old lambs it would not cover his heels; if he
made a cap from the skins of six it would not cover his ears.
Skinny were his arms and thighs, and his long calves were
slender. 'Wield your sword, Prince Kazan!' said he, 'Here I
am!' The next to gallop up was he who saw the Prophet's face,
then came and was his Companion among the Oghuz, from
whose moustaches blood flowed when he was enraged, Bügdüz
Emen,[29] his moustaches covered with blood. 'Wield your sword,
my lord Kazan!' said he, 'Here I am!' Let us see who came
next. Alp Eren son of Ilig Koja, at whose name hounds bayed,
who left his own land and made horses swim the River of
Stallions, who took the keys of fifty-seven castles, who married
the daughter of Agh Melik Cheshme, who made King Sufi
Sandal vomit blood, who wrapped himself in forty robes, stole
away the beloved daughters of the lords of thirty-seven castles,
clasped them round the neck one by one and kissed their faces
and their lips. 'Wield your sword, my lord Kazan!' said he,
'Here I am!'

Of counting the nobles of the Oghuz there could be no end;
they all came. They washed in pure water, they pressed their
white foreheads to the earth, and they prayed.[30] They invoked
blessings on Muhammad of beautiful name, they said 'God is
most great!', then without more ado they charged at the infidel,
they wielded their swords. The thunderous drums were beaten,

the brazen horns, gold-curlicued, were blown. On that day the
manly warriors showed their mettle. On that day the unmanly
spied out roads by which to slink away. On that day there was
a battle like doomsday and the field was full of heads. Heads
were cut off like balls. Falcon-swift horses galloped until they
lost their shoes, pure black steel swords were wielded until they
lost their edges, the three-feathered beech-wood arrows were
shot until they lost their points. Banners were carried off, the
skirmishers fought. Chieftain was parted from retainer, retainer
from chieftain. Wild Dundar with the nobles of the Outer
Oghuz attacked on the right, Kara Budak son of Kara Göne
attacked on the left with his brave warriors. Kazan with the
nobles of the Inner Oghuz attacked the centre. He rushed at
King Shökli and ran him through, he threw him off his horse
and, before he knew what was happening, seized his black head
and cut it off; he hacked at his body and spilled his red blood
on the earth. On the right wing Wild Dundar son of Kiyan
Seljuk met King Kara Tüken and brought him down with a
sword-cut in the right side. On the left wing Kara Budak son of
Kara Göne met King Boghachuk and smashed his head with a
mighty blow of his six-ridged mace. The world became dark in
his eyes, he clutched his horse's neck and toppled to the ground.
Prince Kazan's brother smote the infidels' horse-tail banners and
standards with his sword and laid them low. The infidel broke
and fled over valley and hill, and the crows swarmed over their
carrion. Twelve thousand unbelievers were put to the sword.
Five hundred Oghuz warriors fell. Those who fled, Prince
Kazan did not pursue; those who asked for mercy he did not
kill. The nobles of the teeming Oghuz had their fill of plunder.
Prince Kazan freed his son, his mother and his wife; all those
who had longed for each other found each other once more.
Prince Kazan sat on his high golden throne. He made the
shepherd Karajuk his Master of the Horse. For seven days and
seven nights there was eating and drinking. He freed forty
male slaves and forty female as a thank-offering for his son
Uruz. To the brave young warriors he gave castles and lands,
he gave robes and precious stuffs.

Dede Korkut came and told stories and declaimed; he composed and strung together this tale of the Oghuz.

Where now are the valiant princes of whom I have told,
Those who said 'The world is mine'?
Doom has taken them, earth has hidden them.
Who inherits this transient world,
The world to which men come, from which they go,
The world whose latter end is death?

I shall pray for you, my Khan: may your firm-rooted black mountain never be overthrown, may your great shady tree never be cut down, may your lovely clear-flowing river never run dry, may mighty God never put you in need of unworthy men, may your grey-white horse never stumble as he gallops, may your pure black steel sword never be notched in the fray, may your many-coloured lance never shatter in the thrusting. May your white-bearded father's place be paradise, may your white-haired mother's place be heaven. May the end not find you apart from the pure Faith, may those who say 'Amen' see the Face of God. On your white forehead I invoke five words of blessing;[31] may they be accepted. May your God-given hope never be disappointed, may He grant you increase and preserve you in strength and forgive your sins for the honour of Muhammad the Chosen of beautiful name, O my Khan!

3

TELLS THE STORY OF BAMSI
BEYREK OF THE GREY HORSE,
O MY KHAN!

BAYINDIR KHAN son of Kam Ghan rose up from his place.
On the black earth he pitched his white pavilion, his many-
coloured tents reared up to the face of the sky. In a thousand
places silken rugs were spread. The nobles of the Inner Oghuz
and the Outer Oghuz assembled to Bayindir Khan's gathering.
Bay Büre[32] too had come to Bayindir Khan's gathering. Before
Bayindir Khan there stood Kara Budak son of Kara Göne,
leaning on his bow. On the Khan's right stood Uruz son of
Kazan, on his left stood Prince Yigenek son of Kazilik Koja.
Seeing them, Prince Bay Büre sighed, his wits left his head, he
put his kerchief over his face and wept choking sobs. Thereupon
Salur Kazan, backbone of the teeming Oghuz, son-in-law of
Bayindir Khan, sank onto his great knee, stared into Bay
Büre's face and said, 'Prince Bay Büre, what are you crying and
sobbing for?' He replied, 'Lord Kazan, why should I not cry
and sob, when I have no share of sons, no portion of brothers?
God Most High has humiliated me, my lords. I weep for my
crown and my throne; a day will come when I shall fall and die
and none will be left in my place and in my house.' Prince
Kazan said, 'Is that what you are concerned about?' 'Certainly
it is', replied Prince Bay Büre. 'If I too had a son, who could
stand before Bayindir Khan and serve him, I could look on and
rejoice and be proud and confident.' At these words the nobles
of the teeming Oghuz turned their faces heavenwards, lifted
their hands and prayed, 'May God Most High grant you
a son.'

In those days the nobles' blessings were blessings and their
curses were curses, and their prayers used to be anwered. Prince

Bay Bijan stood up also and said, 'Nobles, pray for me too, that God Most High may grant me a daughter.' The nobles of the teeming Oghuz lifted their hands and prayed, 'May God Most High grant you a daughter.' Then Prince Bay Bijan said, 'Nobles, if God Most High gives me a daughter, be you witnesses that my daughter is to be betrothed in the cradle to the son of Prince Bay Büre.'

Time passed, and God Most High gave Prince Bay Büre a son and Prince Bay Bijan a daughter. The nobles of the teeming Oghuz were glad and joyful at the news. Prince Bay Büre called for his merchants and gave them their orders: 'Now, merchants, God Most High has given me a son; go to the land of Rum[33] and bring my son splendid gifts for when he is grown.' 'Very well, lord', said the merchants; they prepared for the journey and set off, travelling by night and day, until they reached Istanbul. Rare, precious and wonderful gifts they bought. For Prince Bay Büre's son they bought a grey horse, sea-born; a strong bow too they bought, with a white grip; and a six-ridged mace.[34] Then they began the homeward journey. Many years and many months passed before they arrived home. Bay Büre's son reached his fifth year, his tenth, his fifteenth. He became a fine handsome young man, swaggering as he glared about him, brave as an eagle. In those days, my lords, until a boy cut off heads and spilled blood they used not to give him a name. Prince Bay Büre's son mounted his horse and went out hunting. While he was out, he came upon his father's stables. The Master of the Horse met him, invited him to dismount, and entertained him. They sat eating and drinking. Meanwhile, the merchants had come as far as the Black Pass of Pasin and were encamped there. The damned accursed infidels from the castle of Avnik spied on them.[35] As the merchants slept, they were attacked unawares by five hundred unbelievers, who overwhelmed and pillaged them. The great merchants were captured, but a lesser merchant escaped and reached the Oghuz, for this had happened in a place not far from the Oghuz. The merchant saw that a many-coloured tent had been pitched at the edge of the Oghuz land, and a handsome princely young man was sitting with

forty warriors, to his right and to his left. 'A fine young Oghuz
warrior, that's what it is!' said the merchant, 'I'll go up to him
and ask for help.' He went up to him, put his hand on his heart,
gave greeting and said, 'My young prince, my young khan,
understand my words, hear my voice. Sixteen years ago we left
the Oghuz land and we were bringing back rare and precious
infidel goods for the Oghuz nobles. We had climbed to the
Black Pass of Pasin when five hundred infidels from the castle
of Avnik attacked us. My brother was captured, they pillaged
our goods, our lawful livelihood, and went off. I have escaped
with my life and come to you. Help me, young warrior, as an
act of charity, to give thanks for your life.' All this while, the
young man had been drinking, but he stopped drinking, dashed
the gold cup to the ground and said, 'Hey there! Do as I bid;
bring me my equipment and my falcon-swift horse. My young
men who love me, to horse!' The merchant went in front to
lead the way.

Now the infidels had stopped along the road and were divid-
ing the spoils. At that moment the lion of the field of heroes,
the tiger of champions, the grey lad[36] arrived. He did not stop
to argue, he laid into the infidels with his sword and killed those
contumacious unbelievers. He fought well for the Faith and
saved the merchants' goods. The merchants said, 'Young prince,
you have done manfully for us. Come now, take what merchandise you fancy.' The young prince's eye was caught by a
grey horse, sea-born, by a six-ridged mace, and by a bow with
a white grip; these three he fancied. He said, 'Well now, merchants, give me this horse, this mace and this bow.' When he
said this the merchants were dismayed. The young man said,
'Well, merchants, have I asked for too much?' They answered,
'How could it be too much? But we have a prince's son for
whom we were supposed to bring these three things.' 'And
who,' said he, 'is your prince's son?' They replied, 'Bay Büre
has a son ...' They did not know that it was he. The young man
bit his finger in surprise and said, 'Better be given them in my
father's presence ungrudgingly than take them here and leave a
grudge.' He whipped his horse and rode off, the merchants

staring after him and saying, 'A fine young man, by heaven! A chivalrous young man!'

The grey lad came to his father's house. Then news was brought to his father that the merchants who had departed so many years before had returned. His father was delighted. He ordered his council to assemble, he had tents and marquees and many-coloured pavilions pitched, he spread silken carpets, then he took his place and sat down, putting his son at his right hand. The boy did not say a word about the merchants or mention that he had defeated the infidels. Then the merchants appeared. They bowed their heads and gave greeting; and saw that the young man who had cut off heads and spilled blood was sitting at the right of Prince Bay Büre. They came forward and kissed his hand. Prince Bay Büre was furious at this, and said to the merchants, 'You scurvy wretches, does one kiss the child's hand when the father is present?' They answered, 'Khan, is this young man your son?' 'Of course he is my son!' said he. 'Khan', they said, 'don't be angry at us for kissing his hand. If it were not for your son our merchandise would now be in Georgia and all of us would be prisoners.' Prince Bay Büre said, 'Has my son cut off heads and spilled blood?' 'He has indeed cut off heads and spilled blood and laid men low,' said they. 'Enough to give the boy a name?' 'Enough, lord, and more than enough,' they replied.

Prince Bay Büre summoned the nobles of the teeming Oghuz and feasted them. He submitted his son's story to them and they approved. Then Dede Korkut came and gave the boy a name, saying,

'Hear my words, Prince Bay Büre,
God Most High has given you a son; may He preserve him!
When they raise the white banner, may he be the mainstay
   of the Muslims.
When he climbs yonder dark snow-capped mountain,
May the All-powerful grant him a safe passage.
When he crosses the blood-red river,
May He grant him a safe crossing.

When he goes among the multitude of infidels,
May God Most High give him good fortune.
Your pet-name for your son is Bamsa;
Let his name be Bamsi Beyrek of the grey horse.
I have given his name; may God give him his years.'

The nobles of the teeming Oghuz lifted their hands and
prayed, saying, 'May this name be blessed to this young man.'
Then they all mounted to go hunting. Bamsi Beyrek had his
grey horse brought, and mounted him. The many-coloured
host went out to hunt on the many-coloured mountain.[37]

Suddenly a herd of deer appeared before the Oghuz. Away
went Bamsi Beyrek after one of them. He chased it to a place
and what do you think he saw? My Sultan, he saw a red tent
pitched on the green grass. 'Lord!' said he, 'Whose tent can
this be?' He did not know that the tent belonged to the chestnut-
eyed girl he was to marry. He was too polite to advance on the
tent, and he said to himself, 'Whatever it is, at least I'll take
my quarry.' He caught it up and felled it just in front of the
tent. Then he realized that the tent belonged to the Lady
Chichek, who was his cradle-betrothed; she was looking out
from the tent. 'Well, girls,' she said to her ladies-in-waiting, 'I
wonder if this pimp son of a pimp will show us his generosity.
Go and ask him for a share and see what he says.' Among them
was a lady called Kisirja Yenge, who went up to him and
demanded shares: 'Young man,' she said, 'give us a share of this
deer.' Beyrek replied, 'Lady, I am no huntsman; I am a prince
and the son of a prince; you may have it all. But, if it is not
rude to ask, whose tent is this?' Kisirja Yenge answered, 'Young
man, this is the tent of the Lady Chichek, daughter of Prince
Bay Bijan.' Whereupon Beyrek's blood was inflamed, but politely
and in silence he withdrew. The girls took up the deer and
brought it in before the queen of beauties, the Lady Chichek.
She saw that it was a kingly fat sleek stag and she said, 'Well,
girls, who was the young man?' 'Lady,' they told her, 'he was
a handsome young man with a veil over his face.[38] He said he was
a prince, the son of a prince.' The Lady Chichek said, 'Oho,

ladies! My father used to say he had given me to Beyrek of the
veiled face; could this be he? Call him and let's find out.' They
called him and Beyrek came. The Lady Chichek, having veiled
herself, asked him, 'Where are you from, young man?' 'From
the Inner Oghuz,' said Beyrek. 'And who and what are you
among the Inner Oghuz?' 'I am he they call Bamsi Beyrek son
of Prince Bay Büre.' 'And what is your business here?' 'I am
told,' replied Beyrek, 'that Prince Bay Bijan has a daughter,
and I have come to see her.' 'The Lady Chichek is not the sort
of person to show herself to you,' said she, 'but I am her
serving-woman. Come, let us ride out together. We shall shoot
our bows and race our horses and wrestle. If you beat me in
these three, you will beat her too.' 'Excellent!' said Beyrek,
'To horse!' They both mounted and rode out. They spurred
their horses and Beyrek's horse passed the girl's. They shot their
bows and Beyrek's arrow split the girl's arrow. Said she, 'Well,
young man, nobody has ever passed my horse or split my arrow.
Come now, let us wrestle.' At once they dismounted and
grappled; they stood as wrestlers do and grasped each other.
Beyrek picked the girl up and tried to throw her, then she
picked him up and tried to throw him. Beyrek was astonished
and said, 'If I am beaten by this girl they will pour scorn on my
head and shame on my face among the teeming Oghuz.' He
made a supreme effort, grappled with the girl and seized her
breast. She struggled to free herself, but now Beyrek seized her
slender waist, held her tight and threw her on her back. The
girl said, 'Warrior, I am Prince Bay Bijan's daughter, the Lady
Chichek.' Three times he kissed her, once he bit her. He took
the gold ring off his finger and put it on hers, saying, 'Let this
be the token between us, daughter of khans.' 'Now that this has
happened, Prince,' said she, 'we must go.' 'So be it,' said Beyrek,
'as you command.'

Beyrek parted from the girl and went back to his tents. His
white-bearded father came to meet him, saying, 'Son, what re-
markable things have you seen today in the Oghuz land?' 'What
did you expect me to see?' said he, 'The people with sons found
wives for them; the people with daughters found husbands for

them.' 'Son,' said his father, 'ought I to find a wife for you?'
'Indeed you ought.' 'What girl among the Oghuz shall I get for
you?' Beyrek replied, 'Father, find me a girl who will rise before
I get to my feet, who will be on horseback before I mount my
well-trained horse, who before I reach my enemy will bring me
some heads; that's the sort of girl to find for me, father.' His
father replied, 'You don't want a girl, son; you seem to want a
comrade, a fellow-warrior. Son, I wonder, might the girl you
want be Prince Bay Bijan's daughter, the Lady Chichek?' 'That's
right, father,' he replied, 'that's the one I want.' 'Well, son, the
Lady Chichek has a wild brother they call Crazy Karchar, and
he kills anyone who asks for her hand.' 'In that case,' said
Beyrek, 'what are we to do?' Prince Bay Büre said, 'Son, let us
invite the nobles of the teeming Oghuz to our hearthfire and let
us act as they think advisable.'

They invited all the nobles of the teeming Oghuz, they brought
them to their hearthfire, and feasted them. They ate and drank
and began to talk; they took counsel together, saying, 'Who can
go and ask for this girl?' They deemed it advisable that Dede
Korkut should go. Dede Korkut said, 'Friends, since you're
sending me, and you know that Crazy Karchar kills anybody
who asks for his sister, at least bring me two horses from Bayindir Khan's stables; one the champion horse with the goat-head,
the other the lamb-headed bay, so that if there's any running
away and chasing I can mount one and lead the other.' Dede
Korkut's words proved acceptable; they went and fetched those
two horses from Bayindir Khan's stables. Dede Korkut rode one
and led the other. 'Friends,' said he, 'I bid you goodbye,' and off
he went.

Now it seems, my Sultan, that Crazy Karchar had pitched his
white pavilion, his white tent, on the black earth and was sitting
with his comrades; they were shooting at a target. Dede Korkut
came along, he bowed, placed his hand on his heart and gave fair
greeting.[39] Crazy Karchar foamed at the mouth, looked Dede
Korkut full in the face and said, 'And on you be peace, O you
whose works have gone to loss, whose deeds have gone awry, on
whose white forehead God has written doom! No creature on

legs has ever come here, no creature with a mouth has ever drunk
from this river of mine. What ails you? Have your works gone to
loss, have your deeds gone awry, has your appointed hour come?
What are you doing here?' Dede Korkut replied,

'I have come to climb your black mountain yonder,
  I have come to cross your beautiful eddying river,
  I have come to seek refuge in your ample skirts, your close
    embrace.
  By God's command and at the word of the Prophet [40]
  I have come to ask for your sister, the Lady Chichek,
  Purer than the moon, lovelier than the sun,
  For Bamsi Beyrek.'

When Dede Korkut said this, Crazy Karchar said, 'You
there, do as I bid! Bring the black horse and my equipment!'
They did so, and assisted Crazy Karchar to mount. Dede Korkut
mounted the lamb-headed bay and did not wait but rode straight
off, with Crazy Karchar in hot pursuit. The lamb-headed bay
grew weary and Dede Korkut leaped onto the goat-headed champion. Crazy Karchar chased the old man across ten mountain-
peaks and was hard at his heels. The old man did not know
which way to turn; he took refuge in God, he pronounced the
Most Great Name. Crazy Karchar drew his sword and prepared
to bring it down with a furious stroke that would split the old
man in two. Dede Korkut said, 'If you strike me, may your hand
wither.' By command of God Most High, Crazy Karchar's hand
remained suspended aloft, for Dede Korkut was a saint and his
wishes were granted. 'Help! Mercy!' said Crazy Karchar, 'There
is no doubt that God is One! See that my hand mends and by
God's command and at the word of the Prophet I shall give my
sister to Beyrek.' Three times he affirmed this out of his mouth
and repented of his sins. Dede Korkut prayed and by God's
order the crazy one's hand became sound and well. He turned
and said, 'Dede, will you give me whatever I want for my sister?'
'We shall,' said Dede Korkut, 'let's see what you want.' Crazy
Karchar replied, 'Bring me a thousand camel stallions that have
never seen a female camel, bring a thousand horses that have

never mounted a mare, bring a thousand rams that have never
seen a ewe, bring a thousand dogs with no tails or ears. And bring
me a thousand huge fleas. If you bring these things I have said,
good; I give her to you. Otherwise don't let me see you again, for
if I do – I haven't killed you this time but then I shall kill
you.'

Dede Korkut turned back and came to Prince Bay Büre's
tents. Prince Bay Büre said, 'Does Dede Korkut look cheerful or
downcast?' They saw that he was all smiles. 'Dede,' asked Prince
Bay Büre, 'are you a boy or a girl? 'I am a boy,'[41] he replied.
'In that case, how did you escape from Crazy Karchar's hand?'
'It happened by the grace of God and the aid of the saints.' He
told them the story and said, 'In short, I've got the girl.'

The bearer of good tidings came to Beyrek and his mother and
sisters, and they rejoiced and were glad. Prince Bay Büre said,
'How much did the crazy one ask for?' 'Curse him, may he not
prosper!' replied Dede Korkut, 'Crazy Karchar asked for wealth
without end.' 'What did he want, then?' asked Prince Bay Büre.
'A thousand horses that have never mounted a mare, a thousand
camel stallions that have never seen a female camel, a thousand
rams that have never seen a ewe, a thousand dogs with no tails or
ears, and a thousand huge fleas. Then he said, "If you bring
these things I shall give you my sister; if you don't, don't let me
see you, or I shall kill you"'. Prince Bay Büre said, 'Dede, if I
find three of them, will you find two?' 'I shall, lord,' said Dede
Korkut. 'Well, then, Dede, you find the dogs and the fleas.' He
himself went to his stables full of horses and chose a thousand
stallions, he went to his camels and chose a thousand males, he
went to his sheep and chose a thousand rams.

Dede Korkut, for his part, found a thousand dogs without
tails or ears, and came to Prince Bay Büre's house. Then he
took them on to Crazy Karchar's house. Crazy Karchar heard
him approaching and went out to meet him. 'Now let me see
whether you have brought what I told you,' he said. He saw
the horses and approved, he saw the camels and approved,
he saw the rams and approved. At the sight of the dogs he
roared with laughter. Then he said, 'And what about my

fleas, Dede, where are they?' 'Well, Karchar my son,' said Dede Korkut, 'they are as dangerous to a man as those gad-flies. They're savage beasts, I've got them all collected together. Come on, let's go and you can pick out the fat ones and leave the thin ones.' He took Crazy Karchar to a flea-infested sheep-fold, tore the clothes off him and pushed him in. Then he said, 'Take what you want and leave the rest,' and barred the door firmly. The fleas were starving and they swarmed all over Crazy Karchar, who shouted and roared, 'Help, Dede! For the love of God, open the door and let me out!' 'Karchar my son,' said Dede Korkut, 'why the uproar? There are the goods you ordered; I've brought them for you. What's wrong? Why have you gone all stupid? Stop the chatter, take the fat ones and leave the thin ones.' 'Dear Dede,' said Crazy Karchar, 'these are not the kind you can sort into ones you like and ones you don't. For God's sake open the door and let me out!' 'Afterwards you'll quarrel with us again,' said Dede Korkut, 'just you see.' Crazy Karchar reared up to his full height and stamped and bellowed, 'Help, dear Dede! Just you let me out of this door!' Dede opened the door and Crazy Karchar came out, stark naked and swarming with fleas. Dede saw that he was at the end of his tether and scared stiff; his body could not be seen for fleas, and his face and eyes were invisible. He fell at Dede Korkut's feet and said, 'Save me, for the love of God!' 'Go, my son,' said Dede Korkut, 'throw yourself in the river.' It was a cold day, but as if his life depended on it Crazy Karchar trotted to the river and plunged up to his neck in the icy water. The fleas, as fleas will, streamed into the water and left him. 'Dear Dede,' he said, 'may God not be pleased with them, neither the thin ones nor the fat ones.' He put his clothes on, went home, and saw to the preparation of a lavish wedding-feast.

In the days of the Oghuz the rule was that when a young man married he would shoot an arrow and wherever the arrow fell he would set up his marriage-tent. Beyrek shot his arrow and pitched his tent in the place where it fell. From his betrothed came a wedding-gift, a crimson caftan,[42] which he put on. This did not please his friends; they were glum. 'What are you so glum about?' asked Beyrek. 'Why shouldn't we be glum? You are wearing a crimson caftan while we are wearing white.' 'Why be glum over such a little thing? I am wearing it today; tomorrow my groomsman can wear it, and so on for forty days. Then we'll give it to a dervish.' He and his forty young men sat down and feasted.

Now a spy of the infidel (curse him, may he not prosper) spied on them and went and reported to the lord of the castle of Bayburt. 'Why do you sit there, my lord?' said the spy. 'The girl that Prince Bay Bijan was going to give to you he has given to Beyrek of the grey horse.' That damnable unbeliever rode out with a raiding-party of seven hundred infidels, while Beyrek, all unaware, was sitting feasting in his many-coloured marriage-tent. At midnight the infidel attacked the tent. His groomsman drew his sword, saying 'My head be a sacrifice for Beyrek's,' and they killed him. Beyrek was taken prisoner, with thirty-nine young men.

Dawn broke, the sun rose, Beyrek's father and mother saw that the marriage-tent had disappeared. They cried out, they tore their clothes, their wits left their heads. They looked and saw that the tent had been ripped to pieces and the groomsman slain. Beyrek's father took off his great turban and dashed it to the ground, he tugged at the neck of his robe and tore it, and he lamented his son. His white-haired mother sobbed and shed great tears, she scratched her white face with her sharp nails, she dragged at her red cheeks, she tore at her black hair like reeds uprooted and came, weeping and crying, to her tent.

Prince Bay Büre's pavilion with its golden smoke-hole was invaded by mourning. His daughters and daughters-in-law laughed no more, the red henna no more adorned their white hands. Beyrek's seven sisters took off their white dresses and put on black, they lamented and wailed together, saying, 'Alas, my only brother, princely brother, who never attained his heart's desire!' News was brought to his betrothed. The Lady Chichek dressed in black and put away her white caftan, she tore at her cheeks, red as autumn apples, and she mourned, saying,

'Alas, master of my red veil! [43]
Alas, hope of my forehead and head!
Alas, my kingly warrior, my falcon-like warrior!
Warrior at whose face I never gazed my fill!
Where have you gone leaving me alone, my soul, my warrior?
Whom I see when I open my eyes,
Whom I love with all my heart,
With whom I share one pillow, [44]
For whose sake I would die, a sacrifice.
Alas, trusty minister of Prince Kazan!
Alas, darling of the teeming Oghuz!
My lord Beyrek!'

Hearing this, Wild Dundar son of Kiyan Seljuk removed his white clothes and put on black. All Beyrek's friends and comrades did the same. The nobles of the teeming Oghuz mourned greatly for Beyrek, and abandoned hope.

Sixteen years passed, during which they did not know whether Beyrek was alive or dead. One day, the girl's brother, Crazy Karchar, came to the court of Bayindir Khan, bowed the knee and said, 'May the life of the Khan's Majesty be long. If Beyrek were alive, in sixteen years either news of him would have come or he himself would have come. If any man were to bring news that he was alive I would give him richly embroidered robes and gold and silver; to any who brought news of his death I would give my sister.' Thereupon Yaltajuk son of Yalanji (curse him, may he not prosper) said, 'My Sultan, I shall go and bring news of whether he is alive or dead.' Now it seems that Beyrek had given him a shirt, which he never wore but had kept. He went and dipped that shirt in blood, then brought it to Bayindir Khan. 'What is this shirt?' asked Bayindir Khan. 'My Sultan,' he replied, 'it is Beyrek's shirt; they killed Beyrek at the Black Pass, and this is the proof of it.'

Among the Oghuz nobles, lying was unknown; they believed him and wept. But Bayindir Khan said, 'What are you crying for? We do not know this shirt. Take it and show it to his betrothed; she will know it well, for she sewed it and will recognize

it.' They brought it to the Lady Chichek. As soon as she saw it
she knew it and said, 'That's it.' She ripped the neck of her
dress, she drove her sharp nails into her white face, she tore at
her cheeks, red as autumn apples, and she mourned:

> 'Alas for him whom I see when I open my eyes,
> Whom I gave my heart and love!
> Alas, master of my red wedding-veil!
> Alas, hope of my forehead and my head!
> Lord Beyrek!'

The news was brought to her parents, and mourning invaded
their many-coloured encampment; they put off their white
clothes and put on black. The nobles of the teeming Oghuz gave
up hope of Beyrek. Yaltajuk son of Yalanji held his betrothal
feast and appointed a day for his wedding.

Once again Beyrek's father Prince Bay Büre summoned the
merchants and said, 'Merchants, go and search in every land
and bring me news whether Beyrek is dead or alive.' The merchants made preparation for the journey and departed, travelling on without regard for day and night. Eventually they
reached Parasar's castle of Bayburt. Now that day was the infidels' feast-day. Every one of them was eating and drinking. They
brought Beyrek and made him play his lute. Beyrek looked out
from a high platform and saw the merchants. When he saw
them he asked them for news; let us see, my Khan, how he asked.

> 'Caravan, coming from the broad lowlands,
> Caravan, precious gift of the lord my father and my lady
>   mother,[45]
> Caravan, on your long-hooved falcon-swift horses,
> Understand my words, hear what I say, O caravan.
> Among the teeming Oghuz
> If I ask for news of Salur Kazan son of Ulash,
> Does he yet live, O caravan?
> If I ask for news of Wild Dundar son of Kiyan Seljuk,
> Does he yet live, O caravan?
> And Kara Budak son of Kara Göne,

Does he yet live, O caravan?
If I ask for news of my white-bearded father, my white-
   haired mother,
My seven sisters; do they yet live, O caravan?
She whom I saw when I opened my eyes,
Whom I love with all my heart,
The Lady Chichek daughter of Prince Bay Bijan;
Is she yet in her house or has she married another?
Tell me, O caravan,
And my dark head be a sacrifice for you.'

The merchants replied:

'Are you alive, are you well, dear Bamsi?
Sixteen years we have sorrowed over you, lord Bamsi.
If, among the teeming Oghuz, you ask about Prince Kazan,
He lives, Bamsi.
If you ask about Wild Dundar son of Kiyan Seljuk,
He lives, Bamsi.
If you ask about Kara Budak son of Kara Göne,
He lives, Bamsi.
Those nobles have put off their white clothes and put on
   black, Bamsi.
If you ask about your white-bearded father and your white-
   haired mother,
They live, Bamsi.
They have put off their white clothes and put on black for
   you, Bamsi.
Your seven sisters I saw crying at the place where seven
   roads meet, Bamsi.
I saw them tearing their cheeks, red as autumn apples,
I saw them bewailing their brother who had gone and never
   returned.
She whom you saw when you opened your eyes,
Whom you gave your heart and loved,
Prince Bay Bijan's daughter, the Lady Chichek,
Has celebrated her betrothal and appointed the day for her
   wedding.

I saw her on her way to marry Yaltajuk son of Yalanji.
Lord Beyrek, contrive to fly from Parasar's castle of Bayburt,
To reach your many-coloured marriage-tent.
If you do not, you have lost Prince Bay Bijan's daughter,
   the Lady Chichek;
Be sure of this.'

Beyrek, hearing these bitter words, came weeping to his thirty-nine young men. He took off his great turban, hurled it to the ground and said, 'My thirty-nine comrades, do you know what has happened? Yaltajuk son of Yalanji has brought news of my death, mourning has invaded my father's pavilion with the golden smoke-hole, his swan-like daughters and daughters-in-law have put off their white raiment and put on black. She whom I saw when I opened my eyes, whom I gave my heart and loved, the Lady Chichek, is to marry Yaltajuk son of Yalanji.' At these words his thirty-nine young men took off their great turbans and hurled them to the ground, and together they wept and lamented.

Now the infidel lord had a maiden daughter, who loved Beyrek and came every day to visit him. That day again she came. Seeing Beyrek looking downcast, she said, 'Why are you downcast, my kingly warrior? Whenever I have come I have seen you cheerful, smiling and dancing. What has happened now?' 'Why shouldn't I be downcast?' replied Beyrek. 'For the sixteen years that I have been your father's prisoner I have been missing my parents, my people, my sisters, and also I had a black-eyed betrothed. There is a man they call Yaltajuk son of Yalanji who has come and told lies, saying that I was dead. Now she is going to marry him.' When he said this, the girl who was in love with him said, 'If I let you down from the castle by a rope, and if you reach your father and mother safely, will you come back and marry me?' Beyrek swore an oath: 'May I be sliced on my own sword, may I be spitted on my own arrow, may I be slashed like the ground, may I blow in dust like the earth if I reach the Oghuz land safely and do not come back and marry you.'

The girl brought a rope and let Beyrek down from the castle. He looked down and saw that he was on the ground. He gave thanks to God and began to walk, until he came to the infidels' horse-pasture, thinking that he might find a horse, take it and ride. And there he saw his own grey horse, the sea-born, standing and cropping the grass. The grey horse recognized Beyrek too when he saw him; he reared up on his hind legs and whinnied.[46] Then Beyrek praised him; let us see, my Khan, how he praised him.

'Your dear forehead is like a broad open field,
Your dear eyes are like two glowing jewels,
Your dear mane is like rich brocade,
Your dear ears are like twin brothers,
Your dear back brings a man to his heart's desire.
I shall not call you "horse" but "brother" – and better than
   any brother.
"There's work to be done, comrade," I shall say – and better
   than any comrade.'

The horse raised his head, pricked up one ear and came towards Beyrek, who hugged his chest and kissed both his eyes. Then he leaped onto his back and rode towards the castle gate, where he committed his thirty-nine comrades to the infidels' care; let us see, my Khan, how he did so.

'Infidel of filthy religion!
You were for ever casting insults in my mouth; I have not
   had my fill.
You gave me stew to eat, of the black swine's flesh; I have
   not had my fill.
God has given me my freedom and I am on my way.
My thirty-nine young men I commit to your care, O infidel;
If I find one missing I shall kill ten in his place.
If I find ten missing I shall kill a hundred in their place,
   O infidel.
My thirty-nine young men I commit to your care, O infidel!'

Then he rode away. Forty infidels mounted and rode after him; they chased him but they could not catch him, and they rode back.

Beyrek came to the Oghuz land and saw a minstrel [47] journeying. 'Whither away, minstrel?' said he. 'To the wedding, young lord,' the minstrel replied. 'Whose is the wedding?' 'Yaltajuk's, son of Yalanji.' 'And who is the girl he is marrying?' 'The betrothed of the lord Beyrek,' said the minstrel. 'Minstrel,' said Beyrek, 'give me your lute and I shall give you my horse. Keep him till I come and bring you his price and take him.' 'Lo and behold!' said the minstrel, 'I've won a horse, without cracking my voice or straining my throat or breaking my lute! I'll take him and look after him.' And he gave his lute to Beyrek, who took it and made his way to the vicinity of his father's encampment.

There he saw some shepherds lined up at the side of the road, weeping and at the same time ceaselessly piling up stones. 'Shepherds,' said he, 'if anyone finds a stone on the road he throws it away; why are you piling these stones on the road and crying?' The shepherds replied, 'You know about yourself but you know nothing of what ails us.' 'Well, what does ail you?' 'Our lord had a son,' they said, 'but for the last sixteen years no one knew whether he was alive or dead. A man called Yaltajuk son of Yalanji has brought news that he is dead, and they have decided to marry his betrothed to this man. He has to pass this way and we're going to stone him, so that she won't have to marry him but can marry a man worthy of her.' 'All honour to you,' said Beyrek, 'that will be an honest day's work!' Then he came to his father's encampment.

Now before their tents was a great tree, with a fair spring at its foot. Beyrek saw his little sister coming to get water from that spring, and she wept saying, 'My brother Beyrek, how evilly has your wedding-feast turned out!' A mighty grief at his long separation came over Beyrek; he could not endure it and his great tears flowed. He called out to her, declaiming; let us see, my Khan, what he declaimed.

'Girl, why do you cry and sob for your brother?
(I burn within, my heart is aflame.)
So your brother is gone.
Boiling oil has been poured over your heart.
You are racked with inward pain.
Why do you cry and sob for your brother?
(I burn within, my heart is aflame.)
If I might ask, whose summer-pasture is yonder black
    mountain?
Whose drink its cold cold rivers?
Whose mounts those stables full of falcon-swift horses?
Whose beasts of burden those camels, caravan on caravan?
Whose feast the white sheep in the folds?
Whose shade the black and sky-blue tents?
Tell me, maiden, from your own mouth;
My dark head be a sacrifice for you this day.'

The girl replied,

'Play not, minstrel; tell no tales, minstrel!
What use is that, to a wretched girl like me?
If you ask about yonder black mountain,
It was my brother Beyrek's summer-pasture.
Since my brother Beyrek left I have gone to no summer-
    pasture.
If you ask about its cold cold rivers,
They were my brother Beyrek's drink.
Since my brother Beyrek left I have not drunk.
If you ask about the stables full of falcon-swift horses,
They were my brother Beyrek's mounts.
Since my brother Beyrek left I have not ridden.
If you ask about the camels, caravan on caravan,
They were my brother Beyrek's beasts of burden.
Since my brother Beyrek left I have laden no beasts of burden.
If you ask about the white sheep in the folds,
They were my brother Beyrek's feast.
Since my brother Beyrek left I have not feasted.
If you ask about the black and sky-blue tents,

They were my brother Beyrek's shade.
Since my brother Beyrek left I have not migrated.'

Again she spoke,

'Minstrel,
On your way here, when you climbed yonder black mountain,
Did you not meet a man named Beyrek?
On your way here, when you crossed the swollen rivers,
Did you not meet a man named Beyrek?
On your way here, when you passed through famous cities,
Did you not meet a man named Beyrek?
If you have seen him, minstrel, tell me;
My dark head be a sacrifice for you, minstrel.'

Yet again she spoke,

'My black mountain yonder has fallen in ruins;
Minstrel, you are unaware.
My great shady tree has been cut down;
Minstrel, you are unaware.
My only brother in all the world has been taken;
Minstrel, you are unaware.
Play not, minstrel; tell no tales, minstrel.
What use is that, to a wretched girl like me, minstrel?
There is a wedding-feast along the road;
Go to the wedding-feast and sing!'

Beyrek left her and came to where his older sisters were. He
saw them sitting dressed in black, and he called out to them, declaiming; let us see, my Khan, what he declaimed.

'Girls who rise up from your place at early morning,
Who have abandoned the white tent for the black tent,
Who have put off your white clothes and put on black clothes,
Have you any yoghurt, clotting like liver?
Have you any cakes in the black oven?
Have you any bread in the crock?
Three days have I journeyed; give me to eat.'

The girls went and brought food and filled Beyrek's belly. Then he said, 'As charity for your brother's head and eye, if you have a worn-out caftan I might wear to the feast; there they will present me with caftans and I shall return yours.' They went and found a caftan of Beyrek's and gave it to him. He took it and put it on and it fitted him, its length his length, its waist his waist, its arm his arm. His eldest sister noticed how like he was to Beyrek, and her black almond eyes filled with bloody tears. She declaimed; let us see, my Khan, what she declaimed.

> 'Were not your black almond eyes without lustre,
> I should call you my brother Beyrek, minstrel.
> Were your face not covered in black hair,
> I should call you my brother Beyrek, minstrel.
> Were your strong wrists not shrunken,
> I should call you my brother Beyrek, minstrel.
> With your proud swaggering walk,
> Your lion-like stance,
> Your intent gaze,
> You are so like my brother Beyrek, minstrel.
> You have rejoiced me, minstrel; do not cast me down!'

Again she declaimed,

> 'Play not, minstrel, tell no tales, minstrel.
> Since my brother Beyrek left no minstrel has visited us.
> None has taken our caftan from our back,
> None has taken our nightcap from our head,
> None has taken our curly-horned rams.'

Beyrek said to himself, 'Do you see, the girls recognized me by this caftan, and so too will the nobles of the teeming Oghuz. Let me find out who my friends and enemies are among the Oghuz.' He took off the caftan and threw it at the girls, saying, 'Confound you and Beyrek! You gave me an old caftan, you took my head and my brains.'[48] So saying, he went and found an old camel-cloth, poked a hole in it, put his head through and pretended to be mad.

He went on his way and came to the wedding-feast. He saw

the bridegroom shooting arrows, with Budak son of Kara Göne, Uruz son of Prince Kazan, Yigenek the paramount noble, Sher Shemseddin son of Gaflet Koja, and Crazy Karchar, the girl's brother. Every time Budak shot, Beyrek said, 'Luck to your hand!' Every time Uruz shot, Beyrek said, 'Luck to your hand!' Every time Yigenek shot, Beyrek said, 'Luck to your hand!' Every time Sher Shemseddin shot, Beyrek said, 'Luck to your hand!' But when the bridegroom shot, he said, 'May your hand wither, may your fingers rot, pig and son of a pig! May you be a sacrifice for all true bridegrooms!' Yaltajuk son of Yalanji, infuriated, said, 'You rogue and son of a rogue, is it your place to talk to me like this? Come here, you rogue, and draw my bow or I shall cut your head off this instant.' Straightway Beyrek took the bow and drew it; it broke in half at the grip and he threw it down in front of him, saying, 'It'll do for shooting larks at close range.' Enraged that his bow was smashed, Yaltajuk son of Yalanji said, 'There's that bow of Beyrek's; fetch it.' They went and brought it. Seeing the bow, Beyrek was reminded of his comrades, and tears came to his eyes. He said,

'My strong white-gripped bow, which I bought at the price
    of a stallion,
My twisted string, which I bought at the price of a bull.
In a distressful place I abandoned
My thirty-nine comrades, my two messengers.'[49]

Then he said, 'My lords, with your leave I shall draw this bow and shoot an arrow in your honour.' Now they were aiming at the bridegroom's ring,[50] and Beyrek's arrow struck that ring and broke it in pieces. The Oghuz nobles clapped their hands and laughed at the sight. Prince Kazan was looking on and he summoned Beyrek. The crazy minstrel came, bowed his head, placed his hand on his heart and declaimed; let us see, my Khan, what he declaimed.

'You of the white pavilion, pitched afar in the morning
    twilight,
You of the blue parasol made of satin,

You of the falcon-swift horses, drawn up stall on stall,
You of the many officers, who summon and give justice,
You of limitless bounty when the oil is poured,[51]
Prop of forsaken warriors,
Hope of the wretched and the helpless,
Son-in-law of Bayindir Khan,
Chick of the long-plumed bird,
Pillar of the Turkish lands,
Lion of the Emet river,
Tiger of the Karajuk,
Master of the chestnut horse,
Father of Khan Uruz,
My Khan Kazan!
Hear my voice, pay heed to my words.
You rose in the morning twilight,
You entered the white forest,
You passed through the white poplar boughs, shaking them,
You bent down its side-poles,
You threw on its top-struts,
You called it a marriage-bower.[52]
Princes of the right hand, seated on the right!
Princes of the left hand, seated on the left![53]
Ministers at the threshold!
Princes of the entourage, seated at the foot of the throne!
Good fortune on your realm!'

To which Prince Kazan replied, 'Crazy minstrel, what do you
ask of me? Do you want tents and pavilions, slaves and slave-
girls, gold and silver? I shall give them to you.' 'My lord,' said
Beyrek, 'would you permit me to approach the banquet? I am
hungry and would fill myself.' Kazan replied, 'The crazy
minstrel has struck lucky. Nobles! For today my realm is to be
his; let him go where he will, do what he will.' Beyrek came to
the banquet and ate his fill, then kicked the cauldrons, spilt
them and overturned them. He hurled some of the stewed meat
to his right, some to his left. Those on the right got what went
to the right, those on the left got what went to the left. The

righteous wins his just deserts, the unrighteous wins disgrace. The word was brought to Prince Kazan: 'Lord, the crazy minstrel has upset all the food and now he wants to join the girls.' 'Well let him do what he likes; let him go where he wants, let him even join the girls,' said Kazan.

Beyrek upped and went in the direction of the girls. He chased away the pipers, he chased away the drummers. Some he beat, some he split the heads of. He came to the tent where the girls and the ladies were sitting, and he sat down across the threshold. Prince Kazan's wife, Burla the Tall, was furious at the sight and said, 'You crazy rogue and son of a rogue, is it your place to come upon me without ceremony?' 'Lady,' replied Beyrek, 'I have Prince Kazan's orders: none is to interfere with me.' 'Very well,' said the Lady Burla, 'since Prince Kazan has so ordered, let him sit.' Then she turned again to Beyrek and said, 'Crazy minstrel, what do you want?' 'I want the bride to get up and dance while I play the lute.' There was a lady called Kisirja Yenge, and they said to her, 'You stand up and dance, Kisirja Yenge. How will the crazy minstrel know the difference?' Kisirja Yenge stood and said, 'Crazy minstrel, I am the bride. Play your lute and I shall dance.' Beyrek knew who she was and he declaimed; let us see, my Khan, what he declaimed.

'I take my oath I have never mounted a barren mare,[54]
Never have I mounted one and ridden off on foray.
The herdsmen behind the gully watch you;
They follow your footsteps to see which valley you have
   taken,
They watch the road to see which way you come,
Great tears flow from their eyes.
Go to them.
They will give you what you want.
I have no business with you.
Let the girl who is to marry stand,
Let her wave her arms and dance,
And I shall play the lute.'

'Oh dear!' said Kisirja Yenge, 'this accursed madman speaks as if he had seen me!' and she went and sat down again, and all the great khans' wives laughed out loud behind their yashmaks.

There was another lady, called Boghazja Fatima. 'You get up and dance,' they said to her. 'And suppose that crazy nobody says the same sort of impossible things about me?' said she. 'There's no harm in saying you're the bride,' they said, and made her put on the bride's caftan. 'Play, crazy minstrel,' she said, 'and I'll dance. I'm the girl who is to be married.' Beyrek replied,

'This time I take my oath I have never mounted a pregnant mare,[55]
Never have I mounted one and ridden off on foray.
Behind your house was there not a little river?
Was your dog's name not Barak?
Was your name not Boghazja Fatima of the forty lovers?
Go to your place and sit,
Or I shall expose more of your shame; be sure of that.
I do not play with you.
Let the one who is to marry stand,
And I shall play the lute.
Let her wave her arms and dance.'

At that, Boghazja Fatima said, 'Oh dear! The secrets are coming out! The crazy minstrel, coming and spoiling our agreeable party, throwing all our faults in our faces, insulting us and blackening our good name in front of all these people!' She went to the girl and said, 'The things that have happened because of you! Our friends and our enemies have all laughed at us! Now, if you're going to dance, get up and dance! If you won't dance, go and dance in hell!'

Of course the Lady Chichek was wondering what he would say to her, but they said, 'What are you wondering about? We knew you'd have this sort of adventure once Beyrek was gone.' The Lady Burla the Tall said, 'Come girl, get up and dance, make the best of it.' The Lady Chichek put on her red gown, drew her hands inside the sleeves so that they should not show, and prepared to dance, saying, 'Play, crazy minstrel, and I shall dance; I am the girl who is to be married.' Beyrek replied,

'Since I left this place the weather has been icy.
Heavily has the white snow fallen, up to the knee.
In the house of the Khan's daughter there were no more
    slaves or slave-girls,
She herself took the pitcher and went for water,
Her ten fingers were frostbitten from the wrist down.
Bring red gold and I shall make fingers for the Khan's
    daughter.
Bring white silver and I shall fashion fingernails for her.
Shame for a Khan's daughter not to be perfect on her
    wedding-day!'

Angered at this, the Lady Chichek said, 'Crazy minstrel, is there any flaw in me that you should cast shame on me?' She put out her hands, showing her silver-white wrists, and the gold ring which Beyrek had given her was plain to see on her finger. Beyrek recognized the ring and declaimed; let us see, my Khan, what he declaimed.

'Since Beyrek left, have you tramped to the hilltop, maiden?
Have you strained to see on all four sides, maiden?
Have you torn your black hair like reeds uprooted, maiden?
Have you shed bitter tears from your black eyes, maiden?
Have you slashed your cheeks, red as autumn apples,
    maiden?
Have you asked news of Beyrek from every traveller,
    maiden?
Have you cried for Bamsi Beyrek whom you loved, maiden?
You are marrying another; the gold ring is mine.
Give it to me, maiden!'

The girl replied,

'Since Beyrek left, often have I tramped to the hilltop,
Much have I torn my black hair, like reeds uprooted,

Much have I slashed my cheeks, red as autumn apples,
Much have I asked news of travellers,
Much have I shed bitter tears from my black eyes,
Much have I cried for my young prince, my young Khan
    Beyrek,
Who has gone and comes not again.
You are not Bamsi Beyrek my lover, my beloved;
Not yours the golden ring.
In the ring are many tokens;
Tell the tokens if you desire the ring.'

Beyrek said,

'Daughter of Khans, did I not rise up in the morning twi-
    light?
Did I not mount my grey horse?
Did I not fell a stag before your tent?
Did you not summon me to your side?
Did we not race our horses over the plain?
Did my horse not outstrip yours?
When we shot, did I not split your arrow?
Did I not throw you when we wrestled?
Before I put the gold ring on your finger,
Did I not kiss you thrice and bite you once?
Am I not Bamsi Beyrek your lover, your beloved?'

Then the girl recognized him and knew that he was Beyrek,
and she cast herself at his feet. The ladies knew that he was
Beyrek and each went to bring the good news to one of the
nobles, while the serving-maids dressed Beyrek in robes. The girl
leaped up and mounted her horse and galloped off to bring the
good news to Beyrek's parents. When she reached them, she said,

'Your rugged black mountain had fallen; it is risen at last.
Your blood-red rivers had dried up; they are in spate at last.
Your great tree had withered; it is green at last.
Your falcon-swift mare had grown old; she has foaled at
    last.

Your red camel had grown old; she has brought forth at
   last.
Your white ewe had grown old; she has lambed at last.
Your son Beyrek, sixteen years mourned, has come home at
   last.
Father and mother of my husband, tell me,
What will you give me for this good news?'

Beyrek's parents replied,

'Dear daughter-in-law, may I die for your tongue!
May I be a sacrifice for your life!
If your words are a lie, may they prove true!
If he should come, alive and well,
Let yonder black mountains be your summer-pasture,
Let their cold rivers be your drink,
My slaves and slave-girls be your servants,
My falcon-swift horses be your mount,
My caravan on caravan of camels be your beasts of burden,
My white sheep in the folds be your banquet,
My gold and silver be yours to spend,
My white pavilion with its gold smoke-hole be your shade,
My dark head be a sacrifice for you, daughter-in-law!'

At that moment the nobles, having heard the news, were
swarming round Beyrek, and the princes and khans escorted
him to his father. Prince Kazan said, 'Good news, Prince Bay
Büre! Your son has come home.' Now since his son Beyrek
had gone, Prince Bay Büre's eyes had become blind with weeping. Prince Bay Büre said, 'This is how I shall know that he is
my son: let him draw blood from his little finger, smear it on a
towel and wipe my eyes with it. If they open, he is indeed my
son Beyrek.' Beyrek did so; he wiped it across his father's eyes
and they were opened.[56] His parents cried aloud and fell on
Beyrek, saying,

'Son, prop of my white pavilion with its gold smoke-hole!
Son, flower of my swan-like daughters and daughters-in-
   law!

Son, light of my eyes that see!
Son, strength of my hands that hold!
Darling of the teeming Oghuz, my soul, my son!'

They wept and cried together, they gave thanks to mighty God, they sacrificed horses, camels, sheep and cattle, and freed many slaves and slave-girls.

Yaltajuk son of Yalanji heard the news and, fleeing in terror of Beyrek, took to the Calf Woods. Beyrek followed after, chasing him deeper and deeper into the woods. 'Bring fire!' said Beyrek. They did so, and fired the woods. Seeing himself in danger of burning, Yaltajuk left the woods, fell at Beyrek's feet and came beneath his sword, but he escaped, for Beyrek forgave him his crimes.

Prince Kazan said, 'Now you may attain your desire.' But Beyrek replied, 'My Khan Kazan, until I have freed my comrades and taken the castle I shall not attain my desire.' Then Prince Kazan gave a great shout: 'For Beyrek's sake, all the princes and warriors who love me, to horse!' The nobles of the teeming Oghuz mounted and rode off, crying, 'Bayburt Castle, where are you?' The infidels' spies brought the news, the infidel lord gathered his soldiers and went out to meet them. The heroes of the teeming Oghuz performed their ablutions in pure water and prayed. Then they mounted their horses once more and, invoking blessings on Muhammad of beautiful name, they drew their swords, cried 'God is most great!' and charged at the infidel. The drums rolled like thunder and the trumpets brayed, inviting those of good heart to show themselves, and the unmanly to slink away. Lord was separated from retainer and retainer from lord. Doomsday dawned, the field was full of heads. Prince Kazan laid King Shökli low and cut off his head. The Black Lord was felled by a blow from Wild Dundar's sword, Kara Budak felled the Black Lion King. Beyrek and Yigenek smote the infidels' standards with their swords and brought them down. The infidels panicked and fled down the valleys. Seven infidel lords were put to the sword.

Beyrek, Yigenek, Kara Budak, Wild Dundar and Prince

Uruz son of Kazan, with Kazan at their head, advanced on the castle. Beyrek found his thirty-nine warriors and gave thanks to God at seeing them alive and well. They destroyed the infidels' church, they killed its priests and made a mosque in its place. They had the call to prayer proclaimed, they had the invocation recited in the name of the Mighty God. The best of the hunting-birds, the purest of stuffs, the loveliest girls, the heaviest brocades in bundles of nine,[57] they selected as the fifth part of the booty due to Bayindir, the Khan of Khans.

Beyrek had sworn a bargain with the daughter of the infidel King; he took her back to his white pavilion, his white tent, and began the wedding-feast.[58] Prince Kazan found girls for some of the thirty-nine warriors, as did Bayindir Khan. To seven of them Beyrek gave his seven sisters. He set up tents in forty places and shot one arrow for each of the forty girls, for chance to take its course.[59]

For forty days and nights they held the wedding-feast. Beyrek and his warriors attained their desire. Dede Korkut came and played joyful music, he told stories and declaimed, he related the adventures of the heroic fighters for the Faith, and said, 'Let this tale of the Oghuz be Beyrek's.'

I shall pray for you, my Khan: may your firm-rooted black mountains never be overthrown, may your great shady tree never be cut down, may your white-bearded father's place be paradise, may your white-haired mother's place be heaven. May He never part you from your sons and brothers, may the end of days not part you from the pure Faith. May those who say 'Amen' see His face. May He grant you increase and preserve you in strength and forgive your sins for the honour of Muhammad the Chosen of beautiful name, O my Khan!

4
TELLS THE STORY OF HOW PRINCE URUZ SON OF PRINCE KAZAN WAS TAKEN PRISONER, O MY KHAN!

ONE day Salur Kazan son of Ulash, lion of heroes, chick of the long-plumed bird, hope of the wretched and the helpless, prop of forsaken warriors, marshal of the teeming Oghuz, foe of Kan Abkaz,⁶⁰ master of the chestnut horse, brother of Kara Göne, uncle of Kara Budak, father of Khan Uruz, rose up from his place. He had his tents pitched on the black earth. In a thousand places silken carpets were spread. The many-coloured parasol reared towards the sky. Nine hundred thousand young Oghuz assembled to his gathering. Great-mouthed wine-jars were placed around and about, and in nine places vats were set. Golden goblets and ewers were ranged in rows. Nine infidel girls, lovely of face, black of eye, with plaited hair, their hands henna'd from the wrist down, their fingers tattooed, their necks a span long, were circulating the red wine in golden goblets among the nobles of the teeming Oghuz.

Salur Kazan son of Ulash had taken wine from the hands of all of them. He was giving away stacks upon stacks of tents and pavilions, file upon file of camels, black-eyed slaves and slave-girls. His son Uruz stood facing him, leaning on his bow. On his right sat his brother Kara Göne, on his left his maternal uncle Uruz. Kazan looked to his right and laughed aloud, he looked to his left and rejoiced greatly, he looked in front of him and saw his son Uruz; he smote his hands together and wept. This displeased his son Uruz. He came forward, knelt, and declaimed to his father; let us see, my Khan, what he declaimed.

'Hear my voice, understand my words, my lord Kazan.

You looked to your right and laughed aloud,
You looked to your left and rejoiced greatly,
You looked in front of you, saw me, and wept.
Tell me the reason
And my dark head be a sacrifice for you, my father.
If you will not say,
I shall rise up from my place,
I shall take my black-eyed warriors with me,
I shall go to Kan Abkaz's land,
I shall press my hand on the golden cross,
I shall kiss the hand of the black-hatted priest,
I shall marry a dark-eyed infidel girl,
I shall not come before your face again.
Why did you weep? Tell me,
And my dark head be a sacrifice for you, my lord.'

Prince Kazan changed colour, he looked his son full in the face and declaimed in answer; let us see, my Khan, what he declaimed.

'See here, my foal, my son.
When I looked to my right I saw my brother Kara Göne;
He has cut off heads, spilled blood, taken booty, won a
    name.
When I looked to my left I saw my uncle Uruz;
He has cut off heads, spilled blood, taken booty, won a
    name.
When I looked in front of me I saw you.
You have reached your sixteenth year.
This is why I wept: my father died and I was left,
I held his place, I held his lands.
A day will come when I shall die and you be left,
You have not drawn bow, shot arrow, cut off head, spilled
    blood.
Among the teeming Oghuz you have taken no booty.

'I thought of my end and I wept, for on a morrow when time comes round and I die and you are left, they will not give you my crown and my throne.'

Thereupon Uruz declaimed; let us see, my Khan, what he declaimed.

'Lord father,
  You have grown as great as a camel; you haven't the sense
    of a colt.
  You have grown as great as a hill; your brains aren't the
    size of a grain of millet.

'Does a son learn skills by watching his father, or do fathers learn from their children? When have you ever taken me to the infidel frontier, brandished your sword and cut off heads? What have I seen you do? What am I supposed to learn?'

Prince Kazan clapped his hands, laughed loudly and said, 'Nobles, Uruz has spoken well, he has eaten sugar. Nobles, eat and drink; do not break up the party. I shall take this boy and go out hunting. I shall carry a week's provisions, I shall show him the places where I have shot arrows and the places where I have thrust with my lance, wielded my sword, and cut off heads. I shall take him to the infidel frontier, to Jizighlar, to Aghlaghan, to the Blue Mountain.[61] It will come in handy for the boy later on, nobles.'

He had his chestnut horse brought round and he leaped on its back. He took with him three hundred warriors, their mail jewel-studded. Uruz took with him his forty chestnut-eyed young men. Kazan and his son went out to hunt on the bosom of the black mountains. They hunted, they fowled, they brought down the stags. They pitched tents on the green fields, on the beautiful meadows. For several days they feasted with the chieftains. Now the infidels from the fortress of Barehead Dadian, from the fortress of Aksaka,[62] had a spy, who saw them, came to the infidel king, and said, 'Why do you sit still? Kazan, chief of heroes, who does not let your dog bark or your cat miaow, has got drunk, with his young son, and they are asleep.' Sixteen thousand black-mailed infidels mounted their horses and charged down on Kazan. He and his men suddenly noticed that six separate clouds of dust had drawn near to them. Some said, 'It is the dust of a herd of deer'; others said, 'It is the dust of the

enemy.' Kazan said, 'If it were deer there would be one or two
clouds at most; you can be sure it is the enemy that comes.'
The dust parted, there was a gleam like the sun, a surging like
the sea, a blackness like an oak-forest, and sixteen thousand
infidels appeared, with stirrups of rope, with goat-hair caps,
men of savage religion and intemperate speech.

Kazan had his chestnut horse brought and leaped onto its
back. His son Uruz jerked his bridle and made his Arab horse
prance, and came towards him, saying,

'To me, my lord Kazan!
What is this that comes, darkling as the sea?
Gleaming like fire, glittering like the stars?
Speak to me five words from your mouth, your tongue,
And my dark head be a sacrifice for you, father.'

Kazan replied,

'To me, my lion-like son!
That which comes surging like the black sea
Is the host of the unbeliever.
That which comes gleaming like the sun
Is the helmet on the unbeliever's head.
That which comes glittering like the stars
Is the unbeliever's lance.
It is the unbeliever, O my son; the enemy, of savage
    religion.'

The boy inquired, 'What is the meaning of "enemy"?' Kazan
replied, 'My son, the meaning of "enemy" is the people whom
we kill when we catch them, and when they catch us they kill
us.' 'Father,' said Uruz, 'if princes and warriors among the
enemy are killed, does the enemy demand their blood of us?'
Kazan replied, 'My son, if you kill a thousand infidels none will
demand their blood of you.[63] Be that as it may, it is the infidel
of savage religion; it has chanced well that we have met him,
but you are keeping me tarrying in a dangerous place, my son.'
Thereupon Uruz declaimed; let us see, my Khan, what he
declaimed.

'To me, my lord Kazan!
I have risen from my place,
I was keeping my Arab horse for this day;
His day has come.
I shall gallop him over the white field for you.
I was keeping my long-pointed lance for this day;
Its day has come.
On great bellies and broad breasts I shall set it dancing for
    you.
I was keeping my pure black steel sword for this day;
Its day has come.
I shall let it cut off the heads of foul-religioned infidels for
    you.
I was keeping my strong-bodied iron mail for this day;
Its day has come.
I shall have sleeves and collar stitched for you.[64]
I was keeping the strong helmet on my head for this day;
Its day has come.
I shall let it be broken under the great war-club for you.
I was keeping my forty warriors for this day;
Their day has come.
I shall have them cut off infidel heads for you.
I was keeping my lion-name[65] for this day;
Its day has come.
I shall seize the infidel's collar and grapple with him for
    you.
A few words for me from your mouth and tongue,
And my dark head be a sacrifice, my lord, for you!'

Thereupon Kazan declaimed; let us see, my Khan, what he
declaimed.

'My son, my son, O my son!
Hear my voice, understand my words.
That infidel has bowmen who shoot three arrows and do
    not miss once.
He has headsmen who cut off heads in the twinkling of an
    eye.

He has cooks who make stews of human flesh.
He is not the infidel for you to meet.
I shall rise up from my place and stand;
I shall straddle the chestnut horse.
The infidel who comes is mine; I shall meet him,
I shall wield the black steel sword.
It is the infidel of savage religion; I shall cut off his head,
I shall dart hither and yon, and fight and do battle.
Watch me wielding the sword and cutting off heads, and
   learn!
It will be useful when the need falls on your dark head!'

Uruz declaimed in answer; let us see, my Khan, what he
declaimed.

'Lord father, I hear,
But the male lamb is for sacrifice at Arafat.[66]
Fathers have sons for the sake of fame,
And the son girds on the sword out of zeal for his father.
Let my head be a sacrifice for you.'

Kazan then declaimed; let us see, my Khan, what he declaimed.

'My son, my son, O my son!
You have not gone among the enemy and cut off heads,
You have not killed men and spilled blood.
Take your forty chestnut-eyed young men,
Go up to the summit of the great mountains with their
   lovely folds.
While I war and while I fight,
While I struggle and clash my blade,
See! Learn! And lie in wait to help us, son.'

Uruz did not disregard his father's words; he turned and
went back. He took his comrades up to the crest of the high
mountains. In those days a son did not go counter to his father's
words; had one done so, the father would not have acknow-
ledged him as his son. Uruz thrust his spear into the broad
slope and stood.

Prince Kazan saw that the infidel was very close. He dismounted, performed his ablutions with pure water, placed his white forehead on the earth and prayed. He invoked Muhammad of beautiful name, he worked himself up against the infidel of dark religion; he shouted, he spurred his horse and came up to them, he brandished his sword. The drums rolled like thunder, the brazen horns, gold-curlicued, were blown. On that day the gallant and heroic princes wheeled about the field battling. That day the beechwood arrows were shot and the sharp-pointed spears, like many-coloured snakes, were thrust home. On that day the cowards, the unmanly, spied out places where they could skulk.

As Uruz son of Kazan watched the fight, the lust for battle came over him, and he said, 'To me, my forty warriors, and my head be a sacrifice for you! Do you see my lord Kazan has cut off heads and spilled blood? A boy does not become a soldier just by eating his rations. It seems to me my father has been too kind to these infidels; why do you stand there, my young men who love me? Let us attack the infidel flank.' Uruz spurred his horse and charged the infidel right. Well and truly did he scatter them, driving right into left and left into right. You would have thought hail had fallen onto a narrow road or that a falcon had come among the black geese. The infidels of savage religion were bewildered, but they resorted to their arrows. They shot the boy's Arab horse; the boy could not control the reins, his eyes were masked with blood and down he came. The infidels swarmed over Uruz. His forty warriors dismounted, they fastened tightly the straps of their many-coloured shields, they drew their swords and fought mightily over Uruz. The unhorsed warrior has no hope. The infidels surrounded Uruz on all sides, they killed his forty young men before his eyes, they fell on the boy and seized him. They bound his white hands and arms, they tied a hair cord round his neck, they beat him until the blood flowed from his white skin. They made him cry out for his father, they made him wail for his mother. Hands tied, neck tied, they threw him on his face and dragged him off in haste.

Uruz was a captive, but Kazan had no knowledge of this; he thought the enemy had been beaten. He turned his horse's reins and withdrew. He arrived at the place where he had left his son, but could not find him. 'Nobles!' he said, 'Where might the boy have gone?' 'The boy must have become chicken-hearted,' said the nobles, 'he has run off to his mother.' Kazan's face grew dark, and he turned and said, 'Nobles! God has given me a worthless son. I shall go and take him from his mother's side and hack him with my sword. I shall chop him into six pieces and leave him where six roads meet, so that none shall ever again abandon his comrades in a place of danger and run away.' Then he drove his spurs into his chestnut horse and galloped off.

He came home. The daughter of khans, Lady Burla the Tall, heard that Kazan was on his way and she slaughtered of horses the stallions, of camels the males, of sheep the rams. 'It is my son's first hunt; I shall give a feast to the nobles of the Oghuz,' said she. The daughter of khans saw Kazan arriving, and she gathered herself and rose, put on her robe of sables and came out to meet him. She raised her eyebrows and gazed full at Kazan's face; she looked to right and left but did not see her young son Uruz. Her inward parts quaked, her whole heart pounded, her black almond eyes filled with tears of blood. She declaimed to Kazan; let us see, my Khan, what she declaimed.

'My lord Kazan,
  Luck of my head, throne of my house,
  Son-in-law of the Khan my father,
  Loved of the lady my mother,
  He to whom my parents gave me,
  Whom I see when I open my eyes,
  Whom I gave my heart and loved,
  My prince, my warrior, Kazan!
  You rose up from your place and stood,
  With your son you leaped onto your black-maned Kazilik
    horse,
  You went out to hunt over the great mountains with their
    lovely folds,

You caught and laid low the long-necked deer,
You loaded them onto your horses and turned homeward.
Two you went and one you come; where is my child?
Where is my son whom I got in the dark night?
My one prince is not to be seen, and my heart is on fire.
Kazan, have you let the boy fall from the overhanging
   rocks?
Have you let the mountain-lion eat him?
Or have you let him meet the infidel of dark religion?
Have you let them tie his white hands and arms?
Have you let him walk before them?
Have you let him look fearfully around, his tongue and
   mouth dry?
Have you let the bitter tears flow from his dark eyes?
Have you let him cry for his lady mother, the prince his
   father?'

Again she declaimed, saying,

'My son, my son, O my son,
My portion, my son!
Summit of my black mountain yonder, my son!
Light of my dark eyes, my son!
The poison winds are not blowing, Kazan, yet my ears are
   ringing.
I have not eaten garlic, Kazan, yet I burn within.
The yellow snake has not stung me, yet my white body rises
   and swells.
In my breast, which seems dried up, my milk is leaping.
I cannot see my only son, and my heart is aflame.
Tell me, Kazan, about my only son.
If you will not, I shall curse you, Kazan, as I burn with
   fire.'

And again:

'Those who wield the bamboo lance went and have returned;
O Lord, what has become of the wielder of the golden
   lance?

Those who ride the horses of the paddock went and have
  returned;
O Lord, what has happened to a boy who rode an Arab
  horse?
The retainers have returned, and the captains;
O Lord, what has happened to an only son?
Tell me, Kazan, about my only son.
If you will not, I shall curse you, Kazan, as I burn with
  fire.'

Once more she declaimed:

'I threw water into dried-up streams,
  I gave what I vowed to the black-garbed dervishes,
  When I looked to right or left I looked with no evil eye at
    my neighbour,
  I fed all who hoped for food and all who had abandoned
    hope,
  When I saw the hungry, I filled them; the naked, I clothed
    them.
  With prayer and pain I got a son;
  Tell me, Kazan, about my only son.
  If you will not, I shall curse you, Kazan, as I burn with
    fire.'

And again:

'If you have let my only son fall
  Down from yonder black mountain, tell me;
  I shall hurl it in ruins with a spade.
  If you have sent my only son
  Floating down the rapid clear-flowing river, tell me;
  I shall dam its veins.
  If you have left my only son a captive
  With the infidel of savage religion, tell me;
  I shall go to the Khan my father,
  I shall take a great army with plentiful treasure.
  Until I am hacked down from my Kazilik horse,
  Until I wipe away my red blood with my sleeve,

Until I fall dismembered to the ground,
Until I have news of my only son,
I shall not return from the roads of the infidel.
Or shall I cast the high boots from my feet, Kazan?
Drive my dark nails at my white face?
Tear my cheeks, red as autumn apples?
Spill my red blood into my kerchief?
Bring deep mourning on your encampment?
Weep, bewailing "My son, my son"?
The red camels in the herd have passed this way,
Their baby camels with them, whimpering.
I have lost my baby camel; shall I whimper?
The Kazilik horses in the drove have passed this way,
Their little foals with them, whinnying.
I have lost my little foal; shall I whinny?
The white sheep in the fold have passed this way,
Their little lambs with them, bleating.
I have lost my little lamb; shall I bleat?
Shall I bewail "My son, my son"?'

And again:

'I meant to rise up from my place and stand,
To mount my black-maned Kazilik horse,
To go among the teeming Oghuz,
To find a chestnut-eyed daughter-in-law,
To set up white tents on the black earth,
To walk my son to his bridal bower,
To bring him to his heart's desire.
You did not let me attain my wish,
May my dark head's curse seize you, Kazan.
My one prince is not to be seen, and my heart is on fire.
Tell me what you have done,
Or I shall curse you, Kazan, as I burn with fire.'

At these words from the boy's mother, Kazan's wits left his head, his inward parts shook, his whole heart pounded, his dark eyes filled with bloody tears, and he said, 'My beautiful one, if the boy were to come would I hold you responsible?[67] Don't be afraid, don't be anxious; he is hunting, though I thought he had come home. Don't be anxious for a boy who is delayed at the hunt. Give me seven days' grace; if the boy is in the earth I shall bring him out, if he is in the sky I shall bring him down. If I find him then I have found him. If I do not find him, God gave him and God has taken him; what shall I do? I shall come back and mourn with you.' The Khan's daughter replied, 'Kazan, I shall know that the boy is out hunting if you go in search of him with your weary horse and your blunted spear.'

Without letting the boy's mother hear, quietly Kazan gave orders: 'Let ninety thousand young Oghuz follow me; let the nobles know that my son is a prisoner.' He retraced his steps, he took the road by which he had come, he travelled by night and day. He reached the place where the enemy had been beaten. As he roamed among the corpses he saw his son's forty chestnut-eyed young men lying killed there, and his son's Arab horse riddled with arrows. Among the corpses he did not find his dear son's corpse, but he found his gilt whip. He knew without doubt that his son was a prisoner of the infidel. He wept, saying,

'Summit of my black mountain, my son!
Flood of my black river, my son!
My only son, whom in my dotage I let fall captive!'

Then he followed the infidel's traces.

Now the infidel had encamped at the Gated Black Pass. They had dressed the boy in a black shepherd-cloak and put him across the threshold of the gate, so that all who came in or out trod on him. This they had done saying, 'Since the son of our old Tatar enemy[68] has fallen into our hands, let us kill him painfully.' Then Khan Kazan came, reining in his chestnut horse so that it reared on its hind legs. The infidels saw Kazan arrive, and started up. Some mounted their horses, some put on their armour. The boy raised his head and said, 'Infidels, what is happening?' They replied, 'Your father has come and we mean to take him.' The boy said,

'Mercy, infidels, mercy!
There is no doubt that God is one.'

The infidels showed the boy mercy; they loosed his hands and
unbound his eyes. He went to meet his father, declaiming; let
us see, my Khan, what he declaimed.

'To me, my Khan my father, my soul my father!
How did you know I was taken prisoner,
My white hands bound behind my back,
A hair cord tied round my white neck,
My black-eyed young men killed?
Father, before you came the infidels took counsel together:
"Let us take Kazan of the chestnut horse,
Let us tie his white hands and arms,
Cut off his beautiful head before he knows it,
Spill his red blood on the earth's face,
Kill him and his son both together,
Put out his hearth-fire."
My Khan my father, I am afraid.
As you gallop you may let your chestnut horse stumble,
As you fight you may let yourself be taken,
May let your lovely head be cut off before you know it,
May make my white-haired mother, as she mourns her son,
Weep for Kazan, the luck of her head.
Turn round, father, go back;
Be the hope of my aged mother,
Don't make my dark-eyed sister cry,
Don't make my white-skinned mother weep.
Shame it is for a father to die for his son.
Father! For the love of the Creator
Turn round, go back home.
If my old mother comes to meet you,
If she asks you about me,
Tell her the truth, father.
Say, "I saw your son a captive,
His white hands and arms bound,
A cord of hair tied round his neck,

Lying in the black swine's sty,
His dear neck smothered in a hair cloak,
Heavy fetters bruising his ankles,
Burnt barley-bread his food, and bitter onions."
Let my mother not grieve for me;
Let her wait a month.
If I come not in a month, let her wait two months;
If I come not in two, let her wait three;
If I come not in three, she may know I am dead.
Let her slaughter my stallion and give the funeral feast for
    me.[69]
Let her give her freedom to the girl not of our tribe,
Her who should have been my wife.
Another may enter the bower she was keeping for me.
Let my mother dress in blue for me and wrap herself in
    black.
Let them mourn for me in the lands of the teeming Oghuz.
Let my head be a sacrifice for your safe return, father.
Turn back, father!'

Again the boy declaimed:

'If all is well with the black mountains, the people go up to
    the summer-pasture.
If all is well with the blood-red rivers, they overflow in
    blood-red spate.
If all is well with the horses of the paddock, foals are born.
If all is well with the red camels in the stalls, they bring
    forth young.
If all is well with the white sheep in the folds, they bring
    forth lambs.
If all is well with heroic princes, sons are born to them.
Let all be well with you and with my mother,
And God will give you sons better than I.
So that my mother may not think me unworthy of her
    white milk,
Do not give battle, father, but turn round, go back.'

Thereupon Khan Kazan declaimed; let us see, my Khan, what he declaimed.

'My son, my son, O my son!
Summit of my black mountain yonder, my son.
Strength of my strong loins, my soul my son.
Light of my dark eyes, my son.
It was for you that I rose up from my place at daybreak,
I wearied my chestnut horse for you.[70]
My head be a sacrifice, my dear son, for you.
My weeping, which was in the sky,
Since you left has come down to earth.[71]
The thundering drums have not been beaten,
My great solemn court has not been held,
The princes' sons who know you have put aside their white
    raiment and dressed in black,
My swan-like daughters and daughters-in-law have put aside
    their white raiment and dressed in black,
Your old mother has shed tears of blood,
Your white-bearded father is in torment.
Son, if I turn back from here and go home,
If your white-skinned mother comes to meet me
Saying "What of my son?"
Shall I say "His white hands are bound behind him,
A rope of hair is tied round his white neck,
He trails on foot among the infidel"?
Where will my honour be then, my son?'

Again Kazan spoke:

'When yonder black mountains are old,
No grass grows on them, the people do not pasture on them
    in the summer;
When the lovely eddying rivers are old they do not overflow
    their banks;
When the camels are old they give no young;
When the horses are old they give no foals;
When manly warriors are old they get no sons.

Your father is old, your mother is old;
God will give us no better son than you,
Nor could any take your place.
I shall become a black cloud in the sky
And thunder over the infidels;
I shall become a white thunderbolt and blast them;
I shall become a fire and burn them like reeds;
I shall make nine of them count as little as one;
I shall fill the world with battle and slaughter;
God the Creator, lend me Your aid!'

He dismounted from his chestnut horse, he performed his ablutions in clear running water, he placed his white forehead on the earth and prayed. He wept, he asked his need from God the Mighty, he rubbed his face on the ground. He blessed Muhammad, he foamed like a camel, he roared like a lion, he screamed and shouted, and all alone he drove his horse at the infidel, his sword flashing. He turned about and about, and right well did he fight, yet he could not overcome the infidel. Three times in one hour he charged at the infidel. Then suddenly a sword touched his eyelid; his black blood gushed forth, down into his eyes. He hurled himself towards the broken ground. Now let us see what the Creator does.

It seems, my Khan, that the Lady Burla the Tall, thinking about her dear young son, could not sit still. With her forty slender maidens accompanying her, she sent for her black horse, she mounted, and grasped her black sword. 'Kazan, the diadem of my head, has not returned,' she said, and followed in his traces. On and on she went, and eventually came close to him. Kazan did not recognize his wife; he advanced on her and said,

'Give me the rein of your black horse, warrior!
Look well at my face, warrior!
Give me the black horse you ride, warrior!
Give me the black steel sword you hold, warrior!
Be my hope on this day of mine
And I shall give you castles and lands.'

The lady replied,

'Warrior, why confront me wailing?
Why remind me of my bygone days?
Kazan, who rose up from his place;
Kazan, who mounted his chestnut horse;
Kazan, who charged at my black mountain and overthrew it;
Kazan, who cut down my great shady tree;
Kazan, who took a knife and destroyed my wings;
Kazan, who did not spare Uruz my only son,
Kazan, who galloped restlessly about;
Your loins are dead.
Dead is your knee quivering over the stirrup,
Dead is your eye that does not know your wife, the daughter of khans.
You have fallen into dotage; what ails you?
To sword, Kazan, I am here!'

Now the Oghuz nobles had heard that Prince Kazan's son was a prisoner among the infidel and that Kazan had gone after him. They followed Kazan's traces and at this point they arrived. Let us see, my Khan, who they were who arrived. Kara Göne galloped up, he whom the Almighty set at the narrows of the Black Valley, the coverlet of whose cradle was of black bull-hide, who when he was angered made black rock into ashes, whose black moustaches were knotted seven times at the back of his neck, that dragon of heroes, the brother of Prince Kazan. 'Wield your sword, brother Kazan!' said he, 'Here I am!' Let us see who came next. Wild Dundar son of Kiyan Seljuk galloped up, he who kicked in and destroyed the iron gate at the Pass of the Iron Gate, who transfixed men on his sixty-span lance, who three times in one fight unhorsed so great a hero as Kazan. 'Wield your sword, my lord Kazan!' said he, 'Here I am!' Let us see, my Khan, who came next. After him, my Khan, Kara Budak son of Kara Göne galloped up. He it was who smashed the fortresses of Diyarbakr and Mardin, who made King Kipchak of the iron bow vomit blood, who came and won Kazan's daughter by his valour, whom despite his youth the white-bearded Oghuz elders praised whenever they saw him. Red silk trousers he wore, and his horse, born of the sea, was decked with a golden tassel. 'Wield your sword, my lord Kazan!' said he, 'Here I am!' Let us see, my Khan, who came next. Sher Shemseddin son of Gaflet Koja galloped up, with snow still on his grey-white horse's mane, he who swooped down on the enemies of Bayindir Khan without so much as a by-your-leave, who made sixty thousand unbelievers vomit blood. 'Wield your sword, my lord Kazan!' said he, 'Here I am!' Let us see, my Khan, who came next. Beyrek of the grey horse galloped up, he who once flashed forth from Parasar's fortress of Bayburt and arrived in front of his many-coloured bridal tent, darling of the teeming Oghuz, trusty minister of Prince Kazan. 'Wield your sword, my lord Kazan!' said he, 'Here I am!' Next, Prince Yigenek son of Kazilik Koja galloped up, he who swaggered as he glared about him, brave as an eagle, tightly belted, with golden earrings in his ears, who could unhorse the Oghuz nobles one after another. 'Wield your sword, my lord Kazan!' said he, 'Here I am!' Next, Prince Kazan's uncle galloped up, lank-limbed horse-mouthed Uruz Koja. If he made a fur coat from the skins of sixty two-year-old lambs it would not cover his heels; if he made a cap from the skins of six it would not cover his ears .'Wield your sword, my Khan Kazan!' said he, 'Here I am!' Then came Dundar who cosseted his twenty-four tribes, and then Dögür, lord of a thousand men. Next came Aruz, master of the nine elders, and then Emen, backbone of the Oghuz.

Of counting the nobles of the Oghuz there could be no end; Kazan's nobles all came and thronged about him. They washed in pure water, they prayed, they invoked blessings on Muhammad of beautiful name. Then without more ado they charged at the infidel, they wielded their swords. On that day the manly warriors showed their mettle. On that day the unmanly spied out roads by which to slink away. There was a battle like doomsday and the field was full of heads. The skirmishers fought. Chieftain was parted from retainer, retainer from chieftain. Wild

Dundar with the nobles of the Outer Oghuz attacked on the right, Kara Budak with his brave warriors attacked on the left. Kazan with the nobles of the Inner Oghuz attacked the centre. He rushed at the infidel lord, at King Shökli, he made him scream, he unhorsed him and spilled his red blood on the earth. On the right wing Dundar met King Kara Tüken, put him to the sword and brought him down. On the left wing Kara Budak met King Bughachuk, ran him through, and brought him down, then, without giving him a chance to move, he cut off his head. The Lady Burla the Tall aimed a blow of her sword at the infidels' black standard and brought it down. The infidel king was taken and the unbelievers fled. Panic fell on them among the valleys. Of fifteen thousand unbelievers, some were killed and the rest were captured. Of the Oghuz, three hundred warriors fell. Kazan and the Lady Burla came to their son; they dismounted, untied his hands and embraced him. Kazan rescued his son and turned for home. The fight for the Faith was blessed with success. The Oghuz nobles had their fill of plunder.

They came to Aghcha Kala Sürmelü,[72] and Kazan had forty tents pitched. For seven days and seven nights there was feasting. He made forty slaves and forty slave-girls turn about his son and freed them.[73] He gave the brave officers castles and lands, he gave them robes and precious stuffs. Dede Korkut came and played joyful music and strung together this tale of the Oghuz.

> Where now are the valiant princes of whom I have told,
> Those who said, 'The world is mine'?
> Doom has taken them, earth has hidden them.
> Who now inherits this transient world,
> The world to which men come, from which they go,
> The world whose latter end is death?

I shall pray for you, my Khan: may your firm-rooted black mountain never be overthrown, may your great shady tree never be cut down, may your lovely clear-flowing river never run dry, may the tips of your wings never be broken, may God never put you in need of unworthy men, may your grey-white horse never stumble as he gallops, may your pure black steel sword never be notched in the fray, may your God-given hope never be disappointed, may the end not find you apart from the pure Faith. On your white forehead I invoke five words of blessing; may they be accepted. May He grant you increase and preserve you in strength and forgive your sins for the sake of Muhammad of beautiful name, O my Khan!

5

TELLS THE STORY OF WILD DUMRUL SON OF DUKHA KOJA, O MY KHAN!

IT seems, my Khan, that among the Oghuz there was a man they called Wild Dumrul, son of Dukha Koja. He had a bridge built, over a dried-up stream. He took thirty-three silver pieces from all who crossed; those who did not cross he beat soundly and took from them forty silver pieces. Why did he do so? Because he said, 'Is there a man wilder than I, braver than I, to come and fight me? Let word of my manliness, my heroism, my courage, my gallantry, spread abroad as far as the land of the Greeks, the land of the Syrians.'

Now one day a portion of a tribe encamped on the slope of the bridge. In that tribe a fine handsome warrior had fallen ill and by God's command he died. Some mourned their son, some mourned their brother. Great was the black lamentation over that warrior. Suddenly Wild Dumrul hastened up and said, 'You scoundrels, what are you bawling about? What is this uproar by my bridge? Why are you wailing?' 'Lord,' they answered, 'a fine warrior of ours has died; we weep for him.' 'Who has killed your warrior?' said Wild Dumrul. 'By Allah, O Prince,' they replied, 'it was ordered by God Most High; Azrael[74] of the red wings has taken that man's life.' Said Wild Dumrul, 'And who is this person you call Azrael, who takes men's lives? Almighty God, I conjure you by Your Unity and Your Being to show me Azrael, that I may fight and struggle and wrestle with him and save that fine warrior's life – and he will not take any more fine warriors' lives.' Then Wild Dumrul turned away and went back to his house.

Dumrul's words were not pleasing to God Most High. 'See, see!' He said, 'this crazy pimp knows not My Unity, he shows no appreciation of My Unity. Let him swagger and vaunt himself in My great court!' Then He gave orders to Azrael: 'Go, Azrael, appear before the eyes of that crazy pimp; turn his face pale, make his soul yelp and bring it here.'

As Wild Dumrul was feasting with his forty warriors, suddenly Azrael appeared. No steward or gate-keeper noticed him. Wild Dumrul's eyes that saw ceased to see, his hands that held ceased to hold. The wide world became dark in his eye. Wild Dumrul shouted aloud and declaimed; let us see, my Khan, what he declaimed.

> 'Say, what dreadful old man are you?
> The gate-keepers did not see you,
> The stewards did not hear you.
> My eyes that saw have ceased to see,
> My hands that held have ceased to hold,
> My soul is trembling and convulsed,
> My gold cup has fallen from my hand,
> The inside of my mouth is like ice,
> My bones have turned to salt.
> O white-bearded old man,
> Blear-eyed old man,
> What dreadful old man are you? Tell me;
> My doom, my punishment will smite you this day.'

So said he, and Azrael was enraged:

> 'You crazy pimp!
> Does it then displease you that my eye is bleary?
> Many souls have I taken of lovely-eyed maidens and brides.
> Does it then displease you that my beard is white?
> Many souls have I taken of white-bearded and black-bearded
>   warriors.
> That is why my beard is white.'

Then he said, 'Now, you crazy pimp, you have been boasting, you have been saying, "Should red-winged Azrael fall into my hand I would kill him and deliver the soul of the fine warrior." Now, you madman, I have come to take *your* soul. Will you give it up or will you fight me?' 'Are you red-winged Azrael?' said Wild Dumrul. 'Yes,' said he, 'I am.' 'Is it you who takes these fine warriors' lives?' 'It is,' said he. 'Gate-keepers! Shut the gate!' said Wild Dumrul. 'Now, Azrael, I was looking for you in the open; can it be that you have fallen into my hands indoors? I shall kill you and deliver the fine warrior's soul.' He drew his black sword and lunged at Azrael. Azrael became a dove and flew out of the smoke-hole. Wild Dumrul, that dragon of the sons of Adam, clapped his hands, laughed out loud and said, 'My warriors! I terrified Azrael so much that he forgot about the wide door and fled through the narrow chimney; for he turned into a bird like a dove and flew from my grasp. But I shall not let him go without setting my falcon on him.' He rose and mounted his horse. He took his falcon into his hand and followed him. He killed a dove or two, then turned back. But, while he was on the way home, Azrael showed himself to his horse. The horse started and threw Wild Dumrul to the ground. His dark head was stunned and he was in pain. Azrael settled heavy on his white breast. At first he groaned, but then he began to howl:

'O Azrael, mercy!
There is no doubt that God is One!
I did not know that you were like this;
I never heard that you were the stealthy taker of souls.
Mountains we have, with mighty peaks;
On those mountains we have vineyards;
In those vineyards there are grapes in black clusters;
Men press those grapes and the red wine comes;
Those who drink of that wine become drunk.
I was full of wine; I was out of my mind;
I did not know what I said.
I have not tired of being a prince; I have not had my fill of
    being a warrior.
Do not take my soul, Azrael, mercy!'

'You crazy pimp!' Azrael replied, 'why do you beseech me? Beseech God Most High; what can I do? I too am one of His

lackeys.' 'Then is it God Most High who gives and takes souls?'
'Of course it is,' said Azrael. He rounded on Azrael and said,
'Then what good are you, you pest? Get out of the way and let
me talk to God Most High.' Then Wild Dumrul declaimed; let
us see, my Khan, what he declaimed.

'You are higher than the high,
No one knows what You are like,
Beautiful God!
Many the ignorant who look for You in the sky or seek
    You on earth,
But You are in the hearts of the Faithful.
Everlasting, all-powerful God!
Eternal, all-forgiving God!
If You will take my soul, take it Yourself;
Do not let Azrael take it.'

Now Wild Dumrul's words were pleasing to God Most High.
He called Azrael and said, 'Since that crazy pimp has recognized
My Unity, has shown appreciation of My Unity, tell him to
find a soul in place of his own and his own soul can go free.'
Azrael said, 'O Wild Dumrul, God Most High commands thus:
let him find a soul in place of his own and his own soul can go
free.' Said Wild Dumrul, 'How am I to find a soul? But I do
have an old father and mother; come, let's go; one of them
might give his soul, then you take it and leave mine.'

Wild Dumrul went off to his father. He kissed his father's
hand and declaimed; let us see, my Khan, what he declaimed.

'Dear, white-bearded, honoured Father,
Do you know what has befallen?
I spoke blasphemy.
It did not please God Most High.
Above the sky He gave orders to red-winged Azrael, who
    came flying.
He settled heavy on my white breast;
He snarled and was about to take my sweet life.
Father, from you I ask your life; will you give it,
Or will you mourn your son, Wild Dumrul?'

Said his father,

> 'My son, my son, O my son!
> Part of my soul, my son!
> Lion-like son, at whose birth I slew nine bulls,
> Pillar of my gold-topped tent, my son!
> Flower of my swan-like daughters and daughters-in-law,
>   my son!
> There lies my black mountain; if need be,
> Tell Azrael to come and take it for his summer-pasture.
> My cold cold stream, if need be,
> Can be his drink.
> My stables of falcon-swift horses
> Can be his mount.
> Caravan on caravan of camels have I;
> Let them be his beasts of burden.
> My white sheep in the folds, if need be,
> Can be his feast in the dark kitchen.
> If gold and silver and coin are needed,
> He can have them to spend.
> The world is sweet and life is dear;
> I cannot give up my life; this you must know.
> Dearer than I, fonder than I, is your mother.
> Son, go to your mother.'

Finding no indulgence from his father, Wild Dumrul went off to his mother, and said,

> 'Mother, do you know what has befallen?
> Red-winged Azrael flew down from the sky.
> He settled heavy on my white breast;
> He snarled and was about to take my life.
> I asked my father for his life, Mother, but he refused.
> I ask life from you, Mother.
> Will you give me your life,
> Or will you mourn your son, Wild Dumrul?
> Will you dash your bitter nails at your white face?
> Will you tear your hair, Mother, like reeds uprooted?'

Whereupon his mother declaimed; let us see, my Khan, what she declaimed.

'My son, my son, O my son!
Son whom I carried for nine months in my narrow belly,
Whom I brought to the world's face when the tenth moon came,
Whom I swaddled in wrappings of fine linen,
Whom I suckled abundantly with my white milk!
Had you been a prisoner in a white-towered fortress, my son;
Had you been a captive in the hands of the infidel of foul religion,
Gold and silver I should have given to his might, and saved you, my son.
You have come to a dreadful place, to which I cannot come.
The world is sweet and life is dear;
I cannot give up my life; this you must know.'

When his mother too thus refused to give her life, Azrael came to take Wild Dumrul's life. Wild Dumrul said,

'O Azrael, mercy!
There is no doubt that God is One.'

'You crazy pimp,' said Azrael, 'what are you asking mercy for now? You went to your white-bearded father and he would not give his life; you went to your white-haired mother and she would not give her life; who else should give?' 'There is one I long to see,' said Wild Dumrul, 'with whom I would speak.' 'Madman!' said Azrael, 'Whom do you long to see?' 'I have a wife,' said he, 'a girl not of our tribe, by whom I have two small sons; there is a trust I would commit to her, and then you may take my life.' He went off to his wife and said,

'Do you know what has befallen?
Red-winged Azrael flew down from the sky.
He settled heavy on my white breast;
He snarled and was about to take my sweet life.

I asked my father, but ne would not give his life.
I went to my mother, and she would not give her life.
"The world is sweet and life is dear," they said.
Now,
My black mountains, peak on peak, can be your summer-
    pasture.
My cold cold stream can be your drink.
My stables of falcon-swift horses can be your mount.
My gold-topped tent can be your shade.
My caravan on caravan of camels can be your beasts of
    burden.
My white sheep in the folds can be your feast.
If anyone catches your eye,
If your heart loves anybody,
Marry him.
Do not leave the two boys fatherless.'

Thereupon his wife declaimed; let us see, my Khan, what she
declaimed.

'What are you saying? What are you telling?
You whom I see when I open my eyes,
To whom I gave my heart and my love,
My heroic warrior, my kingly warrior,
To whom I gave my sweet mouth and kissed;
With whom I laid my head on one pillow and embraced;
What shall I do after you
With yonder black mountains?
If I should summer there, may they be my grave!
Your cold cold stream
If I should drink may it be my blood!
If I should spend your gold and silver may they be my
    shroud!
Your stables of falcon-swift horses
If I should mount may they be my bier!
If after you I should love a man and lie with him
May he become a many-coloured snake and sting me!
Those cowards, your mother and father!

What is there in a life that they could not show you pity?
May the Dais and the Throne be my witnesses,
May earth and sky be my witnesses,
May mighty God be my witness:
Let my life be sacrificed for yours.'

So she spoke, consenting. Azrael came to take the lady's life.
The dragon of the sons of Adam could not bring himself to let
her suffer, and thereupon he supplicated God Most High; let
us see how he supplicated.

'You are higher than the high,
No one knows what You are like,
Beautiful God!
Many the ignorant who look for You in the sky or seek You
    on earth,
But You are in the hearts of the Faithful.
Everlasting, all-powerful God!
On the great highways
I shall build hospices for Your sake.
When I see the hungry I shall fill them for Your sake.
When I see the naked I shall clothe them for Your sake.
If You will take, take both our lives.
If You will spare, spare both our lives.
Most honoured, mighty God!'

Wild Dumrul's words were pleasing to God Most High, and
He ordered Azrael: 'Take the lives of Wild Dumrul's parents;
I have granted him and his wife a hundred and forty years of
life.' And Azrael straightway took the lives of his father and
mother. Wild Dumrul lived a hundred and forty years more,
together with his companion.

It was Dede Korkut who came and told the story and declaimed. 'Let this story,' said he, 'be known as the Story of Wild
Dumrul. After me let the brave bards tell it and the generous
heroes of untarnished honour listen to it.'

I shall pray for you, my Khan: may your firm-rooted black
mountains never be overthrown, may your great shady tree

never be cut down, may your lovely clear-flowing river never run dry, may mighty God never put you in need of men unworthy of you. On your white forehead I invoke five words of blessing; may they be accepted. May He grant you increase and preserve you in strength and forgive your sins for the sake of Muhammad of beautiful name, O my Khan!

6

TELLS THE STORY OF KAN TURALI
SON OF KANLI KOJA, O MY KHAN!

IN the days of the Oghuz there was a stout-hearted warrior called
Kanli Koja, who had a grown-up son, a dare-devil young man
named Kan Turali. Kanli Koja said, 'Friends, my father died and
I was left; I took his place, I took his lands. Tomorrow I shall
die and my son be left. Come, son, the best thing is for me to get
you married while my eyes still see.' The young man replied,
'Father, you talk of getting me married, but how can there be a
girl fit for me? Before I rise to my feet she must rise; before I
mount my well-trained horse she must be on horseback; before I
reach the bloody infidels' land she must already have got there and
brought me back some heads.' 'I see, my son,' said Kanli Koja,
'you don't want a girl; you want a dare-devil hero to look after
you, and you can eat and drink and be merry.' 'That is so, my
dear father,' he replied, 'but you'll go and get me some pretty
dressed-up doll of a Turcoman [75] girl, whose belly will split if I
should suddenly lean over and fall on her.' 'Son,' said Kanli
Koja, 'finding the girl is up to you; I'll see that you're fed and
provided for.'

Thereupon Kan Turali, that dragon of heroes, rose from his
place and took his forty young men with him. He had a look at
the Inner Oghuz, but could not find a girl; he turned round and
came home again. His father said, 'Have you found a girl, son?'
Kan Turali answered, 'May the Oghuz lands be devastated; I
couldn't find a girl to suit me, father.' 'Well, my son,' said his
father, 'that's not how one goes looking for girls.' 'Indeed?
Then how does one go?' Said Kanli Koja, 'My son, it's no use
leaving in the morning and coming home at noon; it's no use
leaving at noon and coming home in the evening. Son, look after
the property; pile it up and I'll go and find a girl for you.'

Joyful and proud, Kanli Koja rose and gathered his white-

bearded old men around him. He went into the Inner Oghuz but
could find no girl. He wandered on and went into the Outer
Oghuz, but could find no girl. He wandered on and came to
Trebizond.[76]

Now the infidel King of Trebizond had a mightily beautiful
and beloved daughter. She used to draw two bows at once, to her
right and to her left. The arrow she shot never fell to earth. That
girl had three beasts waiting with her dowry.[77] Her father had
promised, 'Whoever subdues those three beasts, conquers and
kills them, to him shall I give my daughter.' But if anyone failed
to kill them, he would cut off his head. Thus the heads of thirty-
two sons of infidel princes had been cut off and hung on the
battlements. One of those three beasts was a raging lion, one a
black bull and one a black camel-stallion. Every one of the three
was a monster. Those thirty-two heads which hung on the battlements had never so much as seen the faces of the raging lion and
the black camel; all they had done was to perish on the horns of
the bull. Kanli Koja saw these heads and these beasts, and the
lice on his head were heaped up round his feet.[78] He said, 'I'll go
straight to my son and tell him that if he's clever enough he can
come and take her; otherwise let him be satisfied with the girls
at home.'

The horse's hoof is fleet as the wind; the minstrel's tongue is
swift as a bird. Kanli Koja made his way back and went up to the
Oghuz land. News was brought to Kan Turali that his father had
come, and he went with his forty young men to meet him. He
kissed his hand and said, 'Dear father, have you found a suitable
girl for me?' 'I have, my son,' said he, 'if you are clever enough.'
Kan Turali replied, 'Does it need gold and silver, or mules and
camels?' 'Son, it is cleverness that's wanted, cleverness.' 'Father,'
said Kan Turali, 'I shall saddle my black-maned Kazilik horse, I
shall raid the bloody infidels' land, I shall cut off heads and spill
blood, I shall make the infidel vomit blood, I shall bring back
slaves and slave-girls; I shall show my cleverness.' 'O my dear
son,' said Kanli Koja, 'that is not what I mean by cleverness.
They keep three beasts for that girl. They will give her to whoever subdues those three beasts. If he does not subdue them and

kill them, they will cut off his head and hang it on a turret.'
'Father,' said Kan Turali, 'you shouldn't have told me this. Now
you have told me, I really must go, lest I bring disgrace on my
head and shame on my face. Lady mother, lord father, farewell!'
Kanli Koja said, 'Do you see what I have brought on myself? I
must tell the boy dread tales, so that he will not go.' Thereupon
Kanli Koja declaimed; let us see, my Khan, what he declaimed.

'Son, in the place where you would go,
  Twisted and tortuous will the roads be;
  Swamps there will be, where the horseman will sink and never
      emerge;
  Forests there will be, where the red serpent can find no path;
  Fortresses there will be, that rub shoulders with the sky;
  A beautiful one there will be, who puts out eyes and snatches
      souls;
  An executioner there will be, whisking heads off in an instant;
  A soldier there will be, with shield dancing on his back.
  To a terrible place have you set your foot; stay!
  Bring not tears to your white-bearded father, your aged
      mother!'

Kan Turali was angered, and replied:

'What are you telling me, what are you saying, dear father?
  Can there be a man who would fear such a task?
  Shame it is to try to frighten a hero!
  If the Almighty will, those twisted tortuous roads
  I shall gallop along by night;
  On that swamp, where the horseman sinks and never emerges,
  I shall spread sand;
  That forest where the red serpent finds no path,
  I shall strike flint and set it ablaze.
  The fortresses that rub shoulders with the sky,
  If the Almighty will, I shall deal with them and destroy;
  The beautiful one who puts out eyes and snatches souls,
  I shall kiss her throat.
  The soldier with shield dancing on his back,

If the Almighty will, I shall cut off his head.
I may get there or I may not,
I may come home or I may not,
Under the black camel I may lie,
On the bull's horns I may be stuck,
I may be shredded in the claw of the raging lion.
I may get there or I may not,
I may come home or I may not;
Until you see me once again
Farewell, lord father and lady mother!'

They saw that for honour's sake he could not stay, and they said, 'Bright be your fortune, son. May you get there and come home safe and well.' He kissed his father's and mother's hand and gathered his forty men about him.

They galloped seven days and seven nights, and reached the infidel frontier, where they made camp. Kan Turali spurred his swift horse and threw his mace towards the sky. Before it fell to earth he caught and held it.

> 'My forty friends, my forty comrades,
>   If there should be a speedy one for me to race,
>   A mighty one for me to wrestle,
>   If God Most High should favour me,
>   If I should slay the three beasts,
>   If I should win the queen of beauties,
>   The Lady Saljan of the yellow robe,
>   If I should return to my parents' house,
>   O my forty friends, my forty comrades,
>   Let my head be a sacrifice for all forty of you.'

Now it seems, my Khan, that even as they were talking thus, news reached the infidel King. 'There is a young man of the Oghuz named Kan Turali,' they said, 'who is on his way to seek your daughter's hand.' The infidels met them seven miles from the city, and asked, 'Warrior princes, what have you come for?' 'To buy and sell,' said they. They did them reverence and honour. They pitched white tents, they spread red carpets, they slew white sheep, they gave them red wine to drink, seven years old. Then they escorted them to the King. The King was seated on his throne; the implacable infidel was inwardly furious. Seven times Kan Turali went round the square then came to him. Now the girl had had a palace built on the square. All the maidens about her wore red; she alone wore yellow, and she watched from above. Kan Turali came and gave greeting to the black-hatted King, who responded. They spread red carpets and he sat down. 'Where do you come from, young man?' said the King. Kan Turali rose from his place and came forward, he strutted about, he bared his white forehead, he rolled up his sleeves to show his white arms, and said,

'I have come to climb your black mountain yonder,
I have come to cross your eddying river,
I have come to seek refuge in your narrow skirts, your broad
   embrace.
By God's command and at the word of the Prophet
I have come to marry your daughter.'

Said the King, 'This young man has a ready tongue; if he has skill in his hand...' Then he said, 'Strip this young man mother-naked.' They did so, and Kan Turali wrapped his fine gold-embroidered linen round his waist. They escorted him on to the square. Kan Turali was a handsome and perfect warrior. Four warriors among the Oghuz used to go about veiled: Kan Turali, Kara Chogur and his son Kirk Kinuk, and Beyrek of the grey horse. Now Kan Turali stripped off his veil. The girl was watching from the palace and she went weak at the knees, her cat miaowed, she slavered like a sick calf. To the maidens by her side she said, 'If only God Most High would put mercy into my father's heart, if only he would fix a bride-price and give me to this man! Alas that such a man should perish at the hands of monsters!'

At that moment they brought on the bull, with a chain of iron. The bull knelt, he kneaded a marble paving-stone with his horns and shredded it like cheese. The infidels said, 'Now he will toss the man; he will lay him low, he will strew him on the ground,

he will tear him to pieces. May the Oghuz lands be devastated!
What difference does it make if forty warriors and a prince's son
die for the sake of one girl?' When the forty warriors heard this,
they all wept. Kan Turali looked to his right and saw his forty
warriors weeping; he looked to his left and saw the same. Said
he, 'Hey, my forty friends, my forty comrades, what are you
weeping for? Bring me my arm-long lute and sing my praises.'
Thereupon the forty warriors praised Kan Turali; let us see, my
Khan, how they praised him.

'My Sultan, Kan Turali,
  Have you not risen from your place and stood?
  Have you not mounted your black-maned Kazilik horse?
  Hunting and fowling, have you not climbed
  The many-coloured mountain that lies askew?
  At the threshold of your father's white pavilion,
  Have you not seen the captive women milk the cows?
  This dread bull of which they speak,
  Is it not the black cow's calf?
  Do gallant heroes quail before their enemy?
  Princess Saljan in her yellow robe watches from the palace;
  Any her glance falls on she inflames with love.
  Glory to God for the love of the girl in yellow!'

'Turn loose your bull and let him come!' said Kan Turali.
They removed the bull's chain and let him loose. His horn was
like a diamond lance as he charged at Kan Turali. Kan Turali
spoke a blessing on Muhammad of beautiful name, and planted
a punch on the bull's forehead that sent him reeling onto his
rump. He pressed his fist onto the bull's forehead, he drove him
up to the end of the square. Greatly did they struggle, neither
gaining the victory. The bull began to pant with heavy thudding
breath and foamed at the mouth. Said Kan Turali, 'It is by intelli-
gence that great men have won this world; let me leap away from
in front of him, and show what skill I have behind him.' He spoke
a blessing on Muhammad of beautiful name, and hurled himself out of the bull's way. The bull planted himself in the earth,
on top of his horn. Kan Turali gave three tugs at his tail and

hurled him to the ground, and his bones were shivered to pieces.
He set his foot on him and throttled him. He brought out his
knife and flayed him. Leaving his flesh in the square, he brought
his skin before the King and said, 'First thing in the morning
you'll give me your daughter.' The King said, 'Oh give him the
girl, expel him from the city and let him clear out.' But the King
had a nephew, who said, 'The lord of beasts is the lion; let him
show his tricks with the lion too, and after that let's give him the
girl.'

They went and brought out the lion and let him into the
square. The lion roared, and every single horse in the square
pissed blood. Kan Turali's young men said, 'He has escaped the
bull; how will he escape the lion?' and they wept together. He
saw his warriors weeping, and said, 'Take up my arm-long lute
and sing my praises. Shall I turn away from a lion, when the love
of the girl in yellow is at stake?' Thereupon his companions declaimed; let us see, my Khan, what they declaimed.

'My Sultan, Kan Turali!
He who falls on the foals when he sees their yellow hides in
    the white thicket,
Who pierces the vein of the quarry and sucks the blood,
Who turns not aside from the pure dark steel sword,
Who fears not the hard white-thonged bow,
Who flinches not from the whistling white-feathered arrow,
Who destroys the raging lion, the lord of beasts;
Does he let the piebald puppy bite him? [79]
Do heroic warriors quail before their enemy on the day of
    battle?
Princess Saljan in her yellow robe watches from the palace;
Any her glance falls on she inflames with love.
Glory to God for the love of the girl in yellow!'

'Hey, infidels!' said Kan Turali, 'turn loose your lion and let
him come! I have no pure black steel sword to slice him in two
with, when he grapples with me. In You I take refuge, Most
Generous of the generous; God, who needs no help, help me!'
They turned the lion loose and he charged. Kan Turali wrapped

a shepherd's cloak round his fist and held it out to the lion's paw.
He spoke a blessing on Muhammad of beautiful name and, fixing
his eye on the lion's forehead, gave it a punch that jarred through
to the jaw and shattered it. He grabbed the lion round the neck,
he broke him in the middle, then he picked him up and threw
him down, and the lion was shivered to pieces.

Kan Turali came before the King and said, 'Tomorrow you'll
give me your daughter.' Said the King, 'Bring the girl and give
her to him. The moment my eye saw this young man my soul
loved him; he may stay or go, as he pleases.' But again his
nephew spoke: 'The commander of beasts is the camel; let him
play his tricks with the camel too, then let us give him the girl.'

By the grace of God, the favour of the nobles and lords was
inclined towards Kan Turali, and the King ordered the camel's
mouth to be bound seven times round. But the jealous infidels did
not do so; they loosened the camel's halters and let him go. Kan
Turali dashed between the camel's forelegs and darted away. The
young man was dazed, having already fought two beasts, and he
slipped and fell. Six headsmen advanced towards the back of his
neck, holding naked swords. Thereupon his comrades declaimed;
let us see, my Khan, what they declaimed.

'Kan Turali, you rose from your place and came.
You mounted your black-maned Kazilik horse,
You took your chestnut-eyed warriors,
By night you climbed the many-coloured mountain that lies
    askew,
By night you crossed its swirling river,
By night you entered the bloody infidels' land.
When the black bull came you smashed him in pieces,
When the raging lion came you broke him in the middle;
When the black camel came, why did you give up?
News will climb the pitch-black mountains,
News will cross the blood-red rivers,
News will reach the teeming Oghuz.
They will say,
"What do we hear of Kanli Koja's son Kan Turali?

When the black bull came he did not even glance over his
    shoulder,
When the raging lion came he broke him in the middle.
When the black camel came, why did he give up?"
None, great or small, but will talk.
None, old woman or elder, but will gossip evilly.
Your white-bearded father will know anguish,
Your aged mother will shed tears of blood.
Lord, if you do not rise and stand,
Six headsmen are holding naked swords at your neck;
Without a thought they will cut off your lovely head.
Will you not look up?
Here is the dappled goose; will you not loose your falcon? [80]
Princess Saljan in her yellow robe is making signs;
Will you not see?
"You!" she says, "the camel's weak spot is his nose!"
Will you not understand?
Princess Saljan in her yellow robe watches from the palace;
Any her glance falls on she inflames with love.
Glory to God for the love of the girl in yellow!'

Kan Turali rose to his feet and said, 'Now if I grab this camel's
nose they'll say I did so because the girl told me to; tomorrow the
news will reach the Oghuz land: "There he was, at the camel's
mercy, and the girl saved him," they'll say. Now play my arm-
long lute and sing my praises; I take refuge in the Creator,
Mighty God. Shall I turn aside from a camel? Lord willing, I
shall cut this one's head off too.'

Kan Turali's young men praised him, declaiming; let us see,
my Khan, what they declaimed.

'The grey-black eagle, who makes his eyrie on the towering
    rocks,
Who flies close to God, the Mighty, the Great,
Who whirrs like a stone from a huge catapult and smashes
    down,
Who screaming snatches the duck from the limpid lake,

Who lifts and breaks the great ring-dove as it walks the
   valley-bottom,
Who rises and flies when his belly hungers,
Sultan of all birds, does he let the magpie brush him with his
   wing?
Do heroic warriors turn from the enemy on the day of battle?
Princess Saljan in her yellow robe watches from the palace;
Any her glance falls on she inflames with love.
Glory to God for the love of the girl in yellow!'

Kan Turali spoke a blessing on Muhammad of beautiful name
and gave the camel a kick. The camel screamed. He kicked it
again and the camel could not stand on its feet but toppled over.
He jumped on it and cut its throat in two places. From its back
he drew out two sinews and put them before the King, saying,
'The raiders' quiver-straps may break, or their stirrup-leathers,
and these will come in handy for sewing.' Said the King, 'By
God, the moment my eye saw this young man my soul loved
him.' In forty places he had tents pitched, in forty places motley
red bridal bowers. They brought Kan Turali and the girl to
their bower and put them inside. The minstrel came and played
the nuptial music. But the young Oghuz flew into a rage, he
drew his sword, he struck and slashed the ground, and said, 'May
I be slashed like this ground, may I blow in dust like this earth,
may I be sliced by my own sword and spitted on my own arrow,
may no son of mine be born or, if he is born, may he not live
to his tenth day if I enter this bridal bower before I see the faces
of my lord father and my lady mother.' [81]

He took down his tent, he set his camels crying, his horses
neighing, he folded his tent by night and took the road. Seven
days and seven nights he galloped until he arrived at the Oghuz
borderland, where he made camp. Then he said,

'My forty friends, my forty comrades,
   Let my head be a sacrifice for you.

'God Most High gave me a road, I went and killed those three
beasts, I won the yellow-robed Princess Saljan and now I have

come home. Tell my father and let him come and meet me.'

Kan Turali looked at this place where they were encamped and saw that swans and cranes, pheasants and partridges were flying about. There were cold cold rivers, meadows, lawns. The Princess Saljan found the place beautiful; it pleased her. They settled down to feasting, they ate and drank. In those days, whatever disaster befell the Oghuz warriors befell them because of sleep.[82] Kan Turali felt sleepy and dozed off. While he slept, the girl thought, 'My suitors are many; they may gallop after us and seize us, and kill my young warrior and take me, the white-skinned bride, and bring me to my parents' house. This must not be.' Quietly she took Kan Turali's horse and saddled it, quietly she dressed herself for battle; she took up his spear and went up to some high ground, on watch.

Now it seems, my Khan, that the King repented of what he had done. 'Just because he killed three beasts he has taken my dear, my only daughter, and gone,' he said. He picked six hundred infidels, black-clad, blue-armoured. They galloped night and day, and without warning they arrived. The girl was ready. She looked and saw that a raiding-party was on them. She spurred her horse, she came to where Kan Turali lay, and she declaimed; let us see, my Khan, what she declaimed.

'Wake up! Raise your dark head, O warrior!
Open your lovely chestnut eyes, O warrior!
Ere your white hands and arms are tied,
Ere your white forehead is trodden into the black ground,
Ere your lovely head is cut off, all unaware,
Ere your red blood is spilled on the earth's face!
The foe has come, the enemy is here!
Why do you sleep? Arise, warrior!
The towering rocks have not stirred but the earth has gaped,
The old lords are not dead but the land is empty.[83]
Milling and swarming the enemy have come down the
    mountain,
Armed and ready they are upon you!

Have you found a place to sleep in? Have you found a hearth
  and home?
What ails you?'

So she cried out, and Kan Turali awoke with a start. He leaped
to his feet and said, 'What are you saying, my lovely one?' Said
she, 'My warrior, the enemy are upon you. My part was to
rouse you; yours, to fight and show your skill.' Kan Turali
opened his eyes, he raised his eyelids and saw his bride on horseback, dressed for battle, spear in hand. He kissed the ground and
said, 'I hold the faith and I believe; my wish has been granted
in the court of God Most High.' Then he performed his ablutions in pure water, put his white forehead on the ground, and
prayed. He mounted his horse, he spoke a blessing on Muhammad of beautiful name, he drove his horse at the black-garbed
infidel and came face to face with them. Princess Saljan spurred
her horse and got in front of Kan Turali, who said, 'My lovely
one, where are you going?' She replied, 'My lordly warrior,
when the head is safe, can the cap be gone? [84] These infidels here
are a great many infidels; let us war and let us fight, let the one
of us who dies die, let the one who lives return to the camp.'
Then Princess Saljan drove her horse forward. She routed their
enemies, but she did not pursue those who fled nor kill those
who asked for mercy.

She supposed the enemy were defeated. Her sword-hilt bloody,
she returned to the camp but did not find Kan Turali. At that
moment Kan Turali's father and mother arrived. They saw that
the sword-hilt of this person who was coming towards them was
covered in blood, while their son was not to be seen. They asked
for news; let us see how they asked. His mother said,

'Mother lady, daughter lady! [85]
You rose and came with the red dawning.
Have you let the boy be captured?
Have you carelessly let them cut off his lovely head?
Have you let him cry for his lady mother, the lord his father?
Here you are, but my one prince is not to be seen
And my heart is on fire.

From your mouth, your tongue, a few words of news for me,
And my dark head be your sacrifice, my daughter-in-law.'

The maiden knew that they were Kan Turali's parents. Point-
ing with her whip, she said, 'Sit down by the campfire. Wherever
dust is falling and swirling, wherever the crow and raven are
dancing, there shall I seek him.' She spurred her horse and rode
up to some high ground and looked out. She saw a valley where
dust was now gathering, now dispersing. She rode towards it and
saw that they had shot Kan Turali's horse and that he himself
had been wounded by an arrow over the eye. Blood had masked
his face, and constantly he was wiping the blood away. The infidels gathered round him, he drew his sword and drove them off.
When Princess Saljan saw him then, fire flamed inside her. Like
a peregrine falcon falling on a flock of geese, she drove her horse
at the infidel; she smashed through them from one end to the
other. Kan Turali looked and saw that someone was chasing the
enemy away. He did not know that it was Saljan and he was
enraged. Thereupon he declaimed; let us see, my Khan, what he
declaimed.

'Warrior, you up there, what warrior are you?
Warrior, mounted on your black-maned Kazilik horse,
What warrior are you?
Warrior, nonchalantly cutting off heads,
Warrior, attacking my enemy without so much as a by-your-
    leave,
What warrior are you?
In my land it is counted shame to attack another man's
    enemy without his leave;
Be off with you!
Shall I turn into a falcon and fly at you?
Shall I grasp you by your beard and throat?
Shall I nonchalantly cut off *your* head?
Shall I spill your red blood on the ground?
Shall I hang your dark head on my saddle?
Doomed warrior, what warrior are you?
Back, I say!'

So he spoke, and Princess Saljan declaimed; let us see, my
Khan, what she declaimed. Said she,

'O my warrior, my lord, my warrior!
Do the camels forsake their young?
Do the Kazilik horses in the paddock kick their foals?
Do the white sheep in the folds gore their lambs?
And do heroic warriors, princely warriors,
Slaughter their beautiful ones?
My warrior, my lord, my warrior,
One wing of this enemy for me and one for you!'

Kan Turali realized that this warrior who was attacking and
scattering the enemy was Princess Saljan. He charged them on
the other flank, he brandished his sword and pressed on, he cut
off infidel heads. The enemy was crushed, the foe was routed.

Princess Saljan rode off on her horse and Kan Turali came
after. As they went, a thought came to Kan Turali's mind, and
he said,

'Princess Saljan, when you rise up,
When you ride the black-maned Kazilik horse,
When you dismount at the threshold of my father's white
    pavilion,
When the chestnut-eyed daughters and daughters-in-law of
    the Oghuz tell their stories,
When everyone says her say,
You will stand there and boast,
You will say, "Kan Turali was helpless;
I led the way on my horse and he followed after."
Anger consumes me, the heart has gone out of me.
I shall kill you.'

So he spoke, and Princess Saljan, knowing what was the
matter, declaimed; let us see, my Khan, what she declaimed.

'Warrior prince,
If a man will boast, let him boast; he is a lion.
For woman to boast is scandalous.
Boasting does not make a woman a man.

I have not embraced you under the many-coloured quilt,
I have not held your sweet mouth and kissed you,
I have not whispered to you through my red bridal veil.
Quickly did you fall in love and quickly did you weary.
You are nothing but a pimp and the son of a pimp!
Mighty God knows I am yours,
Your friend, your lover; spare me!'

'No,' said Kan Turali, 'I must assuredly kill you.' The girl was annoyed, and said, 'Pimp son of a pimp! So you will not meet me half-way! Come over here and let's carry on the discussion; what will you have, arrows or swords?' She spurred her horse and rode up to some high ground. From her quiver she poured her ninety arrows onto the earth. She removed the heads of two arrows; one she nocked and one she kept in her hand, for she could not bring herself to shoot with a pointed arrow. 'Warrior,' said she, 'shoot your arrow.' Said Kan Turali, 'Girls go first; first *you* shoot.' The girl shot an arrow at Kan Turali that sent the lice in his hair scuttling down to his feet. He came forward and took Princess Saljan into his arms and they kissed and were reconciled. Then Kan Turali declaimed; let us see, my Khan, what he declaimed.

'My fine-robed one, like a bright leaping flame,
My waving cypress, who walks without pressing the ground.
The red on your cheek like blood on the snow,
Too tiny your mouth to hold twin almonds,
Your black brows are like lines drawn by scribes,
Your black hair is like forty handfuls of smoke;
Royal maiden, daughter of lions,
Could I bring myself to kill you?
My own soul I might sacrifice, but never yours;
I was but testing you.'

The Princess Saljan declaimed in answer; let us see, my Khan, what she declaimed.

'Oft have I risen from my place and stood,
Mounted my black-maned Kazilik horse,

Ridden from my father's white pavilion,
Hunted over the many-coloured mountain that lies askew,
Chased the dappled stag and roebuck.
When I drew my bow what things I did with my arrow!
With headless arrow, warrior, I was testing you.
Could I bring myself to kill you, warrior?'

They rushed together, they held each other close and embraced, they gave each other their sweet mouths and kissed, and then they mounted their grey-white horses and galloped till they came to the lord his father.

The father saw his dear boy and gave thanks to God. With his son and his daughter-in-law, Kanli Koja went into the Oghuz land. He pitched tents on the lovely grass of varied green. When he had slaughtered of horses the stallions, of camels the males, of sheep the rams, he made a wedding banquet and feasted the chieftains of the mighty Oghuz. A gold-decked pavilion was set up and Kan Turali entered his bridal bower, and attained his wish, his heart's desire.

Dede Korkut came and played joyful music, he told stories, he declaimed, he recounted the adventures of the gallant fighters for the Faith.

Where now are the valiant princes of whom I have told?
Those who said, 'The world is mine'?
Doom has taken them, earth has hidden them.
Who inherits this transient world,
The world to which men come, from which they go,
The world whose latter end is death?

When doom comes, let it not find you apart from the pure Faith. May the Mighty never put you in need of unworthy men, may your God-given hope never be disappointed. On your white forehead I invoke five words of blessing; may they be accepted. May those who say 'Amen' see the Face of God, may He grant you increase and preserve you in strength and forgive your sins for the sake of Muhammad the Chosen of beautiful name, O my Khan!

7

TELLS THE STORY OF YIGENEK
SON OF KAZILIK KOJA,
O MY KHAN!

BAYINDIR KHAN son of Kam Ghan had risen from his place.
He had pitched his white pavilion on the black earth. His many-
coloured parasol had reared towards the sky. In a thousand
places his silken carpets had been spread. The nobles of the Inner
Oghuz and the Outer Oghuz had assembled to the gathering. It
was a feast.

There was a man they called Kazilik Koja, the minister of
Bayindir Khan. The strong wine rose up to his head. He lurched
onto his great knees and asked leave of Bayindir Khan to go on a
raid. Bayindir Khan gave him leave; 'Go where you will,' he
said.

Kazilik Koja was an experienced and competent man. He
gathered his valiant veterans to his side, and with all provision
for the journey they marched out. Many valleys and hills and
mountains they traversed and one day they arrived at Düzmürd
Castle on the Black Sea shore, where they made camp. The castle
had a lord, whose name was King Direk son of Arshuvan. That
infidel was sixty cubits tall.[86] He used to wield a mace that
weighed half a ton, and he drew a mighty strong bow. Kazilik
Koja, when he reached the castle, began hostilities. That King
came out of the castle, entered the field and challenged all comers.
As soon as Kazilik Koja caught sight of him he rose up and
mounted his horse. Like the wind he flew at that infidel of black
religion, and stuck to him like glue. He aimed a blow of his
sword at the back of the infidel's neck but could not make the
slightest scratch. Now it was the infidel's turn. He grasped his
half-ton mace, held it over Kazilik Koja, and smote. The deceitful
world became too narrow for his head; he spouted blood like a

fountain. They seized him, bundled him up and took him off to the castle; his warriors did not stay but fled.

For sixteen full years Kazilik Koja remained a prisoner in the castle. A champion named Emen came six times,[87] but failed to take the castle and free him. Now it seems, my Khan, that when Kazilik Koja kissed Bayindir Khan's hand and set off he had a baby son, one year old.[88] He entered his fifteenth year and became a young man. He supposed that his father was dead, for they had given strict orders to keep it from the boy that he was a captive. They called the boy Yigenek. One day, while he was sitting conversing with the nobles, he fell out with Budak son of Kara Göne. They exchanged words, and Budak said, 'What are you doing, hurling insults here? Since you're looking for people to quarrel with, why don't you go and rescue your father? He has been a captive for sixteen years in the hands of the infidel.' When Yigenek heard this news, his heart pounded, his inward parts shook. He rose and went into the presence of Bayindir Khan. He put his face on the ground and said,

'You of the white pavilion, pitched afar in the morning
  twilight,
You of the blue parasol made of satin,
You of the falcon-swift horses, drawn up stall on stall,
You of the many officers, who summon and give justice,
You of limitless bounty when the oil is poured,
Prop of forsaken warriors,
Hope of the wretched and the helpless,
Pillar of the Turkish lands,
Chick of the long-plumed bird,
Lion of the Emet river,
Tiger of the Karajuk!

'My Khan, I thought my father was dead; I did not know. But now I have learned that he is a captive among the infidel. I ask you by your kingly head to give me soldiers and let me go to the fortress where my father is imprisoned.'

Bayindir Khan ordered the lords of twenty-four provinces[89] to attend him. 'First,' he said, 'let Wild Dundar son of Kiyan

Seljuk go with you, he who holds sway at the Pass of the Iron
Gate, who makes men groan at the point of his lance, who when
he meets the enemy does not ask their names. Let Dölek Evren [90]
son of Ilig Koja go with you, he who made horses swim the
River of Stallions, who took the keys of fifty-seven castles. Let
Ilalmish son of Yaghrinji go with you, whose beechwood arrow
is not stopped by two-fold battlements. Let Rüstem son of Togh-
sun go with you, who weeps blood if for three days running he
does not see an enemy. Let Wild Evren go with you, who
snatches men from the mouths of dragons. Let Soghan Saru go
with you, who says he will travel from one end of the earth to
the other.' Of counting the Oghuz champions there could be no
end. Bayindir Khan dispatched the twenty-four heroic lords of
provinces to accompany Yigenek also. The nobles assembled and
made their preparations.

Now that night Yigenek had a dream, of which he told his
comrades, declaiming; let us see, my Khan, what he declaimed.

'Princes, while my dark head and eyes were oblivious in sleep
    I saw a dream.
Opening my chestnut eyes, I saw the world:
Heroes I saw, galloping grey-white horses,
The white-helmed heroes I rallied to my side.
I took counsel from Dede Korkut,
I climbed the black mountains that lay ahead.
I came upon the Black Sea that lies beyond,
I made a boat, I took off my shirt and hoisted it as a sail,
I passed through the further sea.
I saw a man whose forehead and head were gleaming,[91]
To one side of the far black mountain.
I rose from my place and stood,
I grasped my bamboo-hafted spear,
I advanced towards him.
I faced him and waited my moment to transfix him,
I watched that man stealthily.
It was my mother's brother Emen! I knew him!
I turned and gave him greeting.

"Which of the Oghuz warriors are you?" I said.

He raised his eyelids and looked me in the face;

"Yigenek, my son," he said, "where are you going?"

I said, "I go to Düzmürd Castle,

They say my father lies captive there."

Then my uncle declaimed to me, saying,

"Where my fleet horse reached, the wind could not go;

Like wolves of the tangled slopes were my warriors;

Seven men it took to bend my bow;

Below the feathers my beechwood arrows were solid gold.

The wind blew, the rain came down, it shed its load.

Seven times I went there but failed to take that castle,

So back I came.

You will not prove a better man than I, my Yigenek!

Turn back!" '

In his dream, Yigenek declaimed to his uncle, saying,

'When you rose from your place and stood,

You did not take to your side noble warriors, chestnut-eyed,

You did not ride with princes of famous name;

Mercenaries you chose as comrades, men you had to pay to
     fight.[92]

So you failed to take the castle.'

And again he said,

'Good is stew to eat when it is cut up fine,

Good is the swift horse if on the day of battle it does not
     stumble,

Good is royal state if, when it comes, it abides,

Good is the mind when it does not forget what it knows,

Good is manliness if it does not turn in flight from its enemy.'

That was the dream Yigenek related to his comrades.

Now his uncle Emen was close by at that moment; he joined
the other nobles and off they went. Eventually they came to
Düzmürd Castle; they formed a circle round it and encamped.
When the infidels saw them, they told King Direk son of Arshuvan. That accursed one emerged from the castle, faced them and

challenged all comers. Wild Dundar son of Kiyan Seljuk arose
and couched his sharp-pointed sixty-span lance, meaning to run
that infidel through, but he could not do so. The infidel King
grappled with him and struck him, dragging his lance from his
hand. Then he brought that half-ton mace down on Dundar.
The wide world became too narrow for his head; he wheeled his
Kazilik horse and withdrew. Then Dölek Evren, who did not
know retreat, galloped up with his six-winged war-club and
brought it down in a mighty blow against the infidel, but could
not subdue him. The infidel King grappled with him, took his
club from his hand and smote him also with his mace. He too
wheeled his horse and withdrew. My Khan, why need we prolong
the tale? The lords of twenty-four provinces were helpless in
the infidel King's hand. Then Yigenek son of Kazilik Koja, that
untried young warrior, committed himself to the protection of
God the Creator and gave praise to the Eternal; let us see, my
Khan, how he gave praise.

'You are higher than the high,
 No one knows what You are like,
 Mighty God!
 You were not born of a mother,
 You were not begotten by a father,
 You have eaten no man's sustenance,
 You have done no man wrong.
 In every place You are One,
 You are God the Ever-living,
 You placed the crown on Adam's head,
 You condemned Satan to hell,
 You exiled him from the Court for one sin.
 Nimrod shot his arrows at the sky,
 You opposed with the split-bellied fish.[93]
 There is no limit to Your greatness,
 You have no measure, no dimension,
 You have no body, no ancestor.
 Great God, him whom You strike You lay low;
 Manifest God, him whom You crush You make disappear;

Beautiful God, him whom You raise You bring to heaven;
All-powerful God, him who arouses Your anger You destroy.
I take refuge in Your Unity, my God, my mighty Lord;
Help me!
I shall charge at the black-garbed infidel;
Do You prosper my work.'

So saying, he spurred his horse at the infidel of black religion.
Like the wind he flew at him, and stuck to him like glue. He
aimed a blow of his sword at the infidel's shoulder, which cut
through his armour and his clothing and left a wound six fingers
deep. His black blood spouted, his black leather boots were filled
with blood. His dark head was stunned, he was stupefied. At once
he turned and fled to the castle, with Yigenek at his heels. Just as
they entered the castle gate, Yigenek dealt him such a blow with
his black steel sword on the back of the neck that his head rolled
to the ground like a ball. Then Yigenek wheeled his horse and
came back to the army.

Seeing what had happened, the infidels, hoping to put an end
to the fighting, freed Kazilik Koja from his captivity, and out
he came. 'Warrior princes,' said he, 'who killed the infidel?' Then
he declaimed; let us see, my Khan, what he declaimed.

'I left the she-camel of the herd heavy with young.
  Male or female the foal? Would that I knew!
I left the ewe of my black land heavy with young.
  Male or female the lamb? Would that I knew!
I left my beautiful chestnut-eyed wife heavy with young.
  Boy or girl the child? Would that I knew!
Tell me, warrior princes, for the love of the Creator!'

Then Yigenek declaimed; let us see, my Khan, what he declaimed.

'You left the she-camel of the herd heavy; a stallion was born.
You left your ewe in the black land heavy; a ram was born.
You left your beautiful chestnut-eyed wife heavy; a lion was
  born.'

Then Yigenek went up to his father and fell at his feet. The father clasped his son to his heart and kissed his eyes and embraced him. They withdrew to a place apart, they clung together, they who had longed for each other talked together and howled together like wolves of the wilderness. Then the nobles all together advanced on the castle and sacked it. They destroyed the castle church and built a mosque in its place. They killed the priests and had the call to prayer recited, they had the invocation pronounced in the name of God the Great. The best of the hunting-birds, the purest of stuffs, the loveliest girls, the heaviest brocades in bundles of nine, they selected as the fifth part of the booty due to Bayindir, the Khan of Khans. The rest they bestowed on those who fought for the Faith.[94] Then they returned home.

Dede Korkut came and told stories and declaimed, and he said, 'Let this tale of the Oghuz be Yigenek's. After me let the brave bards tell it and the generous heroes of untarnished honour listen to it.'

I shall pray for you, my Khan: may your great shady tree never be cut down, may your white-bearded father's place be paradise, may your white-haired mother's place be heaven, may the end of days not part you from the pure Faith. On your white forehead I invoke five words of blessing; may they be accepted. May He forgive your sins for the honour of Muhammad the Chosen of beautiful name, O my Khan!

TELLS THE STORY OF HOW BASAT KILLED GOGGLE–EYE, O MY KHAN!

IT is related, my Khan, that once while the Oghuz were sitting in their encampment the enemy fell upon them. In the darkness of night they broke and scattered. As they fled, the baby son of Uruz Koja fell. A lioness found him, carried him off and nursed him. Time passed, and the Oghuz came back and settled in their old home. One day the horse-drover of Oghuz Khan brought him news. 'My Khan, there is a lion comes out of the thicket roaring, but he walks with a swagger, like a man. He attacks the horses and sucks their blood.' Said Uruz, 'My Khan, maybe it is my little son who fell that time when we scattered.' The nobles mounted their horses and came to the lair of the lioness. They drove her off and seized the boy. Uruz took him to his tent. They held a celebration, there was eating and drinking. But for all that they had brought the boy home he would not stay; back he went to the lion's lair. Again they seized him and brought him back. Dede Korkut came and said, 'My boy, you are a human being; do not consort with wild beasts. Come, ride fine horses, amble and trot in company with fine young men. Your elder brother's name is Kiyan Seljuk, your name shall be Basat.[95] I have given you your name; may God give you long life.'

One day the Oghuz migrated to their summer pasture. Now Uruz had a shepherd whom they called Konur Koja Saru Choban. Whenever the Oghuz migrated this man always went first. There was a spring called Uzun Pinar, which had become a haunt of the peris.[96] Suddenly something startled the sheep. The shepherd was angry with the goat which led the flock, and he went forward, to see that the peri maidens had spread their wings and were flying. He threw his cloak over them and caught one. He desired her and straightway violated her. The flock began to scatter; he ran to head them off, and the peri beat her wings and flew away, saying, 'Shepherd, you have left something in trust with me. When a year has passed, come and take it. But you have brought ruination on the Oghuz.' Fear fell on the shepherd's heart and his face turned pale with anxiety at the peri's words.

Time passed, and again the Oghuz migrated to that summer pasture. Again the shepherd came to that spring. Again something startled the sheep and again the shepherd went forward. He saw a brightly glittering shape lying on the ground. The peri appeared and said, 'Come, shepherd, take back your property. But you have brought ruination on the Oghuz.' Seeing this shape, the shepherd was seized with dread. He turned round and began to rain stones on it from his sling. As each stone struck it, it grew bigger. The shepherd abandoned the shape and fled, and the sheep followed him. Now it happened that at that time Bayindir Khan and the nobles had gone out riding, and they chanced on this spring. They saw a monstrous thing lying there, its head indistinguishable from its arse. They surrounded it, and one warrior dismounted and kicked it. At every kick it grew in size. Several other warriors dismounted and kicked it, and still it grew at every kick. Uruz Koja also dismounted and kicked it. His spur drove into it and the shape split down the middle, and out came a child. Its body was that of a man, but it had one eye at the top of its head. Uruz took this child, wrapped it in the skirt of his garment and said, 'My Khan, give this to me and I shall rear it together with my son Basat.' 'Take it,' said Bayindir Khan, 'it's yours.'

Uruz took Goggle-eye and brought him to his house. He ordered a wet-nurse to come, and she put her nipple into the child's mouth. He gave one suck and took all her milk; a second suck, and he took her blood; a third, and took her life. Several other wet-nurses were brought and he destroyed them. Seeing that this was impossible, they decided to feed him on milk, but a cauldronful a day was not enough. They fed him and he grew; he began to walk, he began to play with the little boys. He started to eat the nose of one, the ear of another. The upshot was that the whole camp was greatly upset at him, but there was nothing they could do. They complained and wept in chorus before Uruz. Uruz beat Goggle-eye, he abused him, he ordered him to stop it, but he paid no attention. Finally he drove him from his house.

Goggle-eye's peri mother came and put a ring on her son's finger, saying, 'My son, this is so that no arrow will pierce you or sword cut you.' Goggle-eye left the Oghuz land and came to a high mountain. He infested the roads, he seized men, he became a notorious outlaw. Many men were sent against him; they shot arrows, which did not pierce him; they struck at him with swords, which did not cut him; they thrust at him with lances, which did not penetrate him. No shepherd, no herd-boy was left; he ate them all. Then he began to eat people from the Oghuz. The Oghuz assembled and marched against him. Seeing them, Goggle-eye was angered; he uprooted a tree, threw it, and destroyed fifty or sixty men. He dealt a blow at the prince of heroes, Kazan, and the world became too narrow for his head. Kara Göne, Kazan's brother, became helpless in Goggle-eye's hand. Alp Rüstem son of Düzen was killed. So valiant a man as the son of Ushun Koja died by his hand. His two pure-souled brothers perished at his hand.[97] So too did Bügdüz Emen of the bloody moustaches. White-headed Uruz Koja he made vomit blood, and his son Kiyan Seljuk's gall-bladder split with terror. The Oghuz could do nothing against Goggle-eye, they broke and fled. Goggle-eye hemmed them in and barred their way, he would not let them go, he brought them back to where they were. In all, the Oghuz broke seven times, and seven times he barred their way and brought them back. The Oghuz were totally helpless in Goggle-eye's hand.

They went and called Dede Korkut, they consulted with him and said, 'Come, let us make terms.' They sent Dede Korkut to Goggle-eye. He came and greeted him, then he said, 'Goggle-eye, my son, the Oghuz are helpless in your hand, they are overwhelmed. They have sent me to the dust of your feet; they wish to come to terms with you.' Goggle-eye said, 'Give me sixty men a day to eat.' Dede Korkut replied, 'This way you won't have any men left; you'll exhaust the supply. Let us give you two men and five hundred sheep a day.' 'Very well,' replied Goggle-eye, 'so be it, I agree. And give me two men to prepare my food for me to eat.' Dede Korkut returned to the Oghuz and told them, 'Give Goggle-eye Yünlü Koja and Yapaghilu Koja to cook his food. He also asks for two men and five hundred sheep a day.' They agreed. Whoever had four sons gave one of them, leaving three. Whoever had three gave one of them, leaving two. Whoever had two gave one, leaving one. There was a man called Kapak Kan, who had two sons. One he gave and one was left. His turn came round again. The mother screamed and cried and lamented.

Now it seems, my Khan, that Basat son of Uruz, who had gone on an expedition into the lands of the infidel, returned at this point. The poor woman said to herself, 'Basat has just come back from raiding. I'll go and perhaps he might give me a prisoner so that I can ransom my son.' Basat had pitched his gold-adorned pavilion and was sitting in it, when he saw a lady approaching. She came in, greeted Basat and wept, saying,

'Son of Uruz, my lord Basat,
Renowned among the Inner Oghuz and the Outer Oghuz.
With your flighted arrows that do not stay in your hand,
With your strong bow of the horn of the he-goat,
Help me!'

Said Basat, 'What is it you desire?' The poor woman replied, 'On the face of this treacherous world there has erupted a man who has not let the Oghuz rest in their domain. Those who wield the pure black steel swords have not cut a hair of his that might be cut; those who brandish the bamboo lances have not been able to make them penetrate; those who shoot the hornbeam arrows have achieved nothing. He dealt a blow at Kazan, prince of heroes; Kazan's brother Kara Göne and Bügdüz Emen of the bloody moustaches became powerless in his hand. Your white-bearded father Uruz he made vomit blood; your brother Kiyan Seljuk's gall-bladder burst on the field of battle and he gave up his soul. Of the other nobles of the teeming Oghuz, some he overpowered and some he killed. Seven times he drove the Oghuz from their place. Then he agreed to make terms; he demanded

two men and five hundred sheep a day. They gave him Yünlü
Koja and Yapaghilu Koja to serve him. Whoever had four sons
gave one of them, whoever had three sons gave one of them,
whoever had two sons gave one of them. I had two dear sons and
gave one, and one remained. Now the turn has come round to me
again and they are asking for him too. Help me, my lord!'
Basat's dark eyes filled with tears. He declaimed for his brother;
let us see, my Khan, what he declaimed.

> 'Your tents, pitched in a place apart,
>   Can that pitiless one have overthrown, brother?
> Your swift-running horses from their stalls
>   Can that pitiless one have stolen, brother?
> Your sturdy young camels from their file
>   Can that pitiless one have taken, brother?
> The sheep you would slaughter at your feasting
>   Can that pitiless one have slaughtered, brother?
> Your dear bride I proudly saw you bring home
>   Can that pitiless one have parted from you, brother?
> You have made my white-bearded father mourn his son;
>   Can this be, O my brother?
> You have made my white-skinned mother weep;
>   Can this be, O my brother?
> Brother, pinnacle of my black mountain yonder!
> Brother, flood of my lovely eddying river!
> Brother, strength of my strong back!
> Brother, light of my dark eyes!
> I have lost my brother.'

So saying, he wept and lamented greatly. Then he gave that
lady a captive and said, 'Go, ransom your son.' The lady took the
captive and came and gave him in place of her son. Moreover
she brought Uruz the good news that his son had come home.[98]

Uruz rejoiced, and came with the nobles of the teeming Oghuz
to meet Basat. Basat kissed his father's hand and they cried and
wept together. He came to his mother's house. His mother came
to meet him and pressed her dear son to her heart. Basat kissed
his mother's hand, they embraced and wept together. The Oghuz

nobles assembled and there was eating and drinking. Basat said,
'Princes, I shall meet Goggle-eye for my brother's sake; what do
you say?' Thereupon Kazan Bey declaimed; let us see, my Khan,
what he declaimed.

'Goggle-eye burst forth, a black dragon!
I chased him round the face of the sky but could not catch
   him, Basat.
Goggle-eye burst forth, a black tiger!
I chased him round the darkling mountains but could not
   catch him, Basat.
Goggle-eye burst forth, a raging lion!
I chased him round the dense forests but could not catch
   him, Basat.
Though you be a man, though you be a prince,
You will not be like me, Kazan.
Do not make your white-bearded father cry!
Do not make your white-haired mother weep!'

'I shall surely go,' said Basat, and Kazan replied, 'You know
best.' Then Uruz wept and said, 'Son, do not leave my hearth
desolate. I beg you, don't go.' Basat answered, 'No, my white-
bearded hònoured father, I shall go,' and he would not listen.
He took from his quiver a fistful of arrows and stuck them in his
belt, he girded on his sword, he grasped his bow, he rolled up
his skirts, he kissed his parents' hands, he made his peace with
all, he said 'Good-bye!'

He came to the crag of Salakhana,[99] where Goggle-eye was. He
saw Goggle-eye lying with his back to the sun. He took an arrow
from his belt and shot it at Goggle-eye's back. The arrow did not
penetrate, it broke. He shot another, which also broke. Goggle-
eye said to the cooks, 'The flies here are a bit of a nuisance.'
Basat shot another arrow, and that broke too. One piece fell in
front of Goggle-eye, who leaped up and looked around. When he
saw Basat, he clapped his hands and bellowed with laughter. He
said to the cooks, 'Another spring lamb from the Oghuz!' He
clutched Basat and held him, he dangled him by the throat, he
brought him into his den, he pushed him into the leg of his boot

and said, 'Cooks! This afternoon you will put this one on the spit for me and I'll eat him.' Then he fell asleep again. Now Basat had a dagger, and he cut the boot and slipped out. 'Tell me, men,' said he, 'how can this creature be killed?' 'We do not know,' they answered, 'but there is no flesh anywhere except his eye.' Basat advanced right up to Goggle-eye's head, raised his eyelid and saw that his eye was indeed flesh. 'Come on, men,' he said, 'put the spit in the fire and get it red-hot.' They did so. Then Basat took it in his hand, invoked blessings on Muhammad of beautiful name, and drove the spit into Goggle-eye's eye, which was destroyed.[100] So loud did he scream and bellow that the mountains and rocks echoed.

Basat bounded into the midst of the sheep, down into the cave.[101] Goggle-eye knew Basat was in the cave. He set himself at the entrance, put a foot on each side of it and said, 'Ho billy-goats, leaders of the flock, come one by one and pass through.' They did so, and he patted each one's head. 'My dear yearlings, and you my good fortune, my white-blazed ram, come and pass through.'[102] A ram rose up and stretched itself. At once Basat leaped at it, cut its throat and flayed it. He left the head and tail attached to the skin, and got inside it. Basat came in front of Goggle-eye. Now Goggle-eye guessed that Basat was inside the skin, and said, 'White-blazed ram, you knew through what part I might be destroyed. I shall dash you against the cave-wall so that your tail greases the cave.' Basat gave the ram's head into Goggle-eye's hand, and Goggle-eye grasped it tightly by the muzzle. He lifted it and held the muzzle with the skin hanging. Basat slipped between Goggle-eye's legs and away. Goggle-eye raised the muzzle, dashed it against the ground and said, 'Boy, have you escaped?' Basat replied, 'My God has saved me.' Said Goggle-eye, 'Boy, take this ring which is on my finger and put it on your own finger, and arrow and sword will have no effect on you.' Basat took the ring and put it on his finger. 'Boy,' said Goggle-eye, 'have you taken the ring and put it on?' 'I have,' said Basat. Goggle-eye rushed at Basat, flailing and cutting with a dagger. He leaped away and stood on open ground. He saw that the ring was now lying under Goggle-eye's foot.[103] 'Have you escaped?' asked Goggle-eye. Basat replied, 'My God has saved me.' Said Goggle-eye, 'Boy, do you see that vault?' 'I see it,' he replied. Goggle-eye said, 'I have a treasure; go and seal it so that the cooks don't take it.' Basat entered the vault and saw mounds of gold and silver. Looking at it, he forgot himself. Goggle-eye shut the door of the vault and said, 'Are you inside there?' 'I am,' replied Basat. Goggle-eye said, 'I shall shake it so that you and the vault are dashed to pieces.' There came to Basat's tongue the words 'There is no god but God; Muhammad is the Messenger of God.' Straightway the vault split and doors were opened in seven places, through one of which he came out. Goggle-eye put his hand against the vault and pushed so hard that the vault crumbled to bits. Said Goggle-eye, 'Boy, have you escaped?' Basat replied, 'My God has saved me.' Said Goggle-eye, 'It seems you can't be killed. Do you see that cave?' 'I see it,' said Basat. 'There are two swords in it,' said Goggle-eye, 'one with a scabbard and one without. The one without a scabbard will cut off my head. Go fetch it and cut off my head.' Basat went up to the opening of the cave. He saw a sword without a scabbard, ceaselessly moving up and down. 'I shan't get hold of this,' said he, 'without a bit of trouble.' He drew his own sword and held it out, and the moving sword split it in two. He went and fetched a tree and held it against the sword, which split it in two also. Then he took his bow in his hand, and with an arrow he struck the chain by which the sword was suspended. The sword fell and buried itself in the ground. He put it into his own scabbard and held it firmly by the hilt. He came out and said, 'Hey Goggle-eye! How are you?' Goggle-eye answered, 'Hey boy! Aren't you dead yet?' 'My God has saved me,' replied Basat. 'It seems you can't be killed,' said Goggle-eye. Then crying loudly he declaimed; let us see, my Khan, what he declaimed.

> 'My eye, my eye, my only eye!
> With you, my only eye,
> I once routed the Oghuz.
> Man, you have robbed me of my chestnut eye;
> May the Almighty rob you of your sweet life!

Such pain I suffer in my eye,
May God Almighty give no man pain in the eye.'

Then again he spoke:

'What is the place where you dwell, man, and whence you
migrate in the summer?
If you lose your way in the dark night, what is your
watchword?
Who is your Khan who carries the great standard?
Who is your hero who leads on the day of battle?
What is the name of your white-bearded father?
For a valiant warrior to conceal his name from another is
shameful;
What is your name, man? Tell me.'

Basat declaimed to Goggle-eye; let us see, my Khan, what he
declaimed.

'My place where I dwell, whence I migrate in the summer, is
the southland.
If I lose my way in the dark night, my watchword is God.
Our Khan who carries the great standard is Bayindir Khan.
Our hero who leads on the day of battle is Salur Kazan.
If you ask my father's name, it is Mighty Tree.
If you ask my mother's name, it is Raging Lioness.
If you ask my name, it is Basat son of Uruz.'

'Then we are brothers!' said Goggle-eye, 'Spare me!' Basat replied,

'You filthy scoundrel, you have made my white-bearded father
weep,
You have made my old white-haired mother cry,
You have killed my brother Kiyan,
You have widowed my white-skinned sister-in-law,
You have orphaned her chestnut-eyed babes;
Shall I let you be?
Till I have wielded my pure black steel sword,
Till I have cut off your pointed-capped head,

Till I have spilled your red blood on the ground,
Till I have avenged my brother Kiyan,
I shall not let you be.'

Thereupon Goggle-eye declaimed once more:

'I meant to rise up from my place,
To break my pact with the nobles of the teeming Oghuz,
To kill their newborn young,
To have once more my fill of man-meat.
I meant, when the nobles of the teeming Oghuz massed against
    me,
To flee and shelter at the crag of Salakhana,
To cast rocks from a mighty catapult,
To go down, let the rocks fall on my head, and die.
Man, you have robbed me of my chestnut eye;
May the Almighty rob you of your sweet life!'

Yet again Goggle-eye declaimed:

'I have made the white-bearded old men weep much;
Their white beards' curse must have smitten you, O my eye!
I have made the white-haired old women weep much;
Their tears must have smitten you, O my eye!
Many the dark-moustached youths I have eaten;
Their manhood must have smitten you, O my eye!
Many the maidens I have eaten, their little hands dyed with
    henna;
Their small curses must have smitten you, O my eye!
Such pain I suffer in my eye,
May God Almighty give no man pain in the eye.
My eye, my eye, O my eye, my only eye!'

Basat, enraged, rose up and forced him down on his knees like a
camel, and with Goggle-eye's own sword he cut off Goggle-eye's
head. He made a hole in it, tied his bowstring to it and dragged it
and dragged it until he reached the door of the cave. He sent
Yünlü Koja and Yapaghilu Koja to take the good news to the
Oghuz. They mounted grey-white horses and galloped away.

The news came to the lands of the teeming Oghuz. Horse-mouthed Uruz Koja galloped to his tent and gave Basat's mother glad tidings. 'Good news!' he said, 'Your son has killed Goggle-eye!' The nobles of the teeming Oghuz arrived, they came to the crag of Salakhana and brought out the head of Goggle-eye for all to see. Dede Korkut came and played joyful music. He related the adventures of the valiant fighters for the Faith, and he invoked blessings on Basat:

'When you reach the black mountain may He make a way,
May He give you passage across the blood-red water.'

And he said,

'Manfully have you avenged your brother's blood,
You have saved the nobles of the teeming Oghuz from a
heavy burden;
May Almighty God give you honour and glory, Basat!'

When the hour of death comes may it not part you from the pure Faith, and may He forgive your sins for the sake of Muhammad the Chosen of beautiful name, O my Khan!

9

TELLS THE STORY OF EMREN
SON OF BEGIL

KHAN BAYINDIR son of Kam Ghan had risen from his place.
He had pitched his white pavilion on the black earth. His many-
coloured parasol had reared towards the sky. In a thousand places
his silken carpets had been spread. The nobles of the Inner
Oghuz and Outer Oghuz had assembled.

The tribute came from Georgia of the Nine Provinces;[104] they
brought a horse,[105] a sword, and a mace. Bayindir Khan was
greatly displeased. Dede Korkut came and played joyful music.
'My Khan,' he asked, 'why are you displeased?' 'Why should I
not be displeased?' he replied. 'Every year gold and silver has
been coming; we gave it to the warriors and the nobles and they
were satisfied. Now whom can we satisfy with this?' Dede Korkut
said, 'My Khan, let us give all three things to one warrior and let
him be the warden for the Oghuz land.' 'To whom shall we give
them?' said Khan Bayindir, looking to right and left. None was
willing. There was a warrior called Begil; he looked at him and
asked, 'What do you say?' Begil consented. He rose and kissed
the ground. Dede Korkut girded the sword of divine grace round
his waist, put the mace on his shoulder, the bow on his arm. Begil
called for his falcon-swift horse and leaped onto its back. He took
his family and his people, he struck his tents and migrated from
the Oghuz land. He reached Barda, then Ganja,[106] where he took
some grazing-land. He moved on to the mouth of Georgia of the
Nine Provinces, and there he settled and there he stayed as warden. When strangers and infidels came, he used to send their
heads to the Oghuz as a present. Once a year he would attend
Bayindir Khan's court.

One day again men came from Bayindir Khan, bidding him

come quickly. Begil arrived, offered his gift, and kissed Bayindir Khan's hand. The Khan made him welcome, giving him fine horses, fine clothes, and plenty of money. For three full days he entertained him. 'Princes,' said the Khan, 'let us entertain Begil for three days more with the meat of the chase.' They proclaimed the hunt.

When the preparations were made, one man boasted of his horse, another of his sword, another of his prowess as an archer. Salur Kazan did not boast of his horse or vaunt himself, but told of Begil's skill. If three hundred and sixty-six heroes rode out hunting and attacked the sturdy deer, Begil would not draw his bow or shoot an arrow; he would at once take his bow off from his elbow and hurl it at the neck of the stag, drag it and stop it in its tracks. If it was thin he would pierce its ear to make it recognizable in the hunt, while if it was fat he would kill it. When the nobles caught a quarry, if its ear was pierced they would send it to Begil to give him pleasure. 'This skill,' asked Prince Kazan, 'is it the horse's or the man's?' 'The man's, lord,' they said. 'No!' said the Khan, 'If the horse did not play its part the man could not vaunt himself; the skill belongs to the horse.' These words did not please Begil; he said, 'Before all the heroes you have cast me down from my saddle into the mud.' He threw Bayindir Khan's gifts in front of him, he was enraged against the Khan, and he left the court. They brought his horse, he took his chestnut-eyed warriors and went home. His little sons came to meet him, but he did not caress them, nor did he speak to his whiteskinned lady. The lady declaimed; let us see, my Khan, what she declaimed.

'Lord of my golden throne, my princely warrior,
  You whom I see when I open my eyes,
  Whom I love with all my heart!
  You rose up from your place,
  You took your chestnut-eyed warriors,
  You climbed by night the many-coloured mountain that lies
    askew,
  You crossed by night the lovely eddying river,

You came by night to the court of the honoured Bayindir
  Khan,
You ate and drank with the chestnut-eyed princes.
Was someone at odds with his people?
Was your poor head involved in a quarrel?
And, my lord, you are not on your fine horse; where is he? [107]
Nor are you wearing your golden helmet or the robe that goes
  with it,
You do not caress your chestnut-eyed princes,
You do not talk to your white-skinned beauty;
What ails you?'

Begil declaimed; let us see, my Khan, what he declaimed,

'I rose up from my place,
I leaped onto my black-maned Kazilik horse,
I climbed by night the many-coloured mountain that lies
  askew,
I forded by night the lovely eddying river,
I rode up to the court of the honoured Bayindir Khan,
I ate and drank with the chestnut-eyed princes,
I saw everyone at peace with his people,
I saw our Khan's regard had left me.
Let us move with all our household to Georgia of the Nine
  Provinces;
I have rebelled against the Oghuz, mark this well.'

His wife replied, 'My warrior, my princely warrior! Emperors
are the shadow of God. None who rebels against his emperor
prospers. If there be any tarnish on a pure soul, wine will remove
it. Since you left, there has been no hunting over your many-
coloured mountain which lies askew. Mount your horse and go
hunting, to ease your soul.' Begil saw that the lady's wisdom and
her words were sound. He called for his Kazilik horse, leaped
onto its back, and went hunting.

As he wandered in quest of game, a dappled male elk appeared
in his path. Begil drove his horse at it, came up behind it and
cast his bow-string at its neck. The elk flew through the air and

cast itself down from a high place. Begil could not control his horse's reins and he flew too. His right thigh struck a rock and broke. Begil rose and wept, saying, 'I have no grown son, no grown brother.' Then he took some arrow-shafts from his quiver, tugged at the horse's saddle-girth and twisted it. He bound his leg tightly under his caftan and, with all his strength, mounted and fell forward onto his horse's neck. He was separated from the huntsmen. His turban slipped down to his throat, and so he came to the outskirts of his encampment.

His young son Emren came to meet his brave father. He saw him with his face pale, his turban fallen down to his throat. The boy, seeking news of his comrades, declaimed; let us see, my Khan, what he declaimed.

'You rose from your place and came forth,
   You leaped on to your black-maned Kazilik horse,
   You quested for game to the skirts of the many-coloured
      mountains that lie askew.
   Did you meet the black-garbed infidel?
   Did you let your chestnut-eyed young men be destroyed?
   A few words from your mouth and tongue for me
   And my dark head be a sacrifice, my lord, for you.'

Begil declaimed in answer to his son; let us see, my Khan, what he declaimed.

'My son, my son, O my son!
   I rose up from my place and came forth,
   I rode out to hunt to the foothills of the black mountains,
   I did not meet the black-garbed infidel,
   I did not let my chestnut-eyed young men be destroyed,
   My comrades are safe and sound, son; be not anxious.
   For three days I have been alone.
   Take me off my horse, son, and lay me on my bed.'

The lion's cub is also a lion. He grasped his father, took him off the horse and carried him to his bed. He wrapped his robes over him and closed his door.

The young men for their part having seen that the hunt was

spoiled, everyone went to his own tent. For five days Begil did not go out to the assembly. He told no one that his leg was broken. One night in his bed he groaned and sighed deeply. His wife said, 'My warrior lord, you were never one to turn back, though a throng of enemies came, nor to groan if an arrow struck you in the leg. Can a man possibly not tell his secret to his wife who lies in his bosom? What is the matter?' Begil replied, 'My beautiful one, I fell from my horse and broke my leg.' His wife smote her hands together and told the slave-girl. The slave-girl went out and told the gate-keeper. What came out past thirty-two teeth was broadcast to the whole encampment: 'Begil has fallen from his horse and broken his leg!'

Now the infidel had a spy, who heard this news and went and told the infidel king. The king said, 'Rise up from your places and stand, seize Prince Begil where he lies, bind his white hands and arms, and just cut off his handsome head while you're about it. Spill his red blood on the earth's face, pillage his home, take his daughters and daughters-in-law captive.' Now Begil too had a spy, who was present there. He sent word to Begil: 'Make ready, the enemy is about to attack you.' Begil looked up and said, 'Heaven is a long way off, and the earth is hard.' He sent for his young son and declaimed; let us see, my Khan, what he declaimed.

'My son, my son, O my son!
 Light of my dark eyes, my son!
 Strength of my strong loins, my son!
 See what has befallen now,
 What has broken over my head.
 I rose, my son, from my place,
 I leaped onto the red stallion – may his neck break!
 As I wandered, hunting and fowling,
 He went stupid and stumbled and threw me;
 My right thigh is broken.
 What has befallen my dark head!
 The news has climbed the darkling mountains,
 The news has crossed the blood-red rivers,

The news has reached the Iron Gate Pass.
King Shökli of the dappled horse is ill-tempered;
The smoke of his ill temper has fallen on the black mountains.
"Seize Prince Begil where he lies!" says he.
"Tie his white hands and arms!" says he.
"Pillage his blood-spattered encampment!" says he.
"Take his white-skinned daughters and daughters-in-law
        captive!" says he.
Rise up, my son, and come!
Leap onto your black-maned Kazilik horse,
Climb by night the many-coloured mountain that lies askew,
Arrive by night at the court of the honoured Bayindir Khan,
Give greeting from your mouth and tongue to Bayindir,
Kiss the hand of Kazan, the Prince of Princes,
Say, "My white-bearded father is ill."
Say he said, "At all costs Prince Kazan must come to my aid.
If not, the land will be laid waste and ruined,
My daughters and daughters-in-law captive, be sure of this." '

Thereupon the boy declaimed to his father; let us see, my
Khan, what he declaimed.

'Father, what are you telling me, what are you saying?
Why do you wound me in my inmost heart?
Indeed I shall rise up from my place,
But I shall not mount my black-maned Kazilik horse,
I shall not chase over the many-coloured mountain that lies
        askew,
I shall not go to the honoured Bayindir Khan's court.
Who is Kazan? I shall not kiss his hand.
Give me the red stallion you ride,
I shall gallop him till he sweats blood for you.
Give me your strong-bodied iron mail,
I shall have sleeves and collar stitched for you.
Give me your pure black steel sword,
I shall just cut some heads off for you.
Give me your bamboo-shafted spear,
I shall run men through the breast for you.

Give me your whirring white-flighted arrow,
I shall shoot it through one man and into another for you.
Give me your three hundred chestnut-eyed warriors to bear
    me company,
I shall fight in the cause of Muhammad's religion for you.'

Begil said, 'May I die for your mouth, my son, only do not
remind me of my own bygone days. Here! Bring my armour for
my son to wear, bring my red stallion for my son to ride. Before the people are alarmed, let my son go and take the field.'

They dressed the boy for battle. He came and embraced his
father and mother, and kissed their hands. He took the three
hundred warriors with him and came to the open plain. Whenever the red stallion smelled the enemy he would paw the ground,
and the dust would rise up to heaven. The infidels said, 'That
horse is Begil's; we're off!' Their king replied, 'Look carefully.
If this man who is approaching us is Begil, I shall run away
before you do.' The scout looked closely and saw that although
the horse was Begil's the one on it was not Begil but a boy, skinny
as a bird. He brought the news to the king, saying, 'The horse,
the armour and the helmet are Begil's but it's not Begil inside.'
The king said, 'Pick a hundred men, make a noise and scare the
boy; the boy will be chicken-hearted and leave the field and run.'
A hundred men were picked, who advanced on the boy, and the
infidel declaimed to the boy; let us see, my Khan, what they
declaimed.

'Boy, boy, boy!
Bastard boy!
The red horse you're on is a bag of bones, boy.
Your pure black steel sword is gap-toothed, boy.
The spear in your hand is broken, boy.
Your white-gripped bow is coming apart, boy.
The ninety arrows in your quiver are a bit sparse, boy.
Your comrades are stark naked, boy.
Your dark eyes are far from bright, boy.
King Shökli is very cross with you.
"Seize that boy!" he told us,

"Tie his white hands and arms,
Just cut off his handsome head while you're about it,
Spill his red blood on the ground."
Have you a white bearded father? Don't make him cry!
Have you a white-haired mother? Don't make her weep!
A lone warrior cannot be a hero,
A stalk of mugwort cannot be strong.
Doomed pimp, son of a pimp,
Back, turn back from here.'

Whereupon the boy declaimed; let us see what he declaimed.

'Don't talk rubbish, there's a good infidel dog!
What don't you like about the horse I ride?
He saw you and pranced.
The armour I wear is heavy on my shoulders,
My pure black steel sword slices its scabbard.
What don't you like about my bamboo-shafted spear?
It will stab through your breast and glitter at the sky.
My strong white-gripped bow groans deep,
The arrows are piercing my sable-lined quiver,
My warriors at my side are hungry for battle.
Shame it is to try to frighten a hero!
Come here, infidels, and let us fight!'

The infidel said, 'The cheeky Oghuz is like the crazy Turco-man.[108] Just look at him!' The King said, 'Go and ask what the boy has to do with Begil.' They came and declaimed to the boy; let us see what they declaimed.

'We know the red stallion you ride is Begil's; where is Begil?
Your pure black steel sword is Begil's; where is Begil?
The iron mail on your shoulders is Begil's; where is Begil?
The warriors by your side are Begil's; where is Begil?
Had Begil been here
We would have battled till nightfall,
We would have drawn the strong white-gripped bows,
We would have shot the white-flighted whirring arrows.
What are you to Begil? Tell us, boy!'

Then Begil's son declaimed; let us see, my Khan, what he declaimed.[109] 'Don't you know me, infidel? Salur Kazan, Commander of Commanders of the honoured Bayindir Khan, Salur
Kazan's brother Kara Göne, Dölek Evren who knows not retreat, Alp Rüstem son of Düzen, and Beyrek of the grey horse
were drinking in Prince Begil's house when your spy arrived.
Begil mounted me on his red stallion, gave me his pure black
steel sword for strength, his bamboo-shafted spear for divine
favour, the three hundred warriors of his escort to bear me company. I am Begil's son. Come here, infidel, let us fight!' The
infidel King said, 'Be patient, son of a pimp, I am coming to
you.' He took in his hand his six-winged mace and rode at the
boy. The boy held his shield to ward off the mace. The infidel
dealt a mighty blow down onto the boy, which shattered his
shield and shivered his helmet and shaved his eyebrows, but did
not overcome the boy. They fought with maces, they battled with
pure black steel swords, they exchanged sword-blows all over the
field. Their shoulders were sliced, their swords were shattered,
but neither could bring the other down. They warred with bamboo-shafted spears, they gored at each other over the field like
bulls. Their breast-plates were pierced, their spears broke, but
neither could bring the other down. They dismounted and
grappled with each other, they wrestled. The infidel was the
stronger and the boy became helpless. Calling on God Most High
he declaimed; let us see what he declaimed.

'High God, You are higher than the high;
Beautiful God, no one knows what You are like.
You placed the crown on Adam's head,
You condemned Satan to hell,
You exiled him from the Court for one sin.
You let Abraham be seized,
You, my Khan, let him be bundled up in leather bonds,[110]
Picked up and thrown into the fire;
You made the fire into a garden.
I take refuge in Your Unity,
Dear God, my Master, help me.'

The infidel said, 'Boy, when you have been overcome, do you call on your God? If you have one God, I have seventy-two temples full of idols.' The boy replied, 'You damned heretic! If you call on your idols, I take refuge with my God who made the worlds out of nothing.'

God Most High gave orders to Gabriel, saying, 'Go, Gabriel, I give that slave of mine the strength of forty men.' The boy picked the infidel up and hurled him to the ground. He spouted blood from his nose like a fountain. The boy swooped like a falcon and grasped the infidel's throat. The infidel said, 'Mercy, warrior! What do they call your religion? I accept it.' He raised his finger and pronounced the Profession of Faith and became a Muslim.[111] The rest of the infidels, when they understood what was happening, left the field and ran. The raiders smote the infidels' territory and took captive their daughters and daughters-in-law.

The boy sent bearers of good tidings to his father, to say he had vanquished his enemy. His white-bearded father came to meet him and embraced the boy. Then they came home. He gave the boy pasture-lands on the black mountain that lay before. He gave him stables full of fleet horses. For his white-skinned son he gave a feast of white sheep. For his chestnut-eyed son he found a bride with a red veil. He set aside a fifth of the booty for the honoured Bayindir Khan. He took his son and went to the court of Bayindir Khan. They kissed hands. The emperor indicated a place for him at the right hand of Uruz son of Kazan. He dressed him in robes and fine linen and gold-embroidered stuffs. Dede Korkut came and played joyful music, he strung together this tale of the Oghuz and said, 'Let it be the story of Emren son of Begil.' He related the adventures of the gallant fighters for the Faith.

I shall pray for you, my Khan: may your firm-rooted black mountain never be overthrown, may your great shady tree never be cut down, may your God-given hope never be disappointed, may He forgive your sins for the sake of Muhammad of beautiful name, O my Khan!

10

TELLS THE STORY OF SEGREK
SON OF USHUN KOJA

IN the days of the Oghuz there was a man called Ushun Koja. In his life he had two sons. The name of the elder son was Egrek. He was a brave, reckless, redoubtable warrior. He used to visit Bayindir Khan's court whenever he chose. At the court of Kazan, the Commander of Commanders, he came and went at his own sweet will.[112] He used to push the nobles aside and sit in front of Kazan. He deferred to none. Well, my Khan, one day when he had again pushed the nobles aside and sat down, an Oghuz warrior called Ters Uzamish said, 'Hey, son of Ushun Koja! Everyone of these nobles sitting here has won the place where he sits with his sword and with his bread. Have you cut off heads and spilled blood? Have you fed the hungry and clothed the naked?' Egrek said, 'Ters Uzamish, is cutting off heads and spilling blood a clever thing to do?' 'Of course it is,' he replied. Ters Uzamish's words had their effect on Egrek; he rose and asked Prince Kazan's leave to go on a raid. Leave was given. He sent out the criers and the raiders assembled. Three hundred warriors with polished lances rallied to his side. For five days there was eating and drinking in the wine-shop. Then they raided the land from the borders of Shirakavan as far as the Blue Lake,[113] and took rich booty. Their way lay by Alinja Castle.[114] There the infidel Black King had had a park made, an enclosure which he had filled with geese and hens of the things that fly, and deer and hare of those that walk. This he made a trap for the Oghuz warriors. The son of Ushun Koja happened by this place. They smashed the gate of the park, they killed elk and deer, geese and hens, and they feasted. They unsaddled their horses and they took off their armour. Now the Black King had a spy, who saw them and came and reported: 'A company of horsemen have come from the Oghuz; they have smashed the gate of the park, unsaddled their horses and taken off their armour. What are you waiting for?' Six hundred black-mailed infidels attacked them, killed the warriors, seized Egrek and threw him into the dungeon of Alinja Castle.

The news climbed the darkling mountains, the news crossed the blood-red rivers, the news came to the land of the teeming Oghuz. Mourning began before Ushun Koja's white pavilion. His swan-like daughters and daughters-in-law took off white and put on black. Ushun Koja and Egrek's white-skinned mother wept and lamented together for their son.

Those with ribs get bigger, those with breast-bones grow greater.[115] It seems, my Khan, that Ushun Koja's younger son grew up to be a good, brave, heroic, reckless warrior. One day his way led him to a party. They pitched tents and feasted. Segrek got drunk and went outside to relieve himself. He saw an orphan boy fighting with another. 'What's the matter with you?' he said, and gave each of them a box on the ears. Bitter is the fruit of an old mulberry-tree, and bitter the tongue of an orphan boy. One of them said, 'Isn't it enough for you that we're orphans? What are you hitting us for? If you're so clever, your brother is a prisoner in Alinja Castle; go and set him free.'[116] 'What's my brother's name?' asked Segrek. 'Egrek' was the reply. 'Segrek goes well with Egrek,' said he, 'it seems I have a brother alive and I shall not flinch. I shall not stay among the Oghuz without my brother.' And he wept, saying, 'Light of my dark eyes, my brother!' He went back inside to the party and asked leave to withdraw. 'Farewell!' said the nobles. They brought his horse and he mounted and rode off to his mother's tent. He got off his horse, desiring to learn what his mother could tell him. So Segrek declaimed; let us see, my Khan, what he declaimed.

'Mother, I rose up from my place,
 I leaped onto my black-maned Kazilik horse,
 I reached the skirts of the many-coloured mountain that lies
    askew;

I had heard tell of a party in the land of the teeming Oghuz,
And there I went.
Amidst the eating and drinking,
A messenger came on a grey-white horse.
A warrior named Egrek, he said, had long been captive.
Mighty God had opened a way for him; he had come out
    and was on his way.
Great and small went to meet that warrior.
Mother, shall I go too? What do you say?'

His mother declaimed in answer; let us see, my Khan, what
she declaimed.

'May I die for your mouth, my son!
May I die for your tongue, my son!
Your black mountain yonder
Had fallen in ruin; it has risen at last.
Your beautiful eddying river
Had run dry; it has welled forth at last.
Your branch and twig on the great tree
Had withered; they are fresh and green at last.
If the nobles of the teeming Oghuz go in search of him,
Go you too.
When you meet that warrior,
Alight from your grey-white horse,
Join your hands and salute that warrior.
Kiss his hand and clasp his neck,
Call him, "Summit of my black mountain, brother!"
What are you waiting for, son? Go!'

The boy declaimed to his mother; let us see, my Khan, what
he declaimed.

'Mother, may your mouth dry up!
Mother, may your tongue rot!
So I have a brother of my own! I cannot flinch,
I cannot stay among the Oghuz without my brother.
Were it not that the mother's due is God's due,
I should draw my pure black steel sword,

> I should casually cut off your lovely head,
> I should spill your red blood on the earth's face,
> Mother, wicked mother!'

His father said, 'The news is wrong, son; the one who escaped is not your elder brother but someone else. Do not make your white-bearded father weep, do not make your little old mother cry.' The son declaimed in answer:

> 'If three hundred and sixty-six heroes rode to the hunt,
> If a fight broke out over a stag,
> The men with brothers would rise and stand out;
> The wretch with none, if a fist struck the back of his neck,
> Would weep and look helplessly around,
> Would shed his bitter tears from his chestnut-eyes.
> Until you see your chestnut-eyed son,
> Lord father, lady mother, farewell!'

His parents said, 'The news is wrong, don't go, son!' but he answered, 'Do not keep me from my journey. Until I have reached the castle where my brother is being held, until I know whether my brother is dead or alive and, if he is dead, until I have avenged his blood, I shall not come back to the land of the teeming Oghuz.'

His parents, weeping together, sent a messenger to Kazan to say, 'The boy has bethought himself of his brother and is on his way; what advice can you give us?' Kazan replied, 'Hobble him.' He was already betrothed, so they quickly prepared the wedding-feast. They slaughtered of horses the stallions, of camels the males, of sheep the rams. They put the boy in the bridal bower and he and the girl together climbed onto one bed. The boy drew his sword and placed it between the girl and himself. The girl said, 'Put away your sword, warrior. Give me my heart's desire, take your heart's desire. Let us wrap ourselves in each other's arms.' The boy replied, 'Daughter of a pimp, may I be sliced by my own sword and spitted on my own arrow, may no son of mine be born or, if he is born, may he not live to his tenth year if I enter the bridal bower before I see my brother's face or, if he is dead, before I avenge his blood.' Then he rose, took a falcon-swift horse from the stables and saddled it. He put on his armour, he tied on his greaves and his armlets, and said, 'Girl, wait a year for me. If I do not come in a year, wait two years. If I do not come in two years wait three years. If I do not come then you will know that I am dead. Slaughter my stallion and give a funeral feast for me. If your eye lights on anyone, if your soul loves anyone, marry him.' Thereupon the girl declaimed; let us see, my Khan, what she declaimed.

> 'My warrior, I shall wait a year for you.
> If you come not in a year I shall wait two.
> If you come not in two I shall wait three then four.
> If you come not in four I shall wait five then six.
> I shall pitch a tent where six roads meet,
> I shall ask news of every traveller.
> Whoever brings good news I shall give him horses and
>   raiment,
> I shall clothe him in caftans.
> Whoever brings evil news I shall cut off his head.
> I shall not let a male fly settle on me;
> Give me my heart's desire, take your heart's desire,
> Then go, my warrior.'

Said the boy, 'Daughter of a pimp! I have sworn an oath on my brother's head and I am not turning back.' The girl said, 'So long as they call me "luckless [117] bride", they may as well call me "shameless bride"; I shall speak to my father- and mother-in-law.'
She declaimed:

> 'Father of my husband, better than my father,
> Mother of my husband, better than my mother,
> The male camel of the herd has bolted and is away,
> The cameleers have headed him off but cannot turn him.
> The rams of your fold have bolted and are away,
> The shepherds have headed them off but cannot turn them.

Your chestnut-eyed son has bethought himself of his brother
    and is away,
Your white-skinned daughter-in-law cannot turn him;
This you must know.'

The father and mother sighed deeply. They rose up and said,
'Son, don't go!' but they saw there was no help for it. 'I cannot
stop,' said he, 'until I have been to that castle where my brother
lies captive.' His father and mother said, 'Go, son, and good luck
to you. You will reach there and come home safe and well, if you
are to come.' He kissed his parents' hands, then leaped onto his
well-trained horse.

Away through the night he galloped. For three days and nights
he rode. He passed beyond the limits of Dere-Sham [118] and came
to that park where his brother had been seized. He saw the infidel
horse-drovers pasturing some mares. He drew his sword and
struck down six infidels. Drumming, he stampeded the mares
and shut them in the park. The young man had ridden day and
night for three days, and sleep overcame his dark eyes. He tied
his horse's reins to his wrist, lay down, and slept.

Now the infidels had a spy, who came and told their King: 'A
crazy Oghuz warrior has come and killed the herdsmen, stampeded the mares and shut them in the park.' The King said, 'Pick
sixty men-at-arms; let them go and seize him and bring him
here.' They picked sixty men-at-arms, who went off. Suddenly
sixty iron-clad infidels advanced on the boy. Armour is known by
its jangling as meat is known by its seething. The boy's mount
was a stallion. A horse's ears are sharp, my Khan; it jerked and
awakened the boy. The boy saw a troop of riders approaching; he
leaped to his feet, invoked a blessing on Muhammad of beautiful
name, and mounted. He turned his sword against the black-
garbed infidel and drove them back to the castle. Again he could
not overcome his drowsiness; he went back to his place, lay down
and slept, again putting the horse's reins round his wrist. Such
infidels as were left alive came fleeing to the King. The King
said, 'I spit in your faces! Sixty of you could not take one boy!'
This time a hundred infidels came at the boy. Again his horse

woke him. He saw the infidels coming in an ordered line. He
stood, mounted his horse, invoked a blessing on Muhammad of
beautiful name, set his sword against the infidel, drove them
back and stuffed them into the castle. He turned his horse and
came back to his place. He could not overcome his drowsiness;
once more he lay down and slept. Again he put the reins round
his wrist, but this time the horse slipped away from the boy's
wrist and ran off. Again the infidels came to the King.

The King said, 'This time three hundred of you will go.' The
infidels replied, 'We're not going; he'll wipe us out, he'll kill the
lot of us.' 'Then what is to be done?' said the King. 'Go, release
that captive warrior and bring him here. We'll set a thief to
catch a thief;[119] give him a horse and armour.' They came to
Egrek and said, 'Warrior, our King has shown you grace. There
is a crazy warrior in these parts who is taking the bread of
travellers and wayfarers, of shepherds and children. Seize that
warrior and kill him, and we'll set you free. Now, off you go!'
'Good!' said he. They freed him from his dungeon, they trimmed
his hair and beard, they gave him a horse and sword, and three
hundred infidels to bear him company. They advanced on the
boy.

The three hundred infidels stopped a good way off. 'Where
is that crazy warrior?' asked Egrek. They pointed him out in the
distance. 'Come on!' said Egrek, 'Let's go!' The infidels replied,
'The King's orders were for you; you go.' Egrek said, 'Look, he's
asleep; come on, let's go.' The infidels answered, 'Asleep indeed!
He's watching from under his arm, he'll get up and make the
whole wide plain too narrow for us.' 'All right,' he said, 'I'll go
and tie him hand and foot, then you'll come.' He bounded out
from among the infidels, he rode on and came up to the boy. He
dismounted, and passed the reins over a branch. He saw a handsome chestnut-eyed young man, looking like the fourteenth night
of the moon, sleeping in a muck-sweat, dead to the world. He
circled round him and came right up to him, and saw he had a
lute at his waist. He took it and declaimed; let us see, my Khan,
what he declaimed.

'A young man who rises up from his place,
Leaps onto his black-maned Kazilik horse,
Climbs by night the many-coloured mountain that lies askew,
Fords the lovely eddying river,
Comes to a foreign land and falls asleep;
Can this be?
Lets his white hands and arms be bound like mine,
Lays him down in the pigsty;
Can this be?
Lets his white-bearded father and white-haired mother
Weep and lament;
Can this be?
Why do you sleep, young man?
Be not heedless, raise your handsome head, young man,
Open your chestnut eyes, young man.
Sleep has overcome your sweet God-given soul;
Let not your hands and arms be bound,
Let not your white-bearded father and aged mother weep.
What young man are you, young man from the teeming
    Oghuz land?
For the Creator's sake arise and come!
The infidels are all around you, understand!'

The boy awoke with a start and leaped to his feet. He grasped
his sword-hilt to strike this man. But he saw that he had the lute
in his hand, and he said, 'Infidel! I do not strike you, out of
respect for the lute of Dede Korkut. If you were not holding the
lute, I should have split you in two for my brother's sake.' He
drew the lute from his hand and took it. Then the boy declaimed;
let us see, my Khan, what he declaimed.

'It was for my brother that I rose up at break of day,
For my brother have I worn out the grey-white horses.
Is there a prisoner in your castle? Tell me, infidel,
And my dark head be a sacrifice for you, infidel.'

Thereupon his elder brother Egrek declaimed; let us see, my
Khan what he declaimed.

'What is the place where you dwell, and whence you migrate
  in the summer?
If you lose your way in the dark night, what is your
  watchword?
Who is your Khan who carries the great standard?
Who is your hero who leads on the day of battle?
Young man, who is your father?
For a valiant warrior to conceal his name from another is
  shameful;
What is your name, young man?'

And again he declaimed, saying,

'Are you my cameleer who minds my camels?
  Are you my herdsman who minds my horses?
  Are you my shepherd who minds my sheep?
  Are you my minister who whispers in my ear?
  Are you my little brother whom I left in his cradle?
  Tell me, young man,
  And my dark head be a sacrifice for you this day!

Then Segrek declaimed to his elder brother, saying,

'If I lose my way in the dark night my watchword is God,
  Our Khan who carries the great standard is Bayindir Khan,
  Our hero who leads on the day of battle is Salur Kazan,
  If you ask my father's name, it is Ushun Koja,
  If you ask my name, it is Segrek;
  They say I have a brother, Egrek by name.'

And again he declaimed, saying,

'I am your cameleer who minds your camels,
  I am your herdsman who minds your horses,
  I am your brother whom you left in the cradle.'

Then his elder brother Egrek declaimed; let us see, my Khan,
what he declaimed.

'May I die for your mouth, brother!
May I die for your tongue, brother!
Have you become a man, have you become a warrior, brother?

Have you come to a foreign land in search of your brother,
brother?'

The two brothers embraced. Egrek kissed his younger brother's
neck, and Segrek kissed his elder brother's hand.

The infidels were watching from the ridge opposite. They
said, 'Can they have started wrestling? Let's hope our man wins!'
For they saw them clasping each other and embracing. Then the
brothers mounted their Kazilik horses. They charged at the black-
garbed infidels and set their swords going. They attacked the
infidels and broke them and drove them into the castle. They returned to the park and let the mares out. Drumming, they drove
the mares in front of them. They galloped over the Dere-Sham
river. They joined night to day until they reached the frontiers of
the Oghuz.

He had dragged his dear brother from the clutches of the
bloody infidel. He sent a bearer of good tidings to his white-
bearded father, to tell his father to come and meet him. The
messenger came to Ushun Koja. 'Good news!' he said, 'Bright
be your eyes! [120] Both your sons have come home together, safe
and well.' Hearing this, the old man rejoiced. The thunderous
drums were beaten, the gold and bronze trumpets were sounded.
That day, pavilions and tents of many colours were pitched. Of
horses the stallions, of camels the males, of sheep the rams were
slaughtered. Prince Koja came to meet his sons. He dismounted
and greeted his sons, embracing them. 'Are you all right, are you
well, my sons?' said he. They came to his tent with the gold-
framed window. There was merrymaking, eating and drinking.
He brought a beautiful bride for his elder son too. Each brother
was the other's best man. They galloped off to their wedding
bowers and attained their wish, their heart's desire. Dede Korkut
came and told stories and declaimed.

Sooner or later the end of a life, even a long one, is death.
When the hour of death comes, may it not find you apart from
the pure Faith. May He forgive your sins for the honour of
Muhammad the Chosen. May those who say 'Amen' see the Face
of God, O my Khan!

11

TELLS THE STORY OF HOW SALUR
KAZAN WAS TAKEN PRISONER
AND HOW HIS SON URUZ
FREED HIM

THEY say, my Khan, that the infidel King of Trebizond once
sent a falcon to the Commander of Commanders, Khan Kazan.
One night, as he sat feasting, he said to his chief falconer, 'In the
morning bring the falcons and let us quietly [121] go out hunting.'
They mounted early and rode to the place where game was to be
found. They saw a flock of geese sitting, and Kazan loosed his
falcon. He could not recover it; it flew away. They watched, and
the falcon alighted on Tomanin Castle.[122] Kazan was mightily
displeased and he rode after it. Crossing hill and dale, he came
to the infidel land. The nobles said, 'Lord, let us turn back.' 'Let
us go a little further,' said Kazan. As they went on, Kazan's
dark eyes were overcome by sleep.[123] 'Come, nobles,' said he, 'let
us rest.' The little death seized Kazan and he slept. It seems, my
Khan, that the Oghuz nobles used to sleep for seven days on end.
That is why they used to call it 'the little death'.

Now it chanced that on that day the infidel King of Tomanin
Castle had ridden out hunting. The spies came and told him, 'A
company of mounted men has come and their chief is lying in
their midst asleep.' The King sent men to find out who they
were. They learned that they were Oghuz warriors, and they
brought the news to the King. At once he gathered his army and
advanced on them. Kazan's nobles looked and saw the enemy
approaching. They said, 'If we abandon Kazan and go, we will
be chased away from our home.[124] Better to be killed here.' They
met the infidel and gave battle. The infidels killed Kazan's
twenty-five nobles over him, then they fell on him, seized him as
he slept, firmly tied him hand and foot, and loaded him onto a

cart, to which they bound him with strong ropes. They pulled the cart and rapidly marched off.

On the way, the creaking of the cart woke Kazan. He stretched himself, broke all the ropes that bound his hands, and sat up on the cart. He clapped his hands and roared with laughter. 'What are you laughing at?' asked the infidels. Kazan replied, 'Well, infidels, I thought this cart was my cradle and you were my dear fat cuddly nurse.' Anyway, they brought Kazan in and put him down a pit in Tomanin Castle. Over the mouth of the pit they put a millstone, and they gave him food and water through the hole in the millstone.

One day, the infidel Queen said, 'I'll go and see what sort of person this Kazan is who is supposed to have laid low so many men.' The lady came and had the jailer open the door. She called out, 'Prince Kazan, how are you? Do you prefer life under-ground or overground? And what are you eating and drinking, and what sort of horse do you ride?' Kazan replied, 'When you give food to your dead I take it from their hands, and I ride your liveliest dead and I keep the most sluggish as spare mounts.' [125] The Queen said, 'I adjure you by your religion, Prince Kazan; we had a little daughter, seven years old, who died. Be so kind as not to ride on her.' Kazan replied, 'She is the liveliest of all your dead, I ride her all the time.' 'Alas!' said the Queen, 'I see that neither our live ones on the earth nor our dead under it can escape from your hand.' She came to the King and said, 'Be so kind as to bring that Tatar out of the pit. He is breaking our little daughter's back, he is riding on our little daughter under the ground, he says. He says he is violating our other dead, and taking from their hands the food we give them. Neither our dead nor our living can escape his hands. For the love of your religion, get that man out of that pit!' The King assembled his nobles and said, 'Come, get Kazan out of that pit, and let him praise us and insult the Oghuz. Then let him swear not to come to our land as an enemy.'

They went and got him out of the pit and brought him in, and they said, 'Take an oath not to come to our land as an enemy. And praise us and insult the Oghuz, and then we shall set you free; you may go.' Kazan replied, 'I swear and I swear that so long as I see the straight road I shall never come down the crooked road.' 'By God!' they said, 'Kazan has sworn a fine oath.[126] Now, Prince Kazan, speak, praise us.' Kazan said, 'I praise no man on earth. Bring me a man I can mount and then I shall praise you.' They went and brought an infidel. 'A saddle and a bridle!' said Kazan, and they brought them. He threw the saddle on the infidel's back, he fitted the bridle over his mouth and tightened the girth, then he leaped onto his back. He drove his heels into the man's back [127] and forced his ribs into his belly. He pulled the bridle and split his mouth. He killed the infidel, who collapsed onto the floor. Kazan sat down on him and said, 'Infidels, bring my lute and I shall praise you.' They went and brought his lute. He took it and declaimed; let us see, my Khan, what he declaimed.

'When I saw ten thousand enemies I attended to them,
 When I saw twenty thousand enemies I dented them,
 When I saw thirty thousand enemies I thwarted them,
 When I saw forty thousand enemies I bore it with fortitude,
 When I saw fifty thousand enemies I sifted them,
 When I saw sixty thousand enemies I was never sickly at the
   sight of them,
 When I saw seventy thousand enemies I circumvented them,
 When I saw eighty thousand enemies I castigated them,
 When I saw ninety thousand enemies I was not benign to them,
 When I saw a hundred thousand enemies I thundered at
   them.[128]
 I took up my unswerving sword,
 I wielded it for the love of the Faith of Muhammad;
 In the white arena I cut off round heads like balls;
 Even then I did not boast: "I am a warrior, I am a prince";
 Never have I looked kindly on warriors who boasted.
 Now that you have caught me, infidel, kill me;
 Drive your black sword at my neck; cut off my head.
 I shall not flinch from your sword,
 I do not defame my own stock, my own root.'

Again he declaimed, saying,

'When rocks rolled down from the lofty black mountain,
I was the hero Kazan who held them back with my strong heel
and thigh.
When Pharaoh laden with stakes emerged from the ground,[129]
I was the hero Kazan who restrained him with my strong heel.
When the boisterous sons of nobles quarrelled,
I was the hero Kazan who cracked the whip and quelled them.
When the mist stood on the high mountains,
When the wild black fog arose,
When my horse's ears could not be seen,
When other men without guides missed the way,
I was the hero Kazan who completed the journey with no
guide.
I went and found the seven-headed dragon,[130]
My left eye wept at the awesome sight.
"Eye!" I said, "Cowardly eye, unmanly eye!
What's to fear in a snake?"
Even then I did not boast: "I am a warrior, I am a prince";
Never have I looked kindly on warriors who boasted.
Now that you have caught me, infidel, kill me;
Drive your sword, cut off my head.
I shall not flinch from your sword,
I do not defame my own stock, my own root.
So long as Oghuz heroes stand, I do not praise you.'

Once again Kazan declaimed:

'In a far-off land by the Ocean Sea is poised
The infidel city, built on trackless heights.
Its swimmers dart about to right and left,
Its sailors turn about on the bed of the sea.
Its heretics cry in unison "I am God!" on the bed of the sea.
Its young women turn away from the face and read the back.
The Princes of Sanjidan play with golden knuckle-bones.[131]
Six times the Oghuz went there and could not overcome it;
I, Kazan, went to that fortress with six men,

Before six days were done I had taken it.
I tore down its church, in its place I built a mosque,
I had the call to prayer recited,
I made its daughters and daughters-in-law dance on my white
  breast,
I enslaved its noblemen.
Even then I did not boast: "I am a warrior, I am a prince";
Never have I looked kindly on warriors who boasted.
Now that you have caught me, infidel, kill me;
I shall not flinch from your sword,
I do not defame my own stock, my own root.'

Yet again Kazan declaimed, saying,

  'He whom I routed in the far-off land, infidel, was your
    father,
  Those whose locks I desired were your daughters and
    daughters-in-law.
  At Aghcha Kala Sürmelü I set my horse prancing,
  I galloped to raid the land of-Karun.[132]
  I tore down the tower of Akhisar Castle,
  They brought me white silver; "Dross!" I said.
  They brought me red gold; "Copper!" I said.
  They brought me their chestnut-eyed daughters and
    daughters-in-law;
  I paid no heed.
  I tore down their church, I built a mosque,
  I let my men plunder their gold and their silver.
  Even then I did not boast: "I am a warrior, I am a prince";
  Never have I looked kindly on warriors who boasted.
  Now that you have caught me, infidel, kill me, destroy me;
  I do not defame my own stock, my own root;
  I do not praise you.'

Once again Prince Kazan declaimed, saying,

  'I am kin to the tiger of the white rock,
  He will not let your deer stay in the southland.
  I am kin to the lion of the white thicket,
  He will not let your piebald mares stand.

I am kin to the dun wolf-cub,
He will not let your ten thousand white-fleeced sheep roam.
I am kin to the white falcon,
He will not let your brown ducks and black geese fly.
In the land of the teeming Oghuz I have a son named Uruz,
A brother I have, Kara Göne;
They will not let your newborn live.
Now that you have caught me, infidel, kill me, destroy me;
I shall not flinch from your sword,
I do not defame my own stock.'

And once more he declaimed, saying,

'Greedy Circassian, yapping like a dog,
Whose feast is sucking-pig,
Whose bed is a bag of straw,
Whose pillow is half a brick,
Whose god is carved wood,
Infidel, my dog!
While I see the Oghuz I do not praise you.
So if you will kill me, infidel, kill me.
If you do not kill me, infidel, God willing I shall kill you.'

The infidels said, 'This man has not praised us. Come, let us kill him.' The infidel lords assembled; they said, 'This man has a son and a brother; we cannot kill him.' They took him away and imprisoned him in the pigsty.

The horse's hoof is fleet as the wind; the minstrel's tongue is swift as a bird. None knew whether Kazan was alive or dead. Now it seems, my Khan, that Kazan had a baby son. He grew up and became a young man. One day, as he was riding to the court of the Khan, someone said, 'Hey, aren't you the son of Lord Kazan?' Uruz was angered, and said, 'You pimp, is my father not Bayindir Khan?' 'No,' was the reply, 'he is your mother's father, your grandfather.' 'Then is my father dead or alive?' asked Uruz. 'He is alive,' was the reply, 'he is imprisoned in Tomanin Castle.' At that the boy wept and grieved. He turned his horse and went back. He came to his mother and declaimed; let us see, my Khan, what he declaimed.

'Mother, they tell me I am not the Khan's son,
They tell me I am Kazan's son.
Daughter of a pimp, why have you never told me this?
Were it not that the mother's due is God's due,
I should draw my pure black steel sword,
I should casually cut off your lovely head,
I should spill your red blood on the earth's face!'

His mother wept, and said, 'Son, your father is alive, but I was afraid to tell you, for fear you would go to the infidel and run into trouble and be destroyed; that is why I never told you, my dear son. But send to your father's brother to ask him to come, and we shall see what he says.' He sent a messenger to summon his uncle, and he came. Uruz said, 'I am going to the castle where my father is imprisoned.' They took counsel together. News was sent to all the nobles, saying, 'Uruz is going in quest of his father; equip yourselves and come.' The army assembled and came. The hero Uruz had his tents taken down and his equipment loaded. Kara Göne was appointed marshal of the host. They sounded the trumpets and moved off.

On their way was the infidels' great church,[133] with priests on watch. It was a church very difficult of access. They dismounted and put on traders' garb. Disguised as merchants they came, leading mules and camels. The infidels saw that those who were approaching them did not look like merchants, and they fled into the citadel and barred the gate. They climbed the tower and said, 'Who are you?' 'We are merchants,' they replied. 'You are liars!' said the infidels, and hurled stones at them. Uruz dismounted and said, 'O you who drink from my father's golden goblet, you who love me, dismount, and we shall each strike a blow with our maces at the gate of this place. Sixteen warriors leaped out of the saddle, took up their shields, put their maces on their shoulders and advanced on the gate. Each dealt a blow with his mace and they smashed the gate and entered. The infidels they found, they killed. They spared none to tell the tale. They plundered their treasure, rejoined the host and made camp.

Now the infidel had a herdsman, who saw that they had taken

the citadel, and he ran off and told the King that the great church had been taken. 'Why do you sit there?' he said. 'The enemy is upon you, make ready!' The King summoned his nobles and said to them, 'What device shall we use against them?' The nobles said, 'The device is to turn Kazan loose on them.' All approved this plan. They went and released Kazan and brought him before the King. The King said, 'Prince Kazan, an enemy has attacked us. If you will rid us of this enemy we shall set you free. We shall submit to paying tribute, while you will take an oath not to come to this land of ours as an enemy.' Kazan said, 'I swear and I swear that so long as we see the straight road we shall never come down the crooked road.' The infidels were delighted, saying, 'Kazan has sworn a fine oath.' The King gathered his host, took the field and had the tents pitched. The infidel army assembled round Kazan. They brought him armour, they brought him sword and spear and mace and all the tools of war, and they armed him and equipped him.

Then the Oghuz warriors came, regiment after regiment. The great war-drums and the kettle-drums were beaten and they thundered. Kazan saw that in front of all the host was a man on a grey-white horse, carrying a white banner, wearing strong-bodied iron mail, who led the Oghuz. He saw to the pitching of the tents, he marshalled his regiments and stood. Behind him came Kara Göne, and he marshalled his regiments and stood. Straightway Kazan rode onto the field, challenging the foe. Beyrek of the grey horse spurred on and entered the field. Then Kazan declaimed; let us see, my Khan, what he declaimed.

> 'Warrior, risen from your place and standing,
> What warrior are you?
> Warrior wearing strong-bodied iron mail,
> What warrior are you?
> What is your name? Tell me, warrior?'

Then Beyrek declaimed, saying,

> 'Infidel, do you not know me?
> I am he who flashed forth from Parasar's Bayburt Castle,

Who seized his betrothed and carried her off,
While others tried to take her.
Bamsi Beyrek they call me, son of Bay Büre Khan.
Come here, infidel, and let us fight!'

Kazan said, 'Warrior, a man with a white banner paraded out
before this host and set up his tent before all the people. That
warrior, who rides a grey-white horse, what warrior is he? What
is his family? I adjure you by your head, warrior, tell me.' Beyrek
replied, 'Infidel, what should his family be? He is the son of our
lord Kazan.' Kazan said within his heart, 'Praise be to God! My
baby son has become a grown man.' Beyrek said, 'Infidel, why do
you question me about this and that?' and charged at Kazan. He
took his six-winged mace in hand and swung it at Kazan. Kazan
did not make himself known. He grasped Beyrek round the waist,
dragged the mace from his hand, and aimed a blow with it at the
back of Beyrek's head. Beyrek clutched his horse's neck and
turned and rode off. Kazan said, 'Beyrek! Tell your leader to
come!' Dölek Evren who knew not retreat, son of Ilig Koja, saw
this and took the field. Then Kazan declaimed, saying,

'Warrior rising from your place at daybreak,
  What warrior are you?
Warrior on the prancing Arab horse,
  What warrior are you?
Shame it is for a warrior to hide his name from another;
  What is your name, warrior? Tell me!'

Dölek Evren replied,

'Infidel, do you not know my name?
I am he at whose name the hounds bay, who left his land,
Who took the keys of fifty-seven castles;
Dölek Evren they call me.'

He took his spear in his hand and drove his horse on, meaning
to transfix Kazan, but he could not; he missed. Kazan spurred his
horse, dragged the spear from his hand and struck him on the
head with it; the spear was shattered into pieces. 'Tell your leader

to come, son of a pimp!' he said. He too rode off, and again Kazan challenged them.

Alp Rüstem son of Düzen spurred his horse forward and took the field. Again Kazan declaimed, saying,

'You who rose from your place and stood and came here,
Springing onto your Kazilik horse,
What warrior are you?
What is your name? Tell me!'

Alp Rüstem replied,

'I am he who rose from his place and came,
Wandering in infamy, having killed his two babies;
Alp Rüstem they call me, son of Düzen.'

He too charged at Kazan, meaning to overcome him, but he could not. Prince Kazan dealt him a blow also, and said, 'Go, pimp! Tell your leader to come!' He too turned back. Again Kazan challenged them. Uruz's uncle Kara Göne was holding Uruz's bridle. Uruz suddenly jerked it out of his hand, drew his sword and charged at his father. He gave him no time to dodge but brought his sword down on his shoulder. It cut through his armour and made a wound in his shoulder four fingers deep. His red blood spurted, down onto his chest. Uruz turned to strike again, but now Kazan cried out to his son, declaiming; let us see, my Khan, what he declaimed.

'Summit of my black mountain, my son!
Light of my dark eyes, my son!
My hero Uruz, my lion Uruz,
Spare your white-bearded father, son!'

Uruz's veins of affection swelled, his black almond eyes filled with tears of blood. He dismounted and kissed his father's hand. Kazan too got off his horse, and kissed his son's neck. The nobles galloped up to Kazan and his son, and formed a circle round them. All of them dismounted and kissed Kazan's hand. They advanced and charged at the infidel, smiting with their swords. The infidels were routed, and ran over hill and dale. They seized the fortress, razed the church and built a mosque.

He snatched his father from the bloody infidel's grasp. He came to the land of the teeming Oghuz and went deep into it. He sent the bearer of good tidings to his white-skinned mother. Kazan's swan-like daughters and daughters-in-law came to meet him, they kissed his hand and fell at his feet. Kazan had tents and pavilions pitched on the beautiful meadow. Seven days and seven nights he gave a feast, a banquet, and there was eating and drinking.

Dede Korkut came and played his lute and recounted the adventures of the gallant fighters for the Faith.

> Where are the valiant princes whom we have praised?
> Those who said 'The world is mine'?
> Doom has taken them, earth has hidden them.
> Who inherits this transient world,
> The world to which men come, from which they go,
> The world whose latter end is death?

When the hour of death comes, let it not find you apart from the pure Faith. May the Mighty never put you in need of unworthy men. I invoke five words of blessing; may they be accepted. May those who say 'Amen' see the Face of God, may He forgive your sins for the honour of Muhammad the Chosen of beautiful name, O my Khan!

12

TELLS THE STORY OF HOW THE OUTER OGHUZ REBELLED AGAINST THE INNER OGHUZ AND HOW BEYREK DIED

ONCE every three years, Kazan would assemble the nobles of the Inner Oghuz and the Outer Oghuz,[134] and let them pillage his tent.[135] Kazan's custom was to take his lady's hand and lead her out of the tent, then they would loot whatever furniture and goods were in the tent. One year again Kazan was about to let them do this, but none of the nobles of the Outer Oghuz had arrived. The nobles of the Inner Oghuz began to pillage the tent without waiting. This time, they pillaged when not one of the nobles of the Outer Oghuz was present.

Uruz, Emen, and the other nobles of the Outer Oghuz heard about this and said, 'Just look! Till now, whenever Kazan's tent was being pillaged we have all been there together. What has our offence been this time, that we were not there too?' They all agreed that they would no longer go to salute Prince Kazan; they swore enmity to him.

The horse's hoof is fleet as the wind; the minstrel's tongue is swift as a bird. Kazan had a man called Kilbash, to whom he said, 'Kilbash, those nobles of the Outer Oghuz used to come with my uncle and salute me. Why have they not done so now?' Kilbash replied, 'Do you not know why? When you let your tent be pillaged, the Outer Oghuz were not there, that's why.' 'So!' said Kazan. 'Then they have become my enemies, have they?' 'My lord,' said Kilbash, 'I shall go and find out if they are friend or foe.' 'You know best,' said Kazan, 'Go'.

Kilbash rode off with a few men to the nobles of the Outer Oghuz. When he reached there he stopped at the house of one of them, Uruz, who was Kazan's mother's brother. Uruz was told that a man had come from Kazan. 'All right,' said Uruz, 'let him come.' Uruz had set up his gold-decked parasol and was sitting with his sons. Kilbash came, pressed his hand on his heart and gave greetings. They showed him a place and he sat down. Then he said, 'Kazan Khan prays for your prosperity. He is greatly distressed and says, "My uncle Uruz must come to me. My dark head is bewildered, the enemy has attacked me. He has made my camels scream in their stalls, my Kazilik horses neigh in their paddock. He has made my ten thousand white sheep bleat, my swan-like daughters and daughters-in-law cry out together. See what has befallen my dark head! Let my uncle Uruz come."' Uruz replied, 'See here, Kilbash. When the Üch Ok and the Bez Ok were gathered together, Kazan would let them pillage his tent. What was our offence that this time we were not with the others at the pillaging? Let afflictions ever fall on Kazan's head, so that he always remembers his uncle Uruz. We are enemies of Kazan, let him understand this clearly.' Thereupon Kilbash declaimed; let us see, my Khan, what he declaimed.

'Uruz, Uruz, you pimp Uruz!
Kazan Khan rose from his place and stood,
He pitched his tents on the many-coloured mountain,
Three hundred and sixty-six valiant heroes assembled round
   him.
Amidst the feasting the nobles bethought themselves of you,
"My lord," they said, "your uncle has become your foe."
So I came to learn for sure.
No enemy at all has attacked us;
I came to test whether you were friend or foe.
Now I know you are Khan Kazan's enemy.'

So saying, he rose and immediately departed.
   Uruz was mightily displeased. He sent messengers to the nobles of the Outer Oghuz, saying, 'Let Emen come, and Alp Rüstem, and Dölek Evren who knows not retreat, and all the other nobles.' The nobles of the Outer Oghuz all assembled. He set up the many-coloured tents of state, he had slaughtered of horses the stallions, of camels the males, of sheep the rams. He showed great

honour to the nobles of the Outer Oghuz and entertained them royally.

'Nobles!' he said, 'do you know why I have summoned you?' 'We do not know,' they replied. Uruz said, 'Kazan sent Kilbash to me, to say, "My lands have been ravaged, my dark head is afflicted; let Uruz come to me."' Emen asked, 'And how did you answer?' Uruz replied, 'I told Kilbash, "Whenever Kazan let his tent be plundered, the nobles of the Outer Oghuz used to plunder with the rest, then they would come and salute Kazan and depart. What has our offence been that we were not there this time? You pimp! We are enemies of Kazan!" I said.' 'Well said!' cried Emen. 'Nobles,' said Uruz, 'what do you say?' The nobles replied, 'What should we say? As you have become Kazan's enemy, so are we his enemies.' Uruz brought a Koran and said, 'Now swear.' All the nobles laid their hands on it and swore an oath: 'We are friends of your friend, and enemies of your enemy.' Uruz dressed all the nobles in robes of honour. Then he turned and said, 'Nobles! Beyrek has married my daughter;[136] he is my son-in-law, but he is Kazan's minister. Let us trick him; let us summon him to our hearth to make peace between us and Kazan. When he comes, if he obeys us, well and good. If he does not, I shall grasp his beard while you bring down your swords on him and hack him to pieces. With Beyrek gone, our business with Kazan will be successful.'

They sent a letter to Beyrek. Beyrek was by his hearth-fire, eating and drinking with his young men, when the man came from Uruz and said 'Peace be on you!' 'And on you!' replied Beyrek, 'And what is this?' The man said, 'My lord, Uruz sends you this paper,' and handed it to him. Beyrek opened it and saw that it said, 'Let Beyrek be so kind as to come and make peace between us and Kazan.' 'Good!' said Beyrek. They brought his horse and he mounted and came with his forty warriors to Uruz's tent. The nobles of the Outer Oghuz were sitting there when he came in and gave greeting. 'Do you know why we have summoned you?' said Uruz to Beyrek. 'Why have you summoned me?' said Beyrek. 'All these nobles who are sitting here, and I, have rebelled against Kazan; we have sworn an oath.' They

brought the Koran and said, 'Do you too swear!' 'By God!' said
Beyrek, 'I shall not rebel against Kazan!' and he declaimed; let us
see, my Khan, what he declaimed.

> 'Oft have I enjoyed Kazan's bounty;
>   If I deny this may it blind my thankless eyes.
>   Oft have I mounted his Kazilik horse in the paddock;
>   If I deny this may it carry me to the grave.
>   Oft have I worn his fine caftans;
>   If I deny this may they be my shroud.
>   Oft have I entered his many-coloured tent of state;
>   If I deny this may it be my dungeon.
>   I shall not desert Kazan, be sure of that.'

Uruz, furious, grasped Beyrek's beard and held it, but the
nobles could not bring themselves to harm Beyrek. Beyrek declaimed, saying,

> 'Uruz, my uncle, had I known you would do this,
>   I would have mounted my Kazilik horse in the paddock,
>   Donned my strong-bodied iron armour,
>   Girded on my pure black steel sword,
>   Set on my forehead and head my strong helmet,
>   Taken my spear, its bamboo shaft sixty spans long,
>   Called the chestnut-eyed nobles to my side.
>   Pimp! Had I known, would I have come thus to you?
>   To take a man by deceit is woman's work;
>   Have you learned this from your woman, pimp?'

Uruz said, 'Don't talk nonsense, and don't thirst after your own
blood; come and swear!' Beyrek replied, 'By God I have dedi-
cated myself to Kazan's service and I shall not desert Kazan. If
you must, hack me into a hundred pieces.' Again Uruz was enraged. He clutched Beyrek's beard, he looked at the nobles and
saw that none of them was coming forward. Uruz drew his pure
black steel sword, he smote Beyrek's right thigh and Beyrek was
covered in black blood. Beyrek lost his senses. The nobles all
scattered, each one mounting his horse. Beyrek too they put on
his horse, with a man behind to hold him. They rode away and

brought Beyrek home, and spread his robe over him. Then Beyrek declaimed, saying,

> 'My warriors, rise up from your place,
> Cut off the tail of my grey-white horse,[137]
> Climb by night over the many-coloured mountain that lies askew,
> Ford the lovely eddying river,
> Gallop to Kazan's court,
> Take off your white clothes, put on black,
> Say "Live long! Beyrek is dead." '

'Tell him,' he said, 'a man came from your uncle, the coward Uruz, asking for Beyrek, who went to him. All the Oghuz nobles were assembled there, without our knowing. Amidst the eating and the drinking they brought a Koran and said, "We are rebelling against Kazan; we have sworn. Come, now do you swear too." He did not swear; he said, "I shall not desert Kazan." Your cowardly uncle was enraged and he struck Beyrek with his sword. He was covered in black blood, he lost his senses. To-morrow, on the Day of Resurrection, may my hand be round Kazan's neck, if he lets Uruz have my blood unavenged.' Again he declaimed, saying,

> 'My warriors, before Uruz's son Basat arrives,
> Before my people and my lands are ravaged,
> Before my camels scream in their stalls,
> Before my Kazilik horses neigh in the paddock,
> Before my white sheep bleat,
> Before my white-skinned daughters and daughters-in-law cry,
> Before Uruz's son Basat comes and takes my white-skinned beauty,[138]
> Before he ravages my people and my lands,
> Kazan must come to my aid.
> He must not let Uruz have my blood,
> He must marry my white-skinned beauty to his son,
> He must earn his due in the next world.

Beyrek has gone to God, the King of Kings;
Let him mark well.'

   The news was brought to Beyrek's father and mother, and
lamentation broke out on the threshold of their white pavilion.
His swan-like daughters and daughters-in-law took off their
white clothes and put on black. They cut off the tail of his grey-
white horse. His forty warriors put on black clothes and blue
turbans and came to Prince Kazan. They dashed their turbans
to the ground and wept long for Beyrek. They kissed Kazan's
hand and said, 'Live long! Beyrek is dead. Your cowardly uncle
dealt treacherously; he invited us and we went. The Outer
Oghuz had rebelled against you, though we did not know it; they
brought a Koran and said, "We have rebelled against Kazan.
Obey us! Swear!" Beyrek did not trample upon your bread
which he had eaten; he would not obey them. Your uncle, the
coward Uruz, was enraged; as Beyrek sat, he smote him with his
sword and severed his thigh. Live long, my Khan. Beyrek has
gone to God. He said you must not let Uruz have his blood.'
   At this news Kazan took his kerchief and cried bitterly and
lamented before all the council. All the nobles there wept together. Kazan retired to his own apartments and for seven days
did not come to court but sat weeping. All the nobles assembled
in council. Kazan's brother Kara Göne said, 'Kilbash! Go and
tell my elder brother Kazan to come out to us. Say, "A warrior
is lost from amongst us for your sake, and his dying wish was
that you should not leave his blood unavenged. Let us go and
give the enemy his just deserts."' Kilbash replied, 'You're his
brother; you go.' Eventually the two of them went together and
entered Kazan's quarters. They greeted him, saying, 'Live long,
my Khan! A warrior is lost from amongst us; he gave up his
life for your sake. We must avenge his life-blood. Indeed, he
charged you with this trust, saying, "Let him avenge my blood".
Is anything achieved by weeping? Stand up and come!' Kazan
replied, 'This is what must be done. Quickly let them load the
equipment and let the nobles all mount.' All the nobles mounted.
They brought Kazan's chestnut horse and he mounted. The

trumpets were blown and the drums beaten. Without heed of day or night they advanced.

News reached Uruz and all the nobles of the Outer Oghuz that Kazan was at hand. They too gathered their host and sounded the trumpets, and came out to meet Kazan. The Üch Ok and the Boz Ok met face to face.

Uruz said, 'Let my adversary among the Inner Oghuz be Kazan.' Emen said, 'Let my adversary be Ters Uzamish.' Alp Rüstem said, 'Let my adversary be Okchi son of Ense Koja.' Each of them marked an adversary with his eye. The regiments were drawn up, the squadrons marshalled, the trumpets blown, the drums beaten. Uruz Koja spurred his horse onto the field and called out to Kazan, 'Pimp, you are my adversary! Come over here!' Kazan took up his shield, grasped his spear, turned his head towards him and said, 'You pimp, I shall show you what the end is of killing men by unmanly guile!' Uruz drove his horse at Kazan, and aimed a blow at him with his sword, which did not the least harm but passed him by. Now it was Kazan's turn: he couched his sixty-span lance of many colours and aimed a thrust at Uruz which flashed like lightning through his chest, came out the other side, and hurled him from his horse to the ground. Kazan made a sign to his brother Kara Göne to cut off his head. Kara Göne dismounted and cut off Uruz's head. The nobles of the Outer Oghuz, seeing this, all dismounted and threw themselves at Kazan's feet, begging forgiveness for their crimes and kissing his hand. Kazan forgave them their crimes. He avenged Beyrek's blood on his uncle. He let Uruz's house be sacked and his lands ravaged. Eat, warriors! There was great booty.

Kazan had tents pitched on the green field, the beautiful meadow, and he set up his pavilion. Dede Korkut came and played joyful music, he told stories, he recounted the adventures of the gallant fighters for the Faith.

Where are the valiant princes of whom I have told?
Those who said 'The world is mine'?
Doom has taken them, earth has hidden them.
Who inherits this transient world,

The world to which men come, from which they go,
The world whose latter end is death?

This black earth will eat us too. Finally the termination of a life, even a long one, is death; the end of it is separation. I shall pray for you, my Khan. When the hour of death comes, let it not find you apart from the pure Faith. May your white-bearded father's place be paradise, may your white-haired mother's place be heaven.[139] May the Mighty never put you in need of unworthy men. On your white forehead I invoke five words of blessing; may they be accepted. May those who say 'Amen' see the Face of God, may He grant you increase and preserve you in strength and forgive your sins for the sake of Muhammad the Chosen of beautiful name, O my Khan!

May God the Extolled, the Most High, have mercy on those who remember in their prayers the writer of this book, and may those who say 'Amen, Amen' see the Face of God, O my Khan, O my Prince!

THE WISDOM OF DEDE KORKUT

CLOSE to the time of the Prophet, on whom be peace, there appeared in the tribe of Bayat a man called Korkut Ata. He was the consummate soothsayer of the Oghuz. Whatever he said, happened. He used to bring all kinds of news of things unseen. God Most High used to inspire his heart. Korkut Ata said, 'In time to come the sovereignty will again light on the Kayi and none shall take it from their hands until time stops and the resurrection dawns.' This of which he spoke is the House of Osman and behold it continues yet. And many similar things beside did he say. Korkut Ata used to solve the difficulties of the Oghuz people. Whatever matter arose, they would never act without consulting Korkut Ata. Whatever he ordered they would accept. They would abide by his words and bring them to fruition.[140]

Dede Korkut came to the boil one day and declaimed among the Oghuz nobles; he declaimed to them by way of advice. Now let us see, my Khan, what he said.

'Unless one calls on God, no work prospers; unless God grants, no man grows rich.

'If it is not written from all eternity, no disaster befalls any mortal's head; until the appointed time comes, no man dies.

'The man who dies is not brought to life, the soul which goes out does not come back, until the resurrection.

'When a man has wealth as massive as the black mountain, he piles it up and gathers it in and seeks more, but he can eat no more than his portion.

'Though the rivers rage and overflow, the sea is not filled.[141]

'God does not love the conceited; prosperity does not abide in the vainglorious.

'Though you take care of the son of a stranger he will not become your own son. When he grows he will leave you and go, and never say "I have seen you".

'The lake cannot be a hill, the son-in-law cannot be a son.

'Though you throw a bridle over the black ass's head he does not become a mule; though you dress a captive girl in a robe she does not become a lady.

'Though the snow falls in huge flakes it does not last till summer; the fleecy green grass does not last till autumn.

'Worn cotton does not become cloth; the old enemy does not become a friend.

'If you do not mount the horse, the journey will not be done; if you do not wield the pure black steel sword, the enemy will not turn back; if a man does not spend his wealth, his fame will not go forth.

'A daughter does not take advice except from her mother's example; a son does not become hospitable except from his father's example.

'A son is all a father needs; he is one of his two eyes.

'If a man has a lucky son he is an arrow in his quiver; if he has an unlucky son he is a cinder on his hearth.

'What should the son do if his father dies and no wealth remains? But what profit in a father's wealth if there be no luck on his head? God save you, my Khan, from the evil of the unlucky.[142]

'When going over broken ground the unmanly cannot ride the Kazilik horse; if he does ride him it were better that he did not.

'Better that none should wield the pure sword which strikes and cuts than that the unmanly should wield it.

'To the warrior who knows how to wield it, a club is better than arrow and sword.

'The black tents to which no guest comes were better destroyed.

'Better that the bitter grass the horses will not eat did not grow; better that the bitter water man will not drink did not well forth.

'Better that the loutish son who does not maintain the good name of his father should never come down from his father's loins; if he falls into his mother's womb, better that he be not

born. Best is the fortunate son when he maintains his father's
good name.

'Better that there should be no falsehood in the world; better
that the truth should live thrice thirty years and ten. May your
life be full thrice thirty years and ten; may God bring you no
evil, may your felicity be perpetual, O my Khan!'

Again Dede Korkut declaimed; let us see, my Khan, what he
declaimed.

'The deer as it wanders knows the pasturelands of the earth.
The wild ass knows the meadows of the blue-green land. The
camel knows the tracks of all the different roads. The fox knows
the scents of seven valleys. The lark knows that the caravan
moves off by night. The mother knows who sired the son. The
horse knows the heavy man and the light man. The mule knows
the weariness of the heavy loads. The sufferer knows where the
pains are. The brain knows the ache of the heedless head. The
bard roams from land to land, from prince to prince, carrying
his arm-long lute; the bard knows the generous man and the
stingy man.[143] Let him who plays and recites before you be a
bard.[144] May God ward off the ill-chance that comes raging, O
my Khan.'

Yet again did Dede Korkut declaim; let us see, my Khan, what
he declaimed.

'When I open my mouth and give praise, the God above us is
beautiful.[145] Muhammad the Friend of God, the Prince of the
Faith, is beautiful. Abu Bakr the Veracious, who prayed at
the right hand of Muhammad, is beautiful.[146] The Sura of the
Tidings, which begins the last portion, is beautiful.[147] The Sura
Yā Sīn, when recited correctly, syllable by syllable, is beautiful.[148] Ali, who wielded the sword and gave victory to the Faith,
is beautiful.[149] Hasan and Huseyn, the sons of Ali, two brothers
together, the choice gifts of the Prophet, who were martyred on
the plain of Kerbela at the hands of the Yezidis, are beautiful.[150]
The Koran, the knowledge of God, which was written and set
in order and came down from heaven, is beautiful. Othman son
of Affan, Prince of Scholars, who wrote down the Koran and set
it in order, and who then, when the Ulema had learned it, burned

it and cut it, is beautiful.[151] Built in the lowlands, God's house of Mecca is beautiful. The pilgrim, who has faithfully discharged his duty when he reaches Mecca safely and returns in good health, is beautiful. Friday on the Day of Reckoning is beautiful.[152] The sermon that is delivered on Friday is beautiful. The congregation that gives ear and listens is beautiful. The wise man who calls from the minaret is beautiful. The lawful wife when she kneels and sits is beautiful.[153] The father when his temples go grey is beautiful. The mother who gives her white milk in full measure is beautiful. The black camel-stallion when he approaches and takes the road is beautiful. The dear brother is beautiful. The marriage-bower when it is set up by the mottled tent is beautiful, and beautiful its long ropes.[154] The son is beautiful. God who created all the worlds and resembles none is beautiful.' May the High God I praise be your Friend and give you aid, O my Khan.

The bard speaks, from the tongue of Dede Korkut: 'Women are of four kinds. One is the pillar that upholds the house, one is a withering scourge, one is an ever-rolling ball; and one, whatever you say to her it makes no difference.

'First comes she who is the pillar that upholds the house. If a respected guest comes to the house when her husband is not there, she gives him food and drink, she entertains him and honours him and sends him on his way.[155] She is of the breed of Ayesha and Fatima,[156] O my Khan! May her babies grow up, may such a wife come to your hearth!

'The second is the withering scourge. At break of dawn she rises from her bed and, without washing her hands and face, seeks out nine barley-cakes and a bucket of yoghurt, and stuffs herself full to bursting. Then she clutches her ribs and says, "Since I married this man – may his house fall in ruins! – my belly has never been full, my face has never smiled, my foot has seen no shoe, my face has seen no yashmak. If only he would die, and I could marry someone else and my life could be a good life!" May such a woman's babies never grow up, my Khan, may such a wife never come to your hearth!

'Third is the ever-rolling ball. Early in the morning she wakes and gets up. Without washing her hands and face she scurries round the camp from end to end and back again, gossiping and eavesdropping. She is abroad till noon. Then she comes home and sees that a thieving dog and a calf on the rampage have turned her house upside down, so that it looks like a chicken-run or a cow-shed. She screams at the neighbours, "Zeliha, Zubeyde, Uruveyde, Eyne Melek, Kutlu Melek![157] I hadn't gone out to die and vanish for ever, you know! I still have to sleep in this ruin! Would it have hurt you to keep an eye on my home for an instant? They say the neighbour's due is God's due!" May such a woman's babies never grow up, may such a wife never come to your hearth, O my Khan!

'Fourth is she who whatever you say to her it makes no difference. When a respected guest comes from the plain and the wilds, and her husband is at home and says to her, "Up and bring bread, so that we and this guest may eat; the leftover bread won't do; we must have some proper food," the wife says, "What do you expect me to do? There's no flour and no sieve in this cursed house, and the camel hasn't come back from the mill. Whatever comes, let it come to my rump," and she claps her hand on her behind, turns her side away and her rump towards her husband.[158] If you tell her a thousand things she will not accept one of them; she will not permit her husband's words to enter her ears. She is of the same breed as the Prophet Noah's donkey.[159] May God protect you from her also, my Khan; may such a wife never come to your hearth.'

NOTES

I. BOGHACH KHAN

1. *Khan* means 'Lord' and even 'Emperor'; it is applied, for example, in an eighth-century text to the Emperor of China, and was a title of the Ottoman sultans until the end of the sultanate in 1922. The 'O my Khan!' which prefaces most of the stories and ends all of them is addressed to the bard's royal audience.

2. Among the ancient Turks, male animals were regarded as the most acceptable form of sacrifice. In the Kazak-Kirghiz story of Dudar Kiz, a rich man who wants a child sacrifices 'of horses the stallions, of cattle the bulls, of sheep the rams, of goats the he-goats' (Radloff, *Proben der Volksliteratur der türkischen Stämme Sud-Sibiriens*, III, 310).

3. For the sacred and magical significance of the number forty among the Turks (and the Anatolian Greeks), see F. W. Hasluck, *Christianity and Islam under the Sultans* (Oxford, 1929), 391–402. His examples could be multiplied; thus the pages who guarded the Prophet's Mantle in the palace of the Ottoman sultans numbered forty. For the significance of the number among the English, see Brewer's *Dictionary of Phrase and Fable* (London, 1970), 430–31.

4. He means, presumably, by depriving her of it.

5. Kumis is fermented mare's milk. Marco Polo says of the Tartars (i.e. the Mongols; see note 68), 'Their drink is mare's milk, prepared in such a way that you would take it for white wine; and a right good drink it is, called by them *Kemiz*' (Yule and Cordier, *Travels of Marco Polo* (London, 1929), I, 237, 259–60). 'Let lakes of kumis be drawn' is a concise way of saying 'Let lakes of milk be drawn from the mares and fermented'.

6. The word translated 'wind' might mean 'shadow', while the word translated 'bird' is probably the name of a specific bird. The expression implies 'to cut a long story short'.

7. The reading is that of the Dresden MS. It sounds like a proverbial expression which must mean 'children eventually grow up'.

The Vatican MS reads, 'The months and the years pass, the boy grows.'

8. So Vatican. Dresden: 'he drew the milk of white-haired women'.

9. 'The mountain that lies askew' is identified as Ararat by Kırzıoğlu, who cites evidence that in the tenth century this mountain was not barren as it is now but was well forested and abounding in game. He believes that the word here translated 'askew' means 'lying to the southward'.

10. Kazilik occurs in the stories (a) as a personal name; (b) as the name of a mountain, identified by Kırzıoğlu as Aragats or Alagöz, north-west of Erivan in Soviet Armenia; (c) as the name of a breed of horse, presumably originating at that mountain.

11. Khizir or Khidr is, in Muslim belief, the name of the anonymous 'Servant of God' whose travels with Moses are recounted in Sura (i.e. Chapter) 18 of the Koran. Having drunk the waters of immortality, he roams the earth helping people in distress. In this he resembles the Elijah of Jewish legend, and indeed they appear together in the Turkish word *Hıdrellez* (Khidr + Elias), the name applied to 23 April OS, 6 May in our calendar, regarded as the beginning of spring. For a full account of him, including his curious identification with St George, see Hasluck's book cited in note 3 above, pp. 319–36.

12. The wooden lattice which forms the lower wall of the tent-frame is known as the 'wing', but the 'wings' here are more likely to be metaphorical.

2. SALUR KAZAN'S HOUSE

13. Salur Kazan is addressed in these terms again in Chapter 3, while similar titles are given in Chapter 7 to Bayindir Khan himself. There is probably a relic of totemism in 'chick of the long-plumed bird', as there may be in 'horse-mouthed Uruz Koja' below. The Emet river has not been identified. In the Vatican MS the name appears as Amit, equated by some scholars with Amid, the name by which the city of Diyarbakr was known until the end of the sixteenth century. This seems unlikely, as the city is mentioned later on in this same story under the name Hamid. As for Karajuk, Mahmud Kashghari gives it as a Turkish name for Farab, which was a district and town at the confluence of the Aris and the Syr Darya, in what is now South Kazakhstan. In Kashghari's map of the world,

he shows 'the mountain of Karajuk' as the boundary between the Kipchaks and the Oghuz. If we accept that this mountain is intended, this encourages the belief that the Emet river was far away from Diyarbakr, beyond the Caspian, in the region where the Oghuz fought their battles with the Pecheneks.

14. The word 'gold' should perhaps be inserted before 'capped'.

15. Beyrek's escape from Bayburt is narrated in the next story, in which the infidel king who imprisoned him is not named but must have been Parasar.

16. The name is uncertain, the Dresden MS fluctuating between S and Sh for the initial letter, while the form in the Vatican MS may be read as Sökeli or Sükeli. There may well be a connection with Shawkal, the title of the rulers of the non-Turkish Kazi-Kumuk people of Daghestan, which lies east and north of Georgia.

17. Ali, the fourth Caliph, i.e. Successor of the Prophet (656–61), was the Prophet's cousin and son-in-law, having married his daughter Fatima. He is greatly venerated by all Muslims, particularly those known as Shiites, who hold that he should by rights have succeeded the Prophet in the first place. The caliphate was wrested from him in 661 by Muawiya. Ali's younger son, Huseyn, with his family and a handful of supporters, was massacred in 680 at Kerbela, fifty-five miles south-south-west of Baghdad, by the forces of Muawiya's son and successor Yezid, whom Huseyn had refused to acknowledge. The sufferings of the martyrs of Kerbela are proverbial and include great thirst. Ali's elder son Hasan was not at Kerbela; he had died some years before of poison, administered, according to the Shiites, by order of the usurper Muawiya. He is consequently considered a martyr too, and it may be that as he was poisoned he too suffered from thirst before he died. See also note 150.

18. Water and salt are considered by the Shiites to have been the dowry of Fatima, hence they must not be defiled or refused to anybody who needs them (Henri Massé, *Croyances et coutumes persanes* (Paris, 1938), I, 225). The Sunnites, the non-Shiite majority of Muslims, show great reverence to the family of Ali. With the name of Fatima they couple the name of Ayesha, the Prophet's favourite wife, whom they regard as a model of womanhood. Ayesha however is not generally looked on with favour by Shiites, because of her personal difference with Ali.

19. 'May I be a sacrifice for you' is an expression of admiration and devotion used by many eastern peoples; the reader may recall the recurrent 'May I be thy ransom' of the *Arabian Nights*. It will be noted that Kazan repeats the formula when addressing the wolf but not the dog; this is because of the Islamic view of the dog as unclean, although there is some evidence that this view was not held by the pre-Islamic Turks. The Vatican MS gives as the last line of all three invocations 'Or I shall curse you'; I have preferred the Dresden reading, both because it would be a monstrous blasphemy for a Turk, whether Muslim or not, to curse water, and because Kazan does not in fact do so; nor does he curse the dog or the wolf when they fail to give him information.

20. The wolf, particularly the grey wolf (*bozkurt*) was venerated by the ancient Turks, who according to some legends even gave him a place in their ancestry.

21. Ayran is a drink made of yoghurt and water.

22. Burla has not explicitly recalled Uruz's 'days that are past'; she may have done so implicitly by weeping for him and speaking lovingly of him when he is as good as dead, or the expression may be a poetic cliché, not strictly relevant here.

23. Though Uruz ends by using harsh words to the tree, the passage exhibits the reverence for trees that runs through Turkish legend and still persists. Basat in Chapter 8 tells Goggle-eye that his father was Mighty Tree; compare the legend of the five princes whose parents were trees, in J. A. Boyle, *The History of the World-Conqueror* (Manchester, 1958), I, 55–7.

24. Duldul was the grey mule given by the Governor of Egypt to the Prophet and by him to Ali.

25. The sword Zulfikar was also a gift to Ali from the Prophet. Fine sword-blades were often engraved with the words 'There is no sword but Zulfikar and no hero but Ali'.

26. The Pass of the Iron Gate is the modern Derbent in Daghestan, a few miles inland, halfway down the western side of the Caspian. It was fortified from remote antiquity.

27. It was an ancient Turkish belief that the best horses were those sired by a supernatural stallion which came forth from a mountain, lake, or sea.

28. The wearing of earrings by men was a mark of slavery in Achaemenid Persia but not among the Turks or Mongols. Berke, the first Khan of the Golden Horde to become a Muslim (1256–

66), is said to have worn diamonds in his ears. Timur ('Tamerlane', 1360–1405) wore jewelled earrings, as did his contemporary Kara Yusuf of the dynasty of the Black Sheep.

29. In contrast with the story mentioned in the Introduction, that Dede Korkut was sent on an embassy to the Prophet, is the account of a late sixteenth-century writer known as Osman of Bayburt, to the effect that Bayindir Khan sent Kazan, Dundar and Emen on the same errand. They accepted the Faith, and the Prophet sent Salman the Persian back with them, who taught them and the rest of the Oghuz the practices of Islam and appointed Dede Korkut as their religious leader. This may be no more than an expansion of the present reference to Emen.

30. Here and in four similar passages the text has not 'prayed' but 'performed two *rak'as* of prayer'. A *rak'a* is a series of motions (with accompanying words) consisting of (1) standing erect, (2) bowing, (3) standing, (4) prostration, (5) sitting back on the heels and (6) prostration. For fuller details, with illustrations, see E. W. Lane, *The Manners and Customs of the Modern Egyptians* (Everyman's Library edn), 77–81, and T. P. Hughes, *A Dictionary of Islam* (London, 1855 and reprints), 464–71.

31. What these five words were is not apparent; possibly the expression is deliberately mysterious. They might be the names of the Five Holy Persons in Shiite belief: Muhammad, Fatima, Ali, Hasan and Huseyn.

3. BAMSI BEYREK

32. It can scarcely be anything but coincidence that Bai Bureh was the name of a local chief who came into prominence during the disorders in Sierra Leone in 1898.

33. Rum (pronounced like English 'room' not 'rum') is Asia Minor, the land of the Romans, i.e. the Eastern Roman Empire.

34. The Vatican MS adds 'and a beautiful sword', but three seems a more likely number of gifts than four.

35. Pasin was a district whose name is perpetuated in that of the modern town of Pasinler, twenty-four miles east of Erzurum. Avnik was a great fortress in the vicinity.

36. Beyrek is so called until he is given his name by Dede Korkut. The 'grey' probably anticipates his epithet 'of the grey horse'.

37. There is a mountain of this name, Aladagh, some sixty miles east-north-east of Pasinler.

38. We are told in Chapter 6 that three other Oghuz warriors used to veil their faces.

39. 'Fair greeting' is the Muslim salutation 'Peace be on you', as is shown by the first words of Karchar's response, though he does not seem to have grasped the spirit of it.

40. This formula is still current in Turkey when formally asking for a girl's hand. In Nazim Hikmet's sophisticated modern (1957) comedy of urban life, *Enayi* ('The Idiot'), the girl Ayten's father says to Ahmet, 'To cut a long story short, by God's command and at the word of the Prophet, and with Ayten's wholehearted consent, I give her to you.'

41. In the Vatican MS the question is 'Are you a wolf or a lamb?' and the reply is 'I am a wolf', which rather deprives Bay Büre's next question of its point.

42. Bridegrooms among the Kazak-Kirghiz and the Bashkurts still wear crimson caftans, and the custom is not unknown in rural Turkey.

43. Red is still the colour of the bride's veil at village weddings in Turkey, though urban girls nowadays prefer white.

44. These words are a stock expression used by a wife to her husband, and hence by a bride to her husband-to-be. They are not to be taken as evidence that Chichek and Beyrek had anticipated their wedding.

45. Beyrek calls the caravan 'precious gift' on the assumption that all it contains is intended as a present from his parents to some foreign potentate. He is not suggesting that the merchants have been sent to ransom him.

46. With the hindsight conferred by our knowledge of the several Homeric touches in this story, it is possible to regard this incident as an echo of Odysseus' seeing his faithful old dog again after twenty years, in Book xvii of the *Odyssey*.

47. The Turkish is *ozan*, which elsewhere I translate 'bard'. My use of 'minstrel' in this story was dictated by considerations of rhythm in the ensuing 'declamations' between Beyrek and his sisters.

48. He means 'you have made me act stupidly, in that I was on the point of declaring myself to you and abandoning my plan to go to the feast incognito.'

49. Who the two messengers (the word may also mean 'caravans')

are is not clear; if the text is correct, we can only suppose that
he had two runners in addition to the usual forty warriors. I
have followed the Vatican MS in omitting the three impene-
trably obscure lines with which the Dresden MS begins this
piece of declamation; either they are hopelessly corrupt or
they are part of Beyrek's pretence of being mad.

50. The ring must have been suspended by a string; Yaltajuk could
not have been wearing it, as he too was shooting at it. The
whole passage is strongly reminiscent of Book xxi of the
Odyssey, where the suitors shoot 'through the twelve axes'.

51. The reference might be to the Khan's donating oil for the
people to anoint themselves (though this does not seem to be a
Turkish custom), and indeed the Dresden MS here (but not at
the repetition of the line in Chapter 7) reads, before 'when the
oil is poured', the word *yaykandughinda,* which may mean 'at
the washing'. It could also mean 'when he is agitated', which
gives no discernible sense, or 'when it is storm-tossed', but the
notion of pouring oil on troubled waters is out of the question
in this context. One of the practices of shamanism, the earliest
known religion of the Turks, was to 'feed' idols by rubbing oil
on their mouths; another was to pour libations of oil into a
fire. It may well be that this line preserves a memory of these
ancient customs.

52. The implications of Beyrek's address to Kazan are not clear.
One Turkish authority, Abdülkadir Inan, takes Beyrek to be
mocking Kazan and jeering at Yaltajuk's marriage-tent. But
Kazan is not to be held responsible for this, nor does he seem
anything but delighted at Beyrek's words. It is probably a piece
of deliberate nonsense, in keeping with Beyrek's pose.

53. The princes evidently all had their set places on either side of
Kazan.

54. A play on the lady's name, *kısır* meaning 'barren'.

55. A similar play, *boghaz* meaning 'pregnant'.

56. This episode has been lifted entire from the Koran. In Sura
12, Joseph's father (i.e. Jacob, though he is not named) becomes
blind with weeping for his lost son. When Joseph has made
himself known to his brothers and forgiven them, he says 'Take
this shirt of mine and cast it over my father's face, then his
sight will be restored,' which is what happens.

57. Among the Kirghiz it is still the practice to make ninefold
gifts, and the animals given as bride-price – camels, horses, or

whatever – are still given in multiples of nine, up to a lavish nine times nine.

58. As to what became of the Lady Chichek, the reader's guess is as good as the translator's. It is small consolation for the disappearance of this attractive heroine to say that what we have here is a conflation of several different stories about Beyrek, in one of which he marries her.

59. Each girl was put in a separate tent, and Beyrek shot an arrow for each man, who would take as his bride the girl in the tent nearest to which it fell. 'Forty' must be a slip for 'thirty-nine'.

4. URUZ

60. *Kan* is a by-form of *Khan* (see note 1). By 'Kan Abkaz' is meant the ruler of the Abkhaz, a Caucasian people of the eastern shore of the Black Sea, who became Christian in the sixth century; he is probably the same person as King Shökli. The modern Abkhazia is an Autonomous Soviet Republic, with its capital at Sukhumi.

61. Aghlaghan is a mountain in the north-west corner of Soviet Armenia (41°N, 44°E). Jizighlar lay to the south-west of it. The Blue Mountain is unidentified.

62. 'Barehead' appears in sixteenth-century sources as a title of the ruler of Georgia and as a name for the country of Imeretia, the region round the modern Kutaisi in Transcaucasia. Dadian was the title of the Georgian princes of Mingrelia, immediately north of Imeretia, and was then applied to Mingrelia itself. It rather looks as if our author has conflated the two names to make one geographical area. Aksaka is the modern Akhaltsikhe.

63. This does not mean that the enemy will not seek vengeance, but that they are outside the community within which blood-money, rather than blood, can be exacted.

64. That is, it will need repairing when I have done with it.

65. Uruz may be playing on the resemblance between his name and *urush* meaning 'war'.

66. Arafat, thirteen miles east of Mecca, is the scene of part of the ceremonies of the Pilgrimage, but is not associated with the sacrifice which concludes those ceremonies. Nor is the sacrifice limited to male lambs, or to male animals at all. Traditionally it commemorates Abraham's readiness to sacrifice his son (Ishmael, in Muslim belief, rather than Isaac), and it is to this

that Uruz is referring. Doubtless the ancient Turkish preference for male sacrifices helped dictate the choice of words.

67. This question, omitted by the Vatican MS, appears to be a piece of rather cheap sophistry: it is no more my fault that he has not come than it would be yours if he had come.

68. 'Tatar', once the name of a Mongol tribe, came to be applied to the mixed horde of Mongols and Turks who invaded Russian territory in the thirteenth century. Later it became a generic term for the Turkish-speaking peoples of the Russian Empire and, more broadly, for the Czar's 'Oriental' subjects: Turks, Mongols, even Volga Finns. It is not a precise ethnic term, though there is an Autonomous Tatar Soviet Republic, whose Turkish-speaking inhabitants apply it to themselves. Both here and in Chapter 11, the only other place where it occurs, it is used by an 'infidel', not one of the Oghuz. The western spelling 'Tartar' is due to a confusion with the Latin *Tartarus*, 'Hell'.

69. For the sacrifice of horses at the grave of a dead chief, see J. A. Boyle, 'A Form of Horse-Sacrifice amongst the Thirteenth- and Fourteenth-Century Mongols' (*Central Asiatic Journal* X, Dec. 1965, 145–50). From a passage there quoted it appears that among the Oghuz the horse-flesh formed part of the feast, which is not explicit in this line. Boyle shows that the sacrificed horses were intended as offerings to the Sky-God, which brings to mind Herodotus's statement at the end of Book I of the *Histories* that the Scythians used to sacrifice horses to the Sun.

70. Here the Dresden MS adds the rather bathetic line 'For you my white raiment has been dirtied'.

71. The sense must be that weeping was far from him but suddenly found him.

72. Kırzıoğlu identifies this as Ighdir Karakalası in Kars province. He is on more certain ground when he explains Sürmelü as a corruption of the Armenian Surp Maryam, 'St Mary'.

73. Among the ancient Turks and Mongols it was customary to seek to transfer a sick person's malady to another living being or to a puppet, by turning it around him. There is a story that Babur, the first Mogul Emperor of India, when his son Humayun was dangerously ill, despite the pleas of his ministers turned thrice round the sick-bed, saying, 'I have taken away whatever illness you have; whatever illness you may have, I have taken it away.' Humayun recovered, and Babur fell into a decline, dying

shortly afterwards (1530). Here the slaves who are being freed as a thank-offering are first made to rid Uruz of any evil influences by which he may be threatened.

5. DUMRUL

74. Azrael is the name Muslims give to the Angel of Death.

6. KAN TURALI

75. By 'Turcoman' here Kan Turali refers to the Oghuz or other Turks who have abandoned the proud old nomad ways and settled down as agriculturalists.

76. This city is shown in modern atlases under its Turkish name of Trabzon.

77. Literally, 'had three beasts as her dowry, her trousseau'. The feel of the words can best be given by the impossibly anachronistic 'had three beasts in her bottom drawer'

78. A fine earthy vignette: the lice were dislodged because the old man was quaking with fear.

79. The sense is 'You have killed real lions in your time; this one is only a baby.'

80. Metaphorical for 'Your quarry is at hand; do something about it.'

81. There is a similar incident in the tenth-century Byzantine romance of Digenes Akritas: he has won the hand of his beloved, and her father is about to make preparations for the wedding, but Digenes refuses: 'Let me first go hence to my own mother,/That my father may see his daughter-in-law to be,/And may praise God, and I will soon return' (J. Mavrogordato, *Digenes Akritas* (Oxford, 1956), lines 1830–32).

82. See the end of the first paragraph of Chapter 11. There are other references in the old literature to heroes who kept awake for seven days and nights and would then sleep for a like period. Until a generation ago people round Bayburt would still say, to those overfond of sleeping, 'Have you fallen into the Uguz (i.e. Oghuz) sleep?'

83. The meaning is that things may appear normal but something is very wrong. The idea is reminiscent of Kipling's 'The ancient Front of Things unbroke/But heavy with new wars.'

84. A proverbial expression for inseparables.

85. A paradoxical but touching mode of address; 'Mother' is of course a title of respect.

7. YIGENEK

86. King Direk's giant stature was probably suggested by his father's name, the word for 'cubit' being *arshun*.

87. In Yigenek's dream, Emen says that he came seven times.

88. A more serious inconsistency than the one indicated in the previous note is that it turns out that Yigenek was not yet born when his father left home.

89. With the 'twenty-four provinces', compare the legendary division of the Oghuz into twenty-four tribes.

90. 'Evren' means 'dragon'.

91. The Vatican MS reads 'I saw a man with six heads'.

92. Literally 'five-*akcha* men', *akcha* being a small silver coin.

93. The Biblical Nimrod is several times referred to in the Koran, though not by name, as the persecutor of Abraham. Islamic legend tells how he declared war on the God of Abraham and shot an arrow at the sky which returned covered in blood. Nimrod thereupon claimed to have killed God, but shortly afterwards a gnat penetrated to his brain and tormented him for 400 years until he died. The 'split-bellied fish' refers to the legend that when Nimrod shot his arrow at the sky, God held out a fish which intercepted it and provided the blood.

94. The reference may be to the rank and file as distinct from the princes.

8. BASAT

95. There are many oddities about the construction of this story, which has been analysed by C. S. Mundy in a paper mentioned in the Introduction. But his accusing the author of an inconsistency here is not justified. Mundy says that the ceremonial bestowal of the name Basat is inconsistent with similar incidents elsewhere in the book: 'In the other cases ... the event occurs when the boy has proved his valour ... In the case of Basat there is no justification by valour.' Now it seems unfair to deny the valour, however misdirected, of a boy who attacks a herd of horses and sucks their blood, but, aside from that, Mundy

has missed the point of the incident, which is to provide an etymology for the hero's name: *Bas-at*, 'Attack-horse'.

96. The peris are borrowed from old Persian myth; they are winged beings, originally malevolent, though the term in Persian subsequently came to mean something like our 'fairy' (which has no etymological connection with it). In modern Turkish the derived adjective *perili* still means 'demon-haunted'.

97. Why are the three brothers not mentioned together as 'the three sons of Ushun Koja'? It may be that the words *aruk jandan*, translated 'pure-souled', are a corruption of a proper name.

98. It is perhaps an inconsistency that the suppliant woman knows of Basat's return before his father.

99. To a Turkish ear, the name of Goggle-eye's lair suggests 'slaughterhouse'.

100. The magic ring failed to protect Goggle-eye; perhaps it was proof against arrows and swords but not spits.

101. Tactically this was a crazy thing to do, but it was necessary if the Homeric episode of the cave was to be included; see note 103.

102. Here we have an echo of Polyphemus's affectionate words to his ram in *Odyssey* ix, 447.

103. The only justification Goggle-eye could have had for giving the magic ring to Basat would be to locate him. But the whole business of the ring, which does not help the story much anyway, is made into complete nonsense if Goggle-eye thought he could give it to Basat and still hurt him with a dagger. It is not surprising that the ring fell off Basat's finger; if it fitted the giant it was obviously too big for the giant-killer. Mundy's view is that the story has been dislocated to include the 'Polyphemus episode' of the blinding and the escape from the cave; that in the original form of the story Basat steals the ring from the sleeping giant's finger. The giant then wakes and deals a blow at Basat, which the ring prevents from harming him, but the ring then slips off his finger and rolls under the giant's foot. Basat thereupon runs into the vault for shelter.

9. EMREN

104. The word translated 'Province' is *tümen*, '10,000', which was the name given by the Mongols to administrative divisions large enough to support that many fighting men, though there is

evidence that the figure was not always taken literally.

105. What follows might suggest that this was a slip for 'a bow'. But see note 107.

106. Barda and Ganja are both in Soviet Azerbaijan, some sixty miles apart. Ganja became Elizavetpol and is now Kirovabad.

107. She presumably refers to the horse Begil was given, which he must have returned with the Khan's other gifts.

108. See note 75. The sense is that what distinguishes the cheeky Oghuz from the Turcoman is the sanity of the latter.

109. Emren's words are not rhythmic, unless the 'declaiming' is limited to his first sentence.

110. The use of *Khan* as a title of God is not impossible but is certainly unusual, and the Koranic passages where the story is told (Suras 21:52–70 and 37:85–98) do not specify leather bonds; the text here may be corrupt.

111. The Profession of Faith consists in reciting the formula 'There is no god but God; Muhammad is the messenger of God'. The finger that is raised when making it is the forefinger, which the Turks call 'Profession-finger'.

10. SEGREK

112. Literally 'there was no door or chimney for him', a not very flattering expression, commonly applied to thieves. Doors and chimneys (or 'smoke-holes') being the only openings of nomad tents, 'its door and chimney are open' means 'it is unguarded'. To say there is no door or chimney for the thief implies that he has no need of either, as he can gain an entry without them.

113. Shirakavan is the Armenian name of the fortress known during the Ottoman period as Shüregel, in the administrative region of the same name, on the west bank of the Arpachayi in the province of Kars, just across the frontier from and a little way south of the modern Leninakan. The name appears in the MS as *Sh-ru-k-v-n*; it must be borne in mind that the Arabo-Persian alphabet is deficient in the indication of vowels. The 'Blue Lake' is Lake Sevan in Soviet Armenia. Among the ancient Turks and Mongols 'blue' implied eastern, 'white' western, 'black' northern, 'red' southern.

114. Alinja is an ancient fortress just north of the Soviet-Iranian border, between Nakhichevan and Julfa (the latter name, in the Oxford Atlas, is heavily disguised as Dzhul'fa).

115. See note 7. The present story is not in the Vatican MS.
116. In the Altai folktale of Kan Püdei (Radloff, *Proben*, I, 24), Kan Püdei is born after his father has been killed, but his mother keeps this secret from him. 'Her child asked her, "Where is my father?" His mother did not reply. A number of boys were playing and our boy played too. They struggled and fought, he defeated them all and took their skins from them. The boys said, "You're man enough to take all our skins away; if you're such a hero, why don't you go after your father?" '
117. Literally 'unlucky-footed'; i.e. she must have started off on the wrong foot, as our idiom has it.
118. Dere-Sham lay to westward of Julfa, on the Iranian side of the River Aras (Araxes).
119. This is the sense required. The literal meaning of the words so paraphrased is 'that which gores will tear the [?] which kicks'.
120. This expression is still used to felicitate anybody who is reunited with a loved one.

II. SALUR KAZAN

121. The word translated 'quietly' strictly means 'in solitude'; it was to be a small hunting-party only, not of the whole army.
122. The modern Dmanisi in Georgia, about forty miles south-west of Tiflis.
123. This sentence, in the MS, precedes the sentence beginning 'The nobles said' and is in turn preceded by the words 'He looked and saw a castle'. These words have been omitted from the translation because the most insouciant Oghuz would scarcely have chosen to rest in sight of an enemy stronghold.
124. The text reads 'they will chase us away in his house', which gives no satisfactory sense; it cannot mean 'those in his house will chase us away'.
125. As not even infidels can be supposed to have dropped their beloved dead down a pit, we may assume the 'pit' to have been a shaft leading to a crypt.
126. The infidels thought it a fine oath because they understood Kazan to mean that he would stay on the highroads of his own territory and not take the side-roads leading to theirs.
127. The text has 'heels' instead of 'back'.
128. These lines are a paraphrase intended to convey the effect of the Turkish, where the verb which ends each line is more or less

assonant with the number which begins it. The literal translation is as follows (with 'ten thousand' substituted for the
'thousand thousand' of the MS; it should also be noted that
there is no '70,000' line in the original): 'When I saw ten
thousand enemies I said "My sport!"/... twenty ... I did not
fear/... thirty ... I counted them as ten/... forty ... I looked
daggers/... fifty ... I did not give them my hand/... sixty ...
I did not converse/... eighty ... I did not quail/... ninety ...
I did not put on my armour/... one hundred ... I did not turn
my face.' The last line puns on the word *yüz*, which means
'hundred' or 'face', and the phrase is echoed in the next line:
'I took up my sword which does not turn its face'.

129. In two Koranic passages (38:12 and 89:10) Pharaoh is called
'he of the stakes', for which no convincing explanation is offered.
One suggestion is that he used to punish his victims by staking
them to the ground, but Kazan's words indicate some other
story, now lost.

130. The work called *Shejere-i Terakime* ('Turcoman Genealogy'),
by Abulghazi Bahadur, written in 1660, which incorporates
much Oghuz legend, includes this: 'From the blue sky down
came the living snake. It swallowed every man at sight. Salur
Kazan cut off its head and showed no mercy. You who see
heroes and princes, is there any like Kazan?'

131. Perversity seems to be a characteristic of the people of this
infidel city, including the young women in the mysterious penul-
timate line of the passage. Literally translated, the line runs
'Its daughters and daughters-in-law leave its front and read its
reverse', which sounds like a proverbial expression indicative of
cussedness, as of someone who deliberately chooses the hard
way of reading a written document or perhaps of identifying a
coin. Sanjidan, which might alternatively be read as Sanjida or,
just possibly, Sanjidang, is located by Kırzıoğlu 'in the Kip-
chak-Koman region, i.e. in Daghestan', for no better reason
than that 'the game of knuckle-bones is exclusive to the Turkish
peoples'. Without bothering to give chapter and verse to refute
this surprising assertion, the suggested location of Sanjidan in
Daghestan must be rejected, as it would equate 'Ocean Sea'
(*'ummân dengizi*) with the Caspian, whereas the specific body
of water to which the expression is sometimes applied is the
Indian Ocean.

132. Karun, thrice mentioned in the Koran, is the Biblical Korah

(Num. xvi 1), the wealthy ringleader of the rebellion against
Moses. In Islamic as in Jewish legend his name is proverbial
for vast riches; it is said that the keys of his treasure-houses
formed a load for 300 mules. Kırzıoğlu identifies his land as
the region round Erzurum, the ancient Karin, and he places
Akhisar Castle, mentioned in the next line, to the west of that
city.

133. The word translated 'great church' is *ayasofya*, Hagia Sophia,
which is the name not only of the great St Sophia in Istanbul
but also of a church in Trebizond; there were doubtless others
beside. This church is subsequently referred to as 'the citadel',
so it must have been fortified.

12. THE DEATH OF BEYREK

134. In this sentence, though not in the title, the Dresden MS reads
Üch Ok and *Boz Ok* for Inner and Outer Oghuz, as does the
Vatican MS later in the story. These two divisions of the
Oghuz are known in historic times. Legend tells that Oghuz
Khan gave his golden bow to his three eldest sons and called
them *Boz Ok*, 'Destroying Arrow'; to the youngest he gave his
three golden arrows and the name *Üch Ok*, 'Three Arrows'.

135. This was a well-established Turkish institution. In 1106 or
1107, the Arab ruler of Hilla in Iraq, Seyf al-Dawla Sadaka,
gave a banquet in honour of the Seljuk Sultan Melikshah, after
which the guests were permitted to loot the gold and silver
table-appointments. The same thing happened after the wedding-feast of the Seljuk Sultan Keykavus I (1210–19).

136. This does not necessarily indicate that Beyrek had been faith-
less to the girl he married at the end of Chapter 3 (leaving
aside the tiresome question of whatever became of the Lady
Chichek), because Uruz's reference to Beyrek's beard in the next
sentence but two shows that he was by now advanced in age;
the young Oghuz warriors shaved their beards.

137. The Egyptian historian Ibn Iyas, writing of the funeral of the
Ottoman prince Süleyman, grandson of Sultan Bayezid II, who
died of plague in Egypt in 1513, says 'They brought out his
horses, with their tails cut off and their saddles inverted. On his
bier they put his turban and his bows, which they broke, this
being the custom of their country.'

138. This line is either rhetorical or indicative of carelessness on the

part of the author; as Beyrek's wife was Uruz's daughter she stood in no personal danger from Uruz's son.

139. Here the Vatican MS inserts: 'May Mighty God have mercy on Beyrek, may the Lord let him drink abounding purity in wine from the hand of Ali, Lion of men.' If this had been part of the original it would have appeared in both MSS, since pious wishes may be added by a scribe but scarcely omitted. The next paragraph, with its blessing on the 'writer' (i.e. the scribe, not the author), also occurs only in the Vatican MS and is open to the same objection. But it would be too cruel a pedantry to deny a scribe his meed of blessing.

13. THE WISDOM OF DEDE KORKUT

140. In place of the name Dede Korkut, in this paragraph and nowhere else in the book we find the synonymous Korkut Ata. This fact is enough to make us suspect that the paragraph is an interpolation, and indeed it occurs almost verbatim in the *History of the Seljuks* of Yazijizade Ali, who wrote in the reign of the Ottoman Sultan Murat II (1421–51). It was under this Sultan that an official genealogy was put into circulation which showed the Ottoman dynasty as belonging to the tribe of Kayi. The conclusion seems inescapable that this paragraph, with its prophesy of eternal sovereignty for the Ottomans, the 'House of Osman', was deliberately added to the *Book of Dede Korkut* in support of Sultan Murat's propagandist campaign. For the Kayi were the leading tribe of the Turks, claiming descent from Kayi, the eldest son of Gün ('Sun'), who was the eldest son of Oghuz Khan himself, the ancestor of all the Oghuz and a descendant in the third (or, in other versions of the legend, the fourth, fifth, or twenty-fifth) generation from Japheth son of Noah. Gün's second son was Bayat, from whom were descended the tribe to which Dede Korkut is here said to belong. For a critical analysis of the legend, see Paul Wittek, *The Rise of The Ottoman Empire* (London, 1938).

141. Compare Eccles. i 7.

142. That is, from the evil eye of the unlucky person who is envious of your good fortune.

143. There is a clear purpose behind this string of maxims; it is to remind the prince who is addressed that his reputation depends on how generously he treats the itinerant bard.

144. The meaning is that the prince ought not to allow anyone who is not an accredited bard to perform for him, the next sentence being a thinly-veiled threat of supernatural retribution if he does so.

145. 'Beautiful' in this passage has an overtone of 'holy'.

146. Abu Bakr was among the earliest converts to Islam and on the Prophet's death in 632 became his first successor as leader of the Muslim community. He died in 634.

147. The Sura of the Tidings is the seventy-eighth of the 114 suras of the Koran. It begins the last of the thirty portions into which the Book is divided to enable the reading of the whole to be spread over the thirty days of Ramadan, the month of fasting.

148. Yā Sin is the name of the thirty-sixth sura. The Prophet is said to have called it 'the heart of the Koran', and it is recited to those on their death-bed.

149. For Ali, see note 17.

150. Again see note 17. There are two oddities about this passage: the mis-statement that both brothers died at Kerbela, and the use of the term Yezidis for the troops of Yezid; there may be some confusion with the name of the non-Muslim sect of Yezidis, the so-called devil-worshippers of northern Iraq.

151. This sentence too betokens an unconventional view of early Islamic history. Othman, the third Caliph (644–56), promulgated an official text of the Koran, for the revelations had not been compiled into a book in the Prophet's lifetime. Texts which disagreed with the official version were ordered to be destroyed, an act which made Othman unpopular with many of the pious and may have helped provoke his assassination. That Othman destroyed the Koran only after the Ulema, the religious scholars, had memorized it, is a tale otherwise unknown; it looks like an attempt to reconcile the habitual praises of Othman as one of the 'Rightly-Guided Caliphs' with the well-known criticism of him that 'he found the Korans many and left one; he tore up the Book'.

152. The fact that Friday is the day of congregation, when it is obligatory for all Muslims to come together in prayer, doubtless gave rise to the belief that the Resurrection and Judgement will fall on a Friday.

153. This description of the lawful wife as beautiful when she kneels and sits, i.e. when she is demure and not a gadabout, is far closer to the Islamic ideal than are the heroines of the stories or

the 'pillar that upholds the house'; see note 155, below.

154. Setting up a marriage-tent alongside the tent of the bridegroom's father is a regular Turcoman custom, but is not in accordance with the practice depicted in the stories, where the bridegroom shoots an arrow into the air and sets up his marriage-tent at the spot where it falls to earth. The 'mottled' tent is the father's tent, smoke-blackened and weather-beaten, not a bit like the white tents of the stories.

155. The description of the 'pillar that upholds the house' might well shock a traditionally-minded Muslim, who would consider that a lady has no business showing herself to a stranger, especially in her husband's absence. It is, however, in keeping with Turcoman custom.

156. See note 18.

157. The neighbours' names are all Islamic (the 'Melek' of the last two is the Arabic for 'angel'), quite unlike the names of almost all the ladies in the stories.

158. Though the precise significance of these words and actions is not apparent, they obviously imply a total lack of concern.

159. Noah, like many other Biblical characters, appears in the Koran as a prophet. According to Islamic legend, the ant was the first creature to enter the Ark, the donkey being the last because Iblis was holding its tail. Noah became impatient and cried out, 'Come on, even if the Devil is with you!' whereupon the donkey and the Devil came on board together.

READ MORE IN PENGUIN

In every corner of the world, on every subject under the sun, Penguin represents quality and variety – the very best in publishing today.

For complete information about books available from Penguin – including Puffins, Penguin Classics and Arkana – and how to order them, write to us at the appropriate address below. Please note that for copyright reasons the selection of books varies from country to country.

In the United Kingdom: Please write to *Dept. EP, Penguin Books Ltd, Bath Road, Harmondsworth, West Drayton, Middlesex UB7 ODA*

In the United States: Please write to *Consumer Sales, Penguin USA, P.O. Box 999, Dept. 17109, Bergenfield, New Jersey 07621-0120*. VISA and MasterCard holders call 1-800-253-6476 to order Penguin titles

In Canada: Please write to *Penguin Books Canada Ltd, 10 Alcorn Avenue, Suite 300, Toronto, Ontario M4V 3B2*

In Australia: Please write to *Penguin Books Australia Ltd, P.O. Box 257, Ringwood, Victoria 3134*

In New Zealand: Please write to *Penguin Books (NZ) Ltd, Private Bag 102902, North Shore Mail Centre, Auckland 10*

In India: Please write to *Penguin Books India Pvt Ltd, 706 Eros Apartments, 56 Nehru Place, New Delhi 110 019*

In the Netherlands: Please write to *Penguin Books Netherlands bv, Postbus 3507, NL-1001 AH Amsterdam*

In Germany: Please write to *Penguin Books Deutschland GmbH, Metzlerstrasse 26, 60594 Frankfurt am Main*

In Spain: Please write to *Penguin Books S. A., Bravo Murillo 19, 1° B, 28015 Madrid*

In Italy: Please write to *Penguin Italia s.r.l., Via Felice Casati 20, I–20124 Milano*

In France: Please write to *Penguin France S. A., 17 rue Lejeune, F–31000 Toulouse*

In Japan: Please write to *Penguin Books Japan, Ishikiribashi Building, 2–5–4, Suido, Bunkyo-ku, Tokyo 112*

In Greece: Please write to *Penguin Hellas Ltd, Dimocritou 3, GR–106 71 Athens*

In South Africa: Please write to *Longman Penguin Southern Africa (Pty) Ltd, Private Bag X08, Bertsham 2013*

PENGUIN AUDIOBOOKS

A Quality of Writing that Speaks for Itself

Penguin Books has always led the field in quality publishing. Now you can listen at leisure to your favourite books, read to you by familiar voices from radio, stage and screen. Penguin Audiobooks are ideal as gifts, for when you are travelling or simply to enjoy at home. They are produced to an excellent standard, and abridgements are always faithful to the original texts. From thrillers to classic literature, biography to humour, with a wealth of titles in between, Penguin Audiobooks offer you quality, entertainment and the chance to rediscover the pleasure of listening.

You can order Penguin Audiobooks through Penguin Direct by telephoning (0181) 899 4036. The lines are open 24 hours every day. Ask for Penguin Direct, quoting your credit card details.

Published or forthcoming:

Emma by Jane Austen, read by Fiona Shaw

Persuasion by Jane Austen, read by Joanna David

Pride and Prejudice by Jane Austen, read by Geraldine McEwan

The Tenant of Wildfell Hall by Anne Brontë, read by Juliet Stevenson

Jane Eyre by Charlotte Brontë, read by Juliet Stevenson

Villette by Charlotte Brontë, read by Juliet Stevenson

Wuthering Heights by Emily Brontë, read by Juliet Stevenson

The Woman in White by Wilkie Collins, read by Nigel Anthony and Susan Jameson

Heart of Darkness by Joseph Conrad, read by David Threlfall

Tales from the One Thousand and One Nights, read by Souad Faress and Raad Rawi

Moll Flanders by Daniel Defoe, read by Frances Barber

Great Expectations by Charles Dickens, read by Hugh Laurie

Hard Times by Charles Dickens, read by Michael Pennington

Martin Chuzzlewit by Charles Dickens, read by John Wells

The Old Curiosity Shop by Charles Dickens, read by Alec McCowen

PENGUIN AUDIOBOOKS

Crime and Punishment by Fyodor Dostoyevsky, read by Alex Jennings

Middlemarch by George Eliot, read by Harriet Walter

Silas Marner by George Eliot, read by Tim Pigott-Smith

The Great Gatsby by F. Scott Fitzgerald, read by Marcus D'Amico

Madame Bovary by Gustave Flaubert, read by Claire Bloom

Jude the Obscure by Thomas Hardy, read by Samuel West

The Return of the Native by Thomas Hardy, read by Steven Pacey

Tess of the D'Urbervilles by Thomas Hardy, read by Eleanor Bron

The Iliad by Homer, read by Derek Jacobi

Dubliners by James Joyce, read by Gerard McSorley

The Dead and Other Stories by James Joyce, read by Gerard McSorley

On the Road by Jack Kerouac, read by David Carradine

Sons and Lovers by D. H. Lawrence, read by Paul Copley

The Fall of the House of Usher by Edgar Allan Poe, read by Andrew Sachs

Wide Sargasso Sea by Jean Rhys, read by Jane Lapotaire and Michael Kitchen

The Little Prince by Antoine de Saint-Exupéry, read by Michael Maloney

Frankenstein by Mary Shelley, read by Richard Pasco

Of Mice and Men by John Steinbeck, read by Gary Sinise

Travels with Charley by John Steinbeck, read by Gary Sinise

The Pearl by John Steinbeck, read by Hector Elizondo

Dr Jekyll and Mr Hyde by Robert Louis Stevenson, read by Jonathan Hyde

Kidnapped by Robert Louis Stevenson, read by Robbie Coltrane

The Age of Innocence by Edith Wharton, read by Kerry Shale

The Buccaneers by Edith Wharton, read by Dana Ivey

Mrs Dalloway by Virginia Woolf, read by Eileen Atkins

READ MORE IN PENGUIN

A CHOICE OF CLASSICS

Netochka Nezvanova   Fyodor Dostoyevsky

Dostoyevsky's first book tells the story of 'Nameless Nobody' and introduces many of the themes and issues which dominate his great masterpieces.

Selections from the Carmina Burana
A verse translation by David Parlett

The famous songs from the *Carmina Burana* (made into an oratorio by Carl Orff) tell of lecherous monks and corrupt clerics, drinkers and gamblers, and the fleeting pleasures of youth.

Fear and Trembling   Søren Kierkegaard

A profound meditation on the nature of faith and submission to God's will, which examines with startling originality the story of Abraham and Isaac.

Selected Prose   Charles Lamb

Lamb's famous essays (under the strange pseudonym of Elia) on anything and everything have long been celebrated for their apparently innocent charm. This major new edition allows readers to discover the darker and more interesting aspects of Lamb.

The Picture of Dorian Gray   Oscar Wilde

Wilde's superb and macabre novel, one of his supreme works, is reprinted here with a masterly Introduction and valuable Notes by Peter Ackroyd.

Frankenstein   Mary Shelley

In recounting this chilling tragedy Mary Shelley demonstrates both the corruption of an innocent creature by an immoral society and the dangers of playing God with science.

READ MORE IN PENGUIN

A CHOICE OF CLASSICS

The House of Ulloa   Emilia Pardo Bazán

The finest achievement of one of European literature's most dynamic and controversial figures – ardent feminist, traveller, intellectual – and one of the great nineteenth century Spanish novels, *The House of Ulloa* traces the decline of the old aristocracy at the time of the Glorious Revolution of 1868, while exposing the moral vacuum of the new democracy.

The Republic   Plato

The best-known of Plato's dialogues, *The Republic* is also one of the supreme masterpieces of Western philosophy, whose influence cannot be overestimated.

The Duel and Other Stories   Anton Chekhov

In these stories Chekhov deals with a variety of themes – religious fanaticism and sectarianism, megalomania, and scientific controversies of the time, as well as provincial life in all its tedium and philistinism.

Metamorphoses   Ovid

A golden treasury of myths and legends, which has proved a major influence on Western literature.

A Nietzsche Reader   Friedrich Nietzsche

A superb selection from all the major works of one of the greatest thinkers and writers in world literature, translated into clear, modern English.

Madame Bovary   Gustave Flaubert

With *Madame Bovary* Flaubert established the realistic novel in France while his central character of Emma Bovary, the bored wife of a provincial doctor, remains one of the great creations of modern literature.

READ MORE IN PENGUIN

A CHOICE OF CLASSICS

Aeschylus	**The Oresteian Trilogy**
	Prometheus Bound/The Suppliants/Seven Against Thebes/The Persians
Aesop	**Fables**
Ammianus Marcellinus	**The Later Roman Empire (AD 354–378)**
Apollonius of Rhodes	**The Voyage of Argo**
Apuleius	**The Golden Ass**
Aristophanes	**The Knights/Peace/The Birds/The Assemblywomen/Wealth**
	Lysistrata/The Acharnians/The Clouds
	The Wasps/The Poet and the Women/ The Frogs
Aristotle	**The Art of Rhetoric**
	The Athenian Constitution
	Ethics
	The Politics
	De Anima
Arrian	**The Campaigns of Alexander**
St Augustine	**City of God**
	Confessions
Boethius	**The Consolation of Philosophy**
Caesar	**The Civil War**
	The Conquest of Gaul
Catullus	**Poems**
Cicero	**The Murder Trials**
	The Nature of the Gods
	On the Good Life
	Selected Letters
	Selected Political Speeches
	Selected Works
Euripides	**Alcestis/Iphigenia in Tauris/Hippolytus**
	The Bacchae/Ion/The Women of Troy/ Helen
	Medea/Hecabe/Electra/Heracles
	Orestes/The Children of Heracles/ Andromache/The Suppliant Women/ The PhoenicianWomen/Iphigenia in Aulis

READ MORE IN PENGUIN

A CHOICE OF CLASSICS

Hesiod/Theognis	**Theogony** and **Works and Days/ Elegies**
Hippocrates	**Hippocratic Writings**
Homer	**The Iliad**
	The Odyssey
Horace	**Complete Odes and Epodes**
Horace/Persius	**Satires** and **Epistles**
Juvenal	**Sixteen Satires**
Livy	**The Early History of Rome**
	Rome and Italy
	Rome and the Mediterranean
	The War with Hannibal
Lucretius	**On the Nature of the Universe**
Marcus Aurelius	**Meditations**
Martial	**Epigrams**
Ovid	**The Erotic Poems**
	Heroides
	Metamorphoses
Pausanias	**Guide to Greece** (in two volumes)
Petronius/Seneca	**The Satyricon/The Apocolocyntosis**
Pindar	**The Odes**
Plato	**Early Socratic Dialogues**
	Gorgias
	The Last Days of Socrates (Euthyphro/ The Apology/Crito/Phaedo)
	The Laws
	Phaedrus and **Letters VII and VIII**
	Philebus
	Protagoras and **Meno**
	The Republic
	The Symposium
	Theaetetus
	Timaeus and **Critias**

READ MORE IN PENGUIN

A CHOICE OF CLASSICS

Plautus	**The Pot of Gold/The Prisoners/The Brothers Menaechmus/The Swaggering Soldier/Pseudolus**
	The Rope/Amphitryo/The Ghost/A Three-Dollar Day
Pliny	**The Letters of the Younger Pliny**
Pliny the Elder	**Natural History**
Plotinus	**The Enneads**
Plutarch	**The Age of Alexander** (Nine Greek Lives)
	The Fall of the Roman Republic (Six Lives)
	The Makers of Rome (Nine Lives)
	The Rise and Fall of Athens (Nine Greek Lives)
	Plutarch on Sparta
Polybius	**The Rise of the Roman Empire**
Procopius	**The Secret History**
Propertius	**The Poems**
Quintus Curtius Rufus	**The History of Alexander**
Sallust	**The Jugurthine War** and **The Conspiracy of Cataline**
Seneca	**Four Tragedies** and **Octavia**
	Letters from a Stoic
Sophocles	**Electra/Women of Trachis/Philoctetes/Ajax**
	The Theban Plays
Suetonius	**The Twelve Caesars**
Tacitus	**The Agricola** and **The Germania**
	The Annals of Imperial Rome
	The Histories
Terence	**The Comedies (The Girl from Andros/The Self-Tormentor/TheEunuch/Phormio/The Mother-in-Law/The Brothers)**
Thucydides	**The History of the Peloponnesian War**
Virgil	**The Aeneid**
	The Eclogues
	The Georgics
Xenophon	**Conversations of Socrates**
	A History of My Times
	The Persian Expedition

READ MORE IN PENGUIN

A CHOICE OF CLASSICS

ANTHOLOGIES AND ANONYMOUS WORKS

The Age of Bede
Alfred the Great
Beowulf
A Celtic Miscellany
The Cloud of Unknowing and Other Works
The Death of King Arthur
The Earliest English Poems
Early Irish Myths and Sagas
Egil's Saga
The Letters of Abelard and Heloise
Medieval English Verse
Njal's Saga
Roman Poets of the Early Empire
Seven Viking Romances
Sir Gawain and the Green Knight

READ MORE IN PENGUIN

A CHOICE OF CLASSICS

Basho	**The Narrow Road to the Deep North**
	On Love and Barley
Cao Xueqin	**The Story of the Stone** also known as **The Dream of The Red Chamber** (in five volumes)
Confucius	**The Analects**
Khayyam	**The Ruba'iyat of Omar Khayyam**
Lao Tzu	**Tao Te Ching**
Li Po/Tu Fu	**Li Po and Tu Fu**
Sei Shonagon	**The Pillow Book of Sei Shonagon**

ANTHOLOGIES AND ANONYMOUS WORKS

The Bhagavad Gita
Buddhist Scriptures
The Dhammapada
Hindu Myths
The Koran
The Laws of Manu
New Songs from a Jade Terrace
The Rig Veda
Speaking of Siva
Tales from the Thousand and One Nights
The Upanishads